KATHY HOGAN TROCHECK

TO LIVE & DIE IN DIXIE

A CALLAHAN GARRITY MYSTERY

AVON BOOKS

An Imprint of HarperCollinsPublishers

AVON BOOKS
An Imprint of HarperCollins*Publishers*
195 Broadway
New York, NY, 10007

Copyright © 1993 by Kathy Hogan Trocheck
ISBN: 0-06-109171-5
www.avonmystery.com

First Avon Books paperback printing: December 2004
First HarperPaperback printing: May 1994
First HarperCollins hardcover printing: July 1993

Avon Trademark Reg. U.S. Pat. Off. and in Other Countries,
Marca Registrada, Hecho en U.S.A.
HarperCollins® is a trademark of HarperCollins Publishers Inc.

Printed in the U.S.A.

20 19 18 17 16 15 14 13

Dedicated with love to my mother, Helen Hogan, and to the memory of her mother, Edna Rivers Waymire. Happy Birthday, Mom; miss you, Gram.

Acknowledgments

For their generous gifts of advice, support and informa-
tion, the author wishes to thank the following: Paul
Blatner of Blatner's Antiques, Savannah, Georgia;
Timothy J. Buckley of the Cobb County, Georgia,
District Attorney's Office; Tom Camden, Librarian,
The University of Georgia's Special Collections; Linda
Christian, RPH; Sandie Clark, MSW, program man-
ager of the women's unit at Ridgeview Institute,
Smyrna, Georgia; Jane Cooper, MSW, of New York;
William T. Hankins III; Richard Hansen, M.D.; Lt.
G. D. Hardman of the DeKalb County, Georgia Arson
Unit; Susan Hogan, R.N.; Pradeep Jolly, M.D.; Dennis
Kelly, superintendent of Kennesaw Mountain
Battlefield National Park; Cpl. Tommy Payton of the
Avondale Estates, Georgia Police Department; Dr.
James Roarke, Professor of History at Emory
University; David K. Secrest; C. R. Sheffield; Dr.
Emory Thomas, Regents Professor of History at the
University of Georgia; Jeanne Trocheck; Bob Weeks of
the Weeks Corp.; and Gary Wehner of Cockrell's
Missouri Brigade, C.S.A.

My editor, Eamon Dolan, supplied jokes and his patented cliché-detector, and made the book better. My agent, Sallie Gouverneur, did everything except cook dinner. A special debt is owed my husband, Tom, who loves me even on the bad days, and who does emergency computer retrievals, and to my children, Katie and Andy, who put up with a manic mama when she's on deadline.

1

THE LUMP UNDER THE SHEET stirred, ever so slightly. I poked it with my toe. No response. I poked again. Put my lips up to his ear.

"Give you a hundred dollars if you'll get up and put the coffee on."

The only response was an exaggerated snore.

"A hundred dollars and I'll scratch your back for five minutes."

He pulled the sheet up over his head and turned his back to me.

I sighed. "Okay. A hundred dollars, back scratching, plus . . ."

Before I could finish the offer he turned and put his arms around my neck, lazily running a finger down my bare spine.

I slapped his hand away.

"Forget it, MacAuliffe," I said. "A hundred dollars, back scratching and first dibs on the shower. That's my final offer."

He groaned loudly but sat up, pulling half the covers with him. It was June, but we'd cranked up my air-conditioner the previous night and the room was chilly. I snatched the covers back.

"Deal," he said, then padded, naked, toward the bathroom.

I dozed a few minutes, until the doorbell rang. "Get the door, Mac," I called, but the shower was still running full blast.

"Damn," I muttered, feeling around on the floor for my robe. "Who the hell's here this early in the morning?"

By the time I'd groggily made my way through the hallway to the front door, the bell ringing had been replaced with a persistent knocking. I put one bleary eye to the front door peephole, took a look and tried to shake the cobwebs away.

I looked again, but she was still there. I shot the deadbolt and opened the door a crack, leaving the chain on.

A Southern belle from hell stood on my doorstep. She'd poured her two-hundred-pound-plus self into a long hoop-skirted ball gown made of some kind of white-and-green flowered imitation satin. The sleeves had been pulled down over her shoulders, forcing the double-D bosom forward at a gravity-defying angle. A green velvet sash was wound tight around her waist, so tight that her chubby cheeks were stained an unnatural pink. Her head was wrapped turban style in a faded yellow towel. She fluttered a pair of half-inch-long fake eyelashes and smiled coquettishly at me.

"Hey, Callahan," she said sweetly, trying to push the door open. "Tell your mama I'm here for my comb-out."

I held the door steady. "Edna's still in Swainsboro, at my cousin's wedding, Neva Jean," I said. "What the hell are you doing in that getup at the crack of dawn on a Saturday morning?"

She fluttered the eyelashes again. "Come on and let me in, Callahan," she said plaintively. "It's eighty-five degrees out here already. I don' wanna sweat on my ball gown. Edna promised she'd be back in time to comb me out before I head up to Kennesaw for the big battle. She'll probably be here any minute now."

"I've got company, Neva Jean," I said, tightening my grip on the door. "I'll have Edna call you when she gets in. See you later."

Before I could slam the door an arm snaked around in front of me, unlatching the chain. "What big battle?" Mac asked. I hadn't heard him come up behind me. He opened the door wide, forcing me to step back into the hallway. "Come on in, Neva Jean," he said expansively. "Coffee's on."

She bunched her skirts up tight to her body and squeezed past, treating Mac to another spasm of eyelash fluttering.

I gave Mac a sour look, but he smiled back innocently. "You never heard of Southern hospitality?" he whispered. He doffed an imaginary hat at the swaying backside of Neva Jean McComb, assistant head House Mouse, dressed up as a trailer-park version of Scarlett O'Hara.

Neva Jean doesn't always show up in costume at the front door to the bungalow Edna and I share in Candler Park. Usually, she and the other girls come in the back door. Generally, they wear white slacks and one of our pink or white House Mouse smocks. We run a cleaning business, you see, the best damn cleaning business in Atlanta, I think. We're pricey, but when a Mouse has been in your house, you know it's clean.

In the last year or so, we've acquired a sideline, one I hadn't planned on after I quit the Atlanta Police Department and bought the cleaning business. The new business cards don't mention it, but J. Callahan Garrity, the co-owner and president of House Mouse, has also—

reluctantly—gotten back into the private investigation racket.

Slowly, I trailed Mac and Neva Jean back into the kitchen. As usual, she had her head poked inside the refrigerator. Her voice was muffled, but audible. "Didn't I see a plate of sausage biscuits in here yesterday?"

"Gone," I said. "Mac had a midnight snack off 'em."

Neva Jean stood up straight and waggled a finger at me. "Callahan Garrity, your mama would have a conniption if she knew you were entertaining overnight company while she was out of town."

Mac had the grace to blush, but I waggled my finger right back at her. "Guess again, Neva Jean," I said. "Mac spends just about every Friday night here. It's too far for him to drive back out to Alpharetta."

Neva Jean gasped in horror, but Mac shook his head in agreement. "It's true," he said, handing her a mug of steaming coffee. "These Garrity women are very open-minded."

While Neva Jean drowned her outrage in her coffee I sat down at the oak kitchen table and ran my fingers through my hair, trying to pretty up a bit for my gentleman friend, Andrew MacAuliffe.

"Neva Jean," I said reluctantly, "run that battlefield thing past me again, would you? Just exactly what are you doing on a battlefield and why are you dressed in that tacky getup?"

Neva Jean slurped her coffee loudly. "Tacky. Gawdamighty, Callahan. I had this dress made special. Had to give near sixty dollars just for the material alone."

"It shows," Mac agreed.

"Thank you," she cooed. "Swannelle just loves this dress. He can't keep his hands off me when I wear it."

"Swannelle can't keep his hands off you, period," I groused. "That's the horniest man I ever met."

Neva Jean smiled proudly. "Ain't he, though? He'd be too much man for any normal woman."

"I know that's right," I agreed. "Now what's the deal with the battle?"

"You know, I don't think you listen to a word I say around here," Neva Jean pouted. "I been talkin' about Swannelle's Battle of Kennesaw reenactment for weeks now, and you ain't heard a word. For the last time. It's the Battle of Kennesaw. Remember, the big Civil War deal? Swannelle's unit's been camped up on the mountain for two days."

"What unit?" I said blankly.

She sighed impatiently. "The Gate City Old Guard. Swannelle's in charge of the cannon this year. He got a promotion."

Mac whistled in appreciation. He's a sort of Civil War buff himself, although he's definitely not one of those types who run around with the Confederate Stars and Bars flying from his truck with a bumper sticker that says *'Fergit Hell.*

"That's a big job," he said, setting his coffee cup down. "How long has he been in this outfit?"

"It's his second year," Neva Jean said. "His brother-in-law, Rooney, Rooney Deebs, he's a captain of the outfit. Rooney's got Swannelle so crazy over this reenactment stuff he's give up his slow-pitch softball team."

"All right," I said. "But if it's Swannelle who's doing the reenactment, why are you all tricked out, Neva Jean?"

"I been tryin' to get to that," she said. "Tonight's the CSA Benevolent Society Fancy Dress Ball. I just put the dress on this morning so Edna could envision how I'll look when she combs me out. But now I don't know what to do. It's too late to get a hair appointment."

"Too bad," I sympathized. "Edna will be back, but she said it'd be after noon."

"Damn," she said, stomping her pink fuzzy house slipper. "I'll just have to come back."

"Maybe Callahan could comb you out," Mac suggested.

Neva Jean's eyes swept over my own coiffure. My curly black hair has started to run to gray in the last couple years, and I hadn't had a cut recently. To be honest, my hair looked like the back end of an aging French poodle.

"No, no," she said quickly, edging toward the back door. "I wouldn't want to intrude on you lovebirds. I'll come back later."

"I'd be glad to help out, Neva Jean," I said, with a hint of maliciousness. "I know right where Edna keeps the curling iron and the Aqua Net. In fact, I've been dying to get my hands on your hair."

"No really," Neva Jean said, nervously. "I'll wait." She slid past me and bolted out the back screen door. "Tell your mama I'll be back around one."

2

MAC LEFT SOON AFTER Neva Jean; trout season was in full swing and he wanted to go play with his fishing tackle. I was home alone. Nap time.

The ceiling fan whirred lazily overhead, and as I dozed off I could hear the distant clatter of lawn mowers. When I woke up, Edna was dragging her suitcase into the kitchen from the back door, cursing up a blue streak.

"Hi, Mom, I'm home," I called groggily.

I heard the thump of luggage dropping, then the squeak of our refrigerator door, and shoes being kicked off.

She shuffled barefoot out to the porch, set a glass of iced tea and an ashtray holding a lit extra-long menthol cigarette on the wicker end table, and dropped wearily into the love seat next to my chair. Her hair, which she'd had done before leaving for the wedding Thursday, was toppled to one side, resembling a silver-blue Leaning Tower of Pisa. She wore neatly pressed cotton slacks, a flowered blouse, and an expression that spoke volumes. She leaned forward, slipped her hand behind her back and unsnapped her bra, sighing at the escape from her elastic prison.

"The wedding was that bad, huh?"

"Hellish," she said, dragging on the cigarette. "Your Aunt Olive may never recover. She cried all the way back from Swainsboro."

"Tell," I said, sitting up to get a better grip of the details.

She took a long drink of the tea, smacked her lips and leaned back in the cushions. "Well, it seems Sean forgot to mention to the family that his bride, the delicate Bambi Aurora, was six months pregnant and big as a house."

"Bambi Aurora?" I repeated. "That's her name, for real?"

"Her mother saw a lot of Disney movies during her own pregnancy," Edna said, shrugging.

"Aunt Olive took it pretty hard, huh?"

Edna's sister Olive is the only one in the Rivers family to have married money. She and my Uncle Bebo live in a big brick house in Dunwoody and actually belong to an honest-to-God country club. Appearances count a lot with Aunt Olive.

"Sniveled for four hours straight on the ride home," Edna said. "And she had a cat fit when I lit up a cigarette in that new Coupe de Ville of hers. I ain't had a smoke since we stopped for gas in Dublin. Look at my hand shakin'. My nerves are shot."

She held out a hand, which was actually quavering slightly.

Just then we heard a car shoot up the driveway.

Edna looked at me questioningly.

"Did you forget about promising to fix Neva Jean's hair for some Civil War wingding tonight?"

The kitchen door slammed. "Woo-ooh, Edna, Callahan, where are you?" she sang out.

Edna and I got up and went into the kitchen, where

Neva Jean was hooking a plastic garment bag over the pantry door. The green ball gown must have been in the bag, because Neva Jean had changed to a violently flowered turquoise housecoat.

"Take a look at the dress for inspiration, Edna," Neva Jean ordered, lifting the plastic of the garment bag. She sat herself at the kitchen table, set down a pink train case on the table and flipped open the lid, revealing a mirrored interior packed with combs, brushes, hair spray, mousse, and more cosmetics than I'd owned in my lifetime. She reached inside, pulled out a plastic cape and tied it around her neck, then reached in again and brought out a can of Mountain Dew.

"Go ahead, Edna," she commanded. "I touched up the roots this morning, and I've kept it damp. Make magic."

I should state right here that my mother is not a licensed cosmetologist. But she has worked as a receptionist and part-time bookkeeper at the Salon de Beaute, owned by her good friend Frank, or François, as he insists on being called, for twenty years. You don't hang around a beauty parlor for that many years without learning your way around a set of hot rollers.

Edna let out a loud, martyred sigh, but she stubbed out her cigarette and moved over behind Neva Jean. "All right, let's get this over with," she said, snatching the towel from Neva Jean's head. "You got any particular idea of what kind of style you want?"

Neva Jean glanced up from the mirror and plucked a folded magazine page from the depths of the case. "This is from a back copy of *Southern Coiffure* I been saving for ten years, for a special occasion," she said. "Do me just like this."

The model in the picture was a hollow-cheeked seventeen-year-old wearing black lipstick. Her hair had been piled atop her head and teased into a maelstrom of platinum-colored whorls, ringlets, and terraces.

Edna glanced at the photograph and without batting an eye said "Sure."

While I watched with wonder she divided and subdivided Neva Jean's brassy hair, deftly winding strands onto the rollers until Neva Jean's head sprouted a city-full of pink sponge rollers. The whole operation seemed to take no more than five minutes.

"Good thing I got Dad's curly hair," I said, awed. "I never could get the hang of rolling hair like that."

"It's a gift, Callahan, a gift from God," Neva Jean said. "Your mama never spent a single day at a beauty academy, yet she can just glimpse a picture and instinctively divine just the right setting pattern. It's like Swannelle. He can replace a whole set of points and plugs in the same time most mechanics take to pop the hood. You either got it, or you don't. Your mama and Swannelle, they got it."

Edna looked bored with the whole process. "Don't bother trying to flatter me, Neva Jean," she said. "Now go get under the dryer in my room so I can get you combed out before Swannelle comes charging in here bellowing about your being late."

Neva Jean gathered up her cosmetic kit and started toward Edna's bedroom. "Oh yeah. In all the excitement of the ball I almost forgot, Callahan. I think I lined us up a new customer for the House Mouse."

"Who?"

"Better not be any more of Swannelle's deadbeat cousins," Edna warned. "That crew has laid bad paper on us for the last time. Besides, the House Mouse doesn't do campers."

"Now Edna," Neva Jean said. "I told you those were Swannelle's second cousins. And this man is no kin to anybody I know. He's loaded. He's an antiques dealer. Got a big ol' spooky-looking mansion in Inman Park. You know that redbrick castle-looking place you can see from the MARTA train? That's the place."

"You mean Elliot Littlefield?" Edna asked. "I thought he was still in prison for that murder thing. Just how do you happen to know somebody like that?"

She smiled and waved an imaginary fan in front of her face. "That was years ago. And anyway, Swannelle says he got off on a technicality. I met him at one of Swannelle's last skirmishes. He's the head honcho over Swannelle's unit. When we were introduced, I mentioned where I worked, and I gave him a House Mouse card. He called me this morning and wants you to talk to him right away about cleaning his house."

Edna's eyes had that glint. She pushed the phone across the table toward me. "Call right now," she said. "That house, Eagle's Keep, I think he calls it, is huge. I've always wanted to see the inside of it. I hear it's loaded with gorgeous antiques. And you know they found the body in the tower bedroom in that turret. Call him and tell him we'll both come over to give the estimate."

I reached for the scrap of paper Neva Jean held out and dialed the number.

It rang once, twice, three times before the answering machine picked up. In the background I heard the first few tinny bars of "Dixie." A man's voice, deep and distinctively Southern, identified himself as Elliot Longstreet Littlefield, proprietor of Eagle's Keep Antiques and instructed me to leave a message at the beep. Before I could do so, the phone picked up at the other end. "Wait," the same voice said, live this time. "I'm here. Let me turn this godforsaken machine off.

Just a minute." I heard the receiver drop on the other end and then the sound of glass breaking.

"Damn," he muttered. "That was my last Steuben highball. I'm sorry. This is Elliot Littlefield. Who's calling please?"

"Callahan Garrity, of the House Mouse Cleaning Service," I said crisply. "My associate Neva Jean McComb tells me you're looking for some help."

"That, dear lady, is the understatement of the year," he drawled. "Beulah, the woman who has worked for me for years and my mother before me, has simply gotten too feeble to keep up with things. Now then, Miss . . . what was the name again, please?"

"Garrity. J. Callahan," I prompted.

"Yes, I remembered it was an unusual name. I don't know if Neva Jean told you, Miss Garrity, but I've got a bit of an emergency here. The Eagle's Keep is on the Inman Park Tour of Homes next weekend."

"Next weekend?" I said, relieved. "That's all right then. We can have the girls out by, oh, Tuesday or Wednesday, if we juggle the schedule a little."

"You don't understand," he said, interrupting. "I'm hosting the kick-off brunch for the Inman Park Festival tomorrow. I've got sixty people due at my front door for Bloody Marys and mini-quiches at eleven A.M. tomorrow and this place is a shambles. Can I count on you?"

"Just a minute, please, I need to check with my office manager."

I covered the receiver with my hand and looked over at Edna. "It's got to be cleaned tonight. Big party tomorrow, and the place is a mess. What do you think?"

She wrinkled her brow in thought. Neva Jean shook her head emphatically. "Include me out, ya'll. This ball is the social event of the season. Ya'll just call Baby and Sister and them. I'm not working."

I turned back to the phone before Edna could answer. "Uh, exactly how big is the house, Mr. Littlefield, and how heavy a cleaning are we talking about here?"

"Eight thousand five hundred square feet. Three stories. I need the works. Wood floors waxed, stained-glass windows cleaned, silver buffed, that kind of thing."

I repeated the words after him, while Edna's fingers began to fly over the adding machine keys. I winced. "We can handle it," I said, "but since this is a rush job and we'll have to have several girls, we'll have to charge our deluxe rate."

"Well, how much?"

"Let's see, four girls, plus myself supervising, figure six hours, rush rate . . . "

"Does he sound desperate?" Edna asked in a stage whisper. I shook my head yes. "Tell him nine hundred and fifty. We start at six and we're out by midnight or he pays a two-hundred-dollar-an-hour surcharge."

"That fee will be nine hundred and fifty dollars," I repeated dutifully, "we'll be there at six and—"

"Fine," he said. "Have your people here at four P.M., twenty-seven eleven Jasmine Way. I'll be out but the florist will let you in. I'm assuming your people are bonded. There are a good deal of very valuable collectibles in the home. I don't know if you know this about me, but my specialty is in Civil War artifacts. In fact, I've just acquired an old diary that may prove to be the finest thing in its field—"

"We're bonded," I said, cutting him off. I wasn't really interested in hearing about some rusty pile of old guns and knives. "And my girls have never had any problems with breakage or pilferage. Good-bye."

I hung up the phone. Neva Jean beamed. "Nine hundred fifty bucks. That's some job. Do I get a finder's fee?"

"You get paid one fifty for four hours of work if you show up," I told her. "Otherwise, you know the rules. If we get a callback from Littlefield, you get first shot at it."

I turned to my mother, who had pulled the phone back toward her. "Call Ruby right away before she goes to her missionary society meeting," I told her. "I'll get Jackie on the house phone in my bedroom. What about Baby and Sister? They could help with some of the dusting and the silver polishing."

Neva Jean snorted. "Ruby's church choir left on a bus trip to Jesus World up in Charlotte last night. Remember?"

"Damn," Edna said. "That's right."

"And Jackie's a good worker, but she's too scrawny to push big furniture around or deal with that floor-waxing machine. No way ya'll can clean a house that big in only four hours. Tell you what. The ball don't start till eight o'clock. I'll work from four till seven. Edna, you can comb me out there, and Swannelle can pick me up on the way. He'll want to leave by ten anyway, he always bitches that dancing aggravates his old softball injuries. I'll have him drop me off at Littlefield's on the way home."

"And?" Edna said expectantly.

"And I get paid two hundred. In cash."

Edna and I exchanged glances. Neva Jean had us over a barrel and she knew it. With Ruby gone we'd need Neva Jean's muscle. Jackie is fast and hardworking, but she only weighs about ninety pounds, and the Easterbrooks, Baby and Sister, who are both in their seventies, can only do so much. Sister's legally blind and Baby's almost stone deaf.

"All right," I sighed. "But don't you dare tell the other girls how much you're getting paid. And you better be back from that ball by ten o'clock or I'll come hunting for you myself."

3

EAGLE'S KEEP IS AN ATLANTA landmark: a Victorian Gothic behemoth that commands an entire block of Inman Park, dwarfing the not inconsiderate houses around it. Like every other crime buff in Atlanta, I'd read all about the mansion, its eccentric owner and the sensational murder that had occurred there in the late 1960s.

Elliot Littlefield had been convicted of the murder of a young runaway girl he'd picked up on Atlanta's Tenth Street "Hippie Strip" during the heyday of the city's version of Haight Ashbury. The conviction had been overturned on a technicality so quickly that he'd barely had time to get settled into jail before being set free again.

The murder charge alone would have been enough to make Littlefield unpopular in most neighborhoods. But Littlefield compounded his sins in a number of ways. Neighbors couldn't fail to notice the steady stream of young girls coming and going from the mansion. "Shop assistants," Littlefield called them, and a few of them supposedly had worked in the antiques shop he ran out of the mansion's carriage house.

That antiques shop was a sore subject in Inman Park, whose neighbors had fought a twenty-year-long uphill battle to gentrify what had declined into a seedy slum of broken-down bungalows, boarding houses and dilapidated apartment buildings. Eagle's Keep, with its rose red brickwork and elaborate gingerbread picked out in shades of sand and ivory, should have been the pride of the community, as it had been when a Yankee department store magnate had built it in 1893. But a century later, neighbors claimed Littlefield's clients hogged precious on-street parking, and his practice of renting out the mansion for large fund-raisers and noisy parties also set their teeth on edge.

Twin Confederate flags fluttered in the breeze from flagpoles mounted on either side of the front door of Eagle's Keep that day.

"Uh oh," Baby said, from the back of the van. "I don't like the looks of this."

"Something tells me this ain't the Inman Park NAACP headquarters," Jackie chimed in.

We all piled out of the van and I opened the cargo door to unload the cart full of cleaning gear.

"I wonder which room they found that girl's body in," Edna said, peering up at the twin turrets disappearing into leafy green treetops.

"Somebody say somethin' about a cup of coffee?" Baby asked. "I'd like me a Coca-Cola if it's all the same."

Sister grabbed Baby's arm for guidance and leaned her lips up against Baby's ear. "They talkin' 'bout a body in this here house," Sister shouted. "Right here in this house we fixin' to clean."

"That's nice," Baby replied, patting her sister's arm and guiding her carefully over the curb. "Step up here now so you don't take a fall."

Jackie clasped her arms around herself and shivered, despite the warmth of the late afternoon. "No kiddin', Callahan," she said. "This place gives me the heebie-jeebies. And I ain't even been inside yet."

"Now look ahere, missy," Neva Jean said, addressing herself to Jackie, who stood staring at the flags. "Just because Mr. Littlefield happens to fly the Stars and Bars don't mean he's the Grand Lizard of the Ku Klux Klan. Lots of people who are interested in history fly the Rebel flag. It don't mean nothin' against colored people. Why, me 'n' Swannelle got a Confederate flag on the pickup truck. Jackie, you know how I feel about you. Why, if I had a colored sister, you'd be it."

Jackie glanced over at me and shook her head. "I know, Neva Jean. And if I had to have a redneck bleached-blond honky for a sister, I'd pick you too."

"That's sweet," Neva Jean said, pecking her friend on the cheek. "Come on, let's get in there and get busy before I have to leave for my ball."

We pressed the doorbell, setting off a sonorous set of chimes somewhere inside, and waited. And waited. Finally, a woman pulled the heavily carved door open. A green apron was wrapped around her skeletally thin body. She was short, with spiked mahogany-colored hair and a harried expression. "Yes?" she said, looking expectantly at our tatty little group.

"Callahan Garrity, House Mouse," I said, preparing to enter. The woman's face remained blank. "You know, the cleaning service?" I added. "Mr. Littlefield said someone would be here to let us in."

The woman sighed loudly. "Hi. I'm Danielle DeClerc, the florist. Mr. Littlefield told me the same thing. But when we got here an hour ago, no one was around. I'd have left, but he is a good customer. So I went around to the back of the house and went in through the utility room." Noticing my questioning look, she added, "It was unlocked. I figured his assistant had to run out for something. But if we didn't get in here and get started right away, there'd be no way my arrangements would be ready for this party tomorrow."

I gathered my supplies and motioned to my troops to follow me inside. "Well, if it's all right with you, we'll come in and get started too. We only have a few hours to get it all done."

"You're gonna need all the time you can get," Danielle warned. "This place is a sty. I'm surprised Beulah let things get this out of hand."

She stepped out of the way to allow us to bump the cleaning cart over the raised threshold of the entryway. It wasn't until we were all assembled inside, our cleaning equipment in a pile around us, that we had a chance to notice the surroundings.

"Holy mother," Edna whispered.

"Uh oh," Jackie said.

The entrance hall of Eagle's Keep soared thirty feet above us. The walls had been papered in a forest green moiré, but you couldn't appreciate much of the paper, what with all the stuffed wildlife. A whole jungleful of dead hunting trophies seemed to be emerging from those walls; snarling tigers, glassy-eyed lions, fierce-looking boars, and horned beasts of every description. In between the trophies the walls were dotted with medieval-looking crossbows, muskets, daggers, swords, and other weapons. A chandelier made entirely of animal antlers hung from a heavy gold chain, casting weird shadows on the wall. At our feet, a zebra-skin rug stretched over the white marble floor.

"Wow," Neva Jean said. "Swannelle'd have a fit to see this."

"Just look at that," Jackie said, nodding toward the

wall facing the door. "Thought you said Confederate flags didn't mean nothing."

The fancifully carved Victorian sideboard was eight feet long and covered with a collection of military headgear. I recognized the mashed kepi of the Confederate foot soldier, a dull gray-green metal doughboy's helmet from World War I, some plumed and gilt-covered hats of a vaguely Eastern European flavor, a World War II leather flying ace helmet, and yes, holding pride of place in the display, the distinctive spiked helmet of a Nazi SS officer.

Danielle noticed our stares. "Make sure your girls are careful," she said crisply. "I don't want to be blamed for any breakage. If you need me, Rodney, my assistant and I will be in the kitchen. We should be cleared out of here in another hour or so. We'll try not to leave it a bigger mess than it was when we got here."

"Good," Edna muttered. She'd been walking around the entry hall, taking a grunge inventory. A heavy film of dust covered the sideboard and its millinery display. The lower drawers of the cabinet stood ajar, and papers and more hats spilled out. Cobwebs stretched from antler to antler of the hunting trophies and the floor beneath my feet felt sticky in places. Beside the sideboard, a sagging cardboard carton overflowed with old newspapers, crumpled circulars and empty wine bottles.

"Cat piss," Edna said, sampling the air like a sommelier sniffs a Bordeaux cork. "I smell cat piss." As she said it, an ancient one-eyed Siamese slunk from the entry hall and disappeared toward the back of the house.

With Edna kicking at imaginary hair balls and denouncing the urinary habits of incontinent felines, the girls and I did a quick survey of the downstairs. Things were as bad or worse in the other rooms. Each was stuffed with magnificent, ornate Victorian furniture, musty-looking oil paintings, tarnished silver, assorted gewgaws and spotty Oriental rugs, and an appalling amount of plain old dirt.

"We look hard enough, we'll probably find poor old Beulah the cleaning lady in here," Edna griped. "Cleaning this mess probably killed her."

"How many hours did you say we have to get this place clean?" Jackie demanded.

"Midnight," Neva Jean volunteered. "But it'll never get done with ya'll standing around like statues."

"She's right," I said. "It's bad, but we've seen worse."

"Don't know when," Edna said under her breath.

"Let's get started," I continued. "Jackie, you and Sister and Baby get started down here." I lowered my voice a notch. "Watch Sister, for God's sake, and don't let her get near the crystal or china. In fact, you better sit her down somewhere and let her get started on the silver. Baby can tell her if she's missing any spots."

Jackie nodded her head in agreement. "Right," she said. Then, louder, "Ladies, we're gonna start downstairs, in the dining room. Miss Baby, we need you to dust, and Miss Sister, you do such a fine job on the silver, would you take care of that for me, please?"

Neva Jean ran ahead of us up the heavily carved oak stairway to the second floor. "Ya'll bring the cart up," she called. "I don't want to break a nail."

"I'll break her nails and her neck," Edna said, but she started to push the trolley toward the stairs.

"Let's leave it down here so the sisters don't have to climb these stairs," I said, grabbing a mop, a bucket and a plastic caddy full of cleaning sprays and powders.

Edna got the broom and dustpan and a gallon jug of Pine Sol. "If Littlefield doesn't have a vacuum upstairs, Neva Jean is hauling ours up the stairs, nail or no nail," she declared.

At the top of the stairs, I paused to catch my breath while Edna stopped and lit a cigarette. I glared at her, but she waved aside my silent protest. "Cigarette smoke is a natural deodorizer," she said, blowing a puff in the air to demonstrate. "It's a scientific fact."

"Littlefield said there were four bedrooms and two baths on this floor," I said, trying not to gasp. Some day soon I've got to start working out. "You take the north end, Edna, and I'll take the south. We'll meet in the middle."

"What about Neva Jean?" Edna said suspiciously. "Where's that girl gotten to?"

"Up here," a muffled voice called from above our heads. "There's a bunch more rooms up here," she wailed. "I ain't even looked at 'em all, but the one I'm in now looks like a library of some kind. Books all thrown on the floor, papers everywhere. More of those animal heads and statues and shit. And it don't look like it's been cleaned since Christ was a corporal."

"Too bad," Edna said, stubbing her cigarette in an ashtray that was sitting on a small table in the hallway. "Come down about six-thirty and I'll comb you out."

Reluctantly, I headed for the door at the end of the hallway, and pushed open the paneled wood door.

A carved gilt mirror took up one whole wall of what had to be the master bedroom suite and the damndest bed I'd ever seen took up most of the other. It was a four-poster affair, each poster made of a grinning blackamoor holding aloft a palm frond that supported a swagged and fringed gold brocade canopy. A pedestal on either side of the bed held marble busts; one of Robert E. Lee, the other reminded me of Jefferson Davis.

The room was in total disarray. Clothes were strewn about, chairs overturned and the drawers of a massive carved and inlaid chest of drawers had been pulled out and the contents dumped on the floor. The door to a walk-in closet stood ajar. Inside, most of the clothes had been tossed in a heap.

"What a pig," I moaned.

Edna appeared at the doorway. "That's an understatement," she snapped. "My rooms look this bad or worse. I don't care what you told this Littlefield character. Forget midnight. If we get this place sorted out by eight A.M. it'll be a miracle."

"I know," I admitted. "I had no idea it'd be this bad. How does one man living alone make such a mess?"

"He's a man," Edna shrugged.

A scream cut short her diatribe. It was followed by a series of short, hiccupy shrieks that sounded like they were coming from the third floor.

"Must be even worse upstairs," Edna said. "You know Neva Jean's got a high tolerance for crud."

"Call-A-Han," Neva Jean screeched. "Ed-Na. Come Here. Come Here. It's Aw-Fulll."

"I don't think this is about dirt," I said uneasily. "We better get up there."

We raced up the stairs, sidestepping books, papers, and what looked like a month's worth of dirty laundry.

Neva Jean sat on the floor in the third-floor hallway, slumped against a doorway. Her hands covered her face and she was gasping.

"Don't look. Don't. Go. In . . . Girl . . . dead . . . She's dead . . . Oh my God, the blood."

Edna had her hand on the doorknob. "Don't, Ma," I said sharply. "Take Neva Jean down to the kitchen and get her something to drink."

My mother's face got that stubborn look, her lower lip pooching out, her eyes glittering dangerously. "Fuck that," she said. "I'm having a look. You forget, I was almost killed in an alley underneath Rich's." She stepped over the slumped woman at her feet and started into the room. From where I stood I could see only a glimpse of the room, but the glimpse included the sight of a spatter of blood on the light blue sprigged wallpaper, and out of the corner of my eye I thought I saw a very pale, very lifeless woman's hand flung across the bed.

I glanced at Edna. Her lips moved silently, forming the words to a Hail Mary. I grasped the doorknob and pulled the door shut before Edna could see more. Before she could see what I wished I hadn't.

"Get Neva Jean downstairs," I ordered. "Give her a drink and call Swannelle. Tell the others to stay put. Don't let the florists leave. And call nine one one."

4

EDNA SPRAYED A HEAVY MIST of window cleaner on the stainless-steel sink for the third time in five minutes. In the thirty minutes since we'd discovered the body of a young girl on the third floor and herded everyone into the kitchen to wait for the cops, she'd managed to sweep and mop the floor, de-crud the countertops and cabinet fronts, and clean the oven.

"Would you stop," I said sharply. "You're making us all nervous." In answer, she stepped toward the refrigerator door and attacked the door with a soapy sponge. "If we keep busy, we can still finish up and get paid," she said. "This is too big a job to lose, Jules."

I moved quickly across the floor, took the sponge out of her hands and flipped it into the sink. Then I steered her toward the long marble-topped table where the others were gathered. "Sit," I directed. "The cops aren't going to let us do any more cleaning tonight. It'd be destroying evidence. No telling what we'd already done before we found that girl."

"Oh," she said meekly. "I didn't think about that. Anybody got a deck of cards?" The other girls shook their heads mutely. Neva Jean worried at a microscopic nail polish chip on her left hand.

The doorbell rang then. The girls, the florist, and her helper looked at me expectantly.

"That'll be the cops," I said. "Guess I'll get it."

Through the leaded-glass fanlights on either side of the front door I could see the swirling blue lights that told me Atlanta's finest had arrived on the scene. At least three patrol cars were pulled up to the curb, and a crowd of blue uniforms stood on the other side of the door.

I straightened my smudged smock and pulled the door open. "Upstairs, third floor, first door at the top of the hallway," I said. Four young uniformed officers shouldered past me and raced for the stairs.

They left behind two plainclothes detectives. One of the detectives was a familiar face. C. W. Hunsecker's grizzled close-cropped hair had gone grayer since I'd last seen him at a retirement dinner for my former commander in the Atlanta P.D.'s burglary unit two years previously. And he'd shaved his legendary mustache. But the blue-green eyes, so memorable in a black man with such a dark complexion, crinkled in a warm grin. There'd been a Hunsecker on the Atlanta Police Force ever since a "Negro Force" had been authorized to patrol the city's black neighborhoods in 1948. That first force hadn't been allowed to carry guns or arrest white citizens, but the Hunseckers, starting with C. W.'s grandfather and continuing with his father, and various brothers, cousins and uncles, had all served in the force in varying capacities ever since. All the Hunseckers, C. W. included, were tall, at least six foot three, and almost all of them had those odd blue-green eyes.

Before I could say a word, C. W. folded me into a suffocating bear hug. "Callahan Garrity," he drawled, hitting heavily on the last syllable of both names. "I might have known when they said a cleaning lady discovered the body it'd be you. Girl, you got to stop making work for us."

"I know, C. W., I know," I said, wriggling out of his iron grasp. "Actually, it wasn't me who discovered the body. It was one of my employees, Neva Jean McComb. She's in the kitchen with the rest of my girls, plus the florist and her helper. They were here when we got here."

"Ya'll didn't touch anything, did you?" he asked sternly.

I shot him a look that told him he should have known better. "I went in quickly, felt for a pulse to make sure the girl was dead, then I shut the door and came downstairs and called you," I said. "Nobody's been upstairs since."

"What else?" he said.

"The room was a mess," I told him. "Papers and books and junk thrown everywhere. It's a guess, but maybe she surprised a burglar. I'm no homicide expert, C. W., but it looked to me like she'd been hit on the left side of the head with something heavy. Blood spatters on the wall. Oh yeah." I swallowed hard. The memory of the gruesome murder scene was one I wouldn't easily lose. "I think she'd been stabbed. There's blood all over the bed, and what looks like a puncture wound in her chest."

He sighed loudly. "Let me get up there and take a look," Hunsecker said to himself. He gestured to the younger woman who'd been standing silently at his side during our impromptu reunion. "Callahan, meet Detective Linda Nickells. Linda, this here is an old girlfriend, Callahan Garrity. She's been chasing my butt since I taught her criminal investigation back at the academy. Left the department a couple years ago, now she can't decide whether she wants to be a cleaning lady or a private detective."

"Detective Nickells will take your statement, Callahan. I'll be back down in a minute, but I want to get a look at that body."

Linda Nickells was dwarfed by C. W.'s bulk. She was maybe five foot three, with tan skin several shades lighter than C. W.'s. She had large dark eyes framed with the longest lashes I'd ever seen, and her hair had been pulled back into a sleek knot at the nape of her neck. Silvery hoop earrings dangled from her earlobes and brushed her shoulder tops. She was dressed in a pair of size nothing knife-creased stone-washed blue jeans and wore a crisp white oversize man's dress shirt and a pair of high-heeled lizard-skin cowboy boots. She looked like something off a *Vogue* magazine cover.

She grabbed my hand and pumped it. "Nice to meet you," she said, betraying what sounded like a Chicago accent. "Sorry about the sloppy attire. C. W. and I were going over some old case files over Chinese takeout when the call came in."

"I'll excuse you if you'll excuse me," I said, gesturing toward my own spattered ensemble. "Where do you want me?"

She turned and her gaze lighted on the living room, a corner of which Baby and Sister had managed to halfway clean before the shit had hit the fan. "Let's sit in there," she said, gesturing through the arched doorway. "When you and I are done you can take me to the kitchen and we'll get started on the others' statements."

We sat in a pair of matching carved armchairs near the fireplace and Linda dug into the waistband of her jeans, pulling out a tiny mini-cassette tape recorder. She pushed the button and I started to recount the evening's events. We hadn't gotten far before C. W. came lumbering back down the stairs. He pulled up a nearby ottoman and sat down heavily, listening without saying much.

"It's possible my girls and I might have destroyed some evidence," I admitted, "but if we did, it was purely unintentional. See, Mr. Littlefield told me on the phone that the place was a mess. So we just figured the guy was a slob. It never occurred to us that the house had been ransacked until after Neva Jean found the girl on the third floor."

"Littlefield," Hunsecker said, looking around the hallway with newfound interest. "Not Elliot Littlefield?"

I nodded. "Same one. I thought you knew that."

"Shit," Hunsecker said. "Goddamn. I thought there was something familiar about this place."

"You worked the Sunny Girl murder?" I asked.

"Surprised you remember it," Hunsecker said.

"I was a kid, but even then I was fascinated with murder. I used to sneak downstairs to listen to the eleven o'clock news every night to hear the latest development in the case," I said.

Hunsecker turned to Linda Nickells. "You wouldn't have heard about it up north, I don't guess. But the Sunny Girl murder case was a big one. I was just a young twerp with big ideas back then. First black detective in homicide," he said, with a touch of pride. "'Course, I didn't do all that much. Took statements, interviewed some hippie chicks down on the Strip, that kind of thing."

Linda shook her head to signal her ignorance. "Sunny Girl? What kind of name was that? Who was she? What's she got to do with this homicide?"

"Sunny Girl was the only name anybody in Atlanta ever knew her by," I explained. "She was what, about seventeen?" I asked, looking to Hunsecker for confirmation. He nodded.

"It was the same summer as Woodstock, so it must have been 1969," I said. "Anyway, this girl who called herself Sunny had run away from home. All she ever told people was that her name was Sunny and she was from nowheresville. She'd been living with a bunch of bikers in an apartment above a poster shop at Tenth and Peachtree."

Nickells looked blank.

"The Strip, everybody called it," I said. "It was a magnet for kids from all over the South. Atlanta and the Strip, which was Peachtree and Tenth Street, was it. Sex, drugs, and rock and roll. Cheap rent, cheap dope, good tunes. Led Zeppelin, Jimi Hendrix, Iron Butterfly, Janis Joplin. Sunny met a guy when he came into the poster shop. She went to live with him, in his mansion."

"This mansion," Linda said. She was starting to catch on.

Hunsecker picked up the story where I'd left off. "Elliot Longstreet Littlefield came to Atlanta to work as a hairdresser. The only place he could afford to live was Inman Park. It was a slum in those days, not ritzy like it is now. He saved his money, bought a little shotgun house on Edgewood. Sold it, bought a couple more. Sometimes he bought houses from old ladies with the furniture still in it. That's how he got into the antiques business."

"And one day he met Sunny, brought her here and killed her," Linda prompted. The young have such short attention spans these days.

"Littlefield had a reputation for having the best reefer in town. Lots of young ladies were in and out of his house. Including Sunny. After a dope party one night, a guest who was too stoned to leave stumbled into the master bedroom to sleep it off. He found Sunny, nude, in the master bedroom. She was in Littlefield's bed. Been strangled to death. Never forget that bed," he said, his usually cheerful face clouding over. " 'The pickaninny bed,' my sergeant called it. Had these carved slave figures holding up palm fronds that made up the top part of the bed."

"He's still got the bed," I prompted. "Still sleeping in it too, from what I could see."

"Yuck," Linda said. "Did they arrest Littlefield?"

"He was arrested, tried, and convicted," Hunsecker said.

"And?" Linda insisted.

"And he hadn't even gotten down to Reidsville, that's where they had Death Row back then, hadn't even been transferred out of the Fulton County Jail before the verdict was reversed on appeal."

"On what grounds?" she wanted to know.

"The usual, a technicality," Hunsecker said, shrugging. "A rookie detective fucked up the chain of evidence. Untied the stocking from the girl's body, instead of cutting it off. Then somehow, the stocking got cut later. I forget all the ins and outs of it. Right after he was convicted, Littlefield appealed it, and some judge decided the evidence had been tampered with."

"And Littlefield got off?" Nickells asked. "He went scot-free?"

"Not quite," said a deep voice behind us. "The courts set me loose from prison, but I've never really been free of that murder charge. Not really."

Beside me, I heard Hunsecker suck in his breath quickly. A tall balding man in his late forties stood with his back to the front door. He'd let himself in so quietly we hadn't heard a thing. He was dressed in a pair of tight black designer jeans and a black polo shirt.

"Elliot Littlefield," the man said, nodding politely. "Would someone please tell me what's going on here? Why are all these police here? Not another burglary, I hope."

Hunsecker stood up, walked into the entry hall, pulled a small leather folder from the breast pocket of his blue denim work shirt and flipped it open to display a gold shield. "Captain C. W. Hunsecker, Atlanta Homicide," he said coolly. "There's been a murder here, Mr. Littlefield."

"My God," Littlefield said, paling. "Who?"

"That's what we'd like you to tell us," Hunsecker said. "The body of a young woman was found by a member of the cleaning crew you hired. She's in a bedroom on the third floor. Let's go upstairs and take a look, all right?"

Littlefield headed for the stairs, then glanced back at me. "Are you with the cleaning service?"

"Callahan Garrity," I said, not bothering to extend my hand for a proper how-do. "I own the House Mouse. Neva Jean McComb, who I believe you know, she was the one who found the body."

"Oh dear," he said, clinging to the stair rail. "Please don't let it be Bridget. Not Bridget."

"Bridget?" Hunsecker said sharply.

"Bridget Dougherty, my shop assistant," Littlefield said. "I couldn't bear it if it's my little Bridget."

He glanced at me again. "Jesus. I'm sorry about Neva Jean finding the body. I hope she wasn't too upset."

"She'll live," I said dryly.

"Let's go," Hunsecker said, stepping back to allow Littlefield to precede him up the stairs. "Top floor." Hunsecker caught my eye and held it. "Detective Nickells will want to take the statements from the rest of your people now, Callahan."

I nodded agreement.

"And Callahan?"

"What?"

"Don't even think about it."

5

THE DOORBELL RANG AGAIN. I looked around for someone to get it. Linda Nickells was still in the kitchen, questioning the girls, and Hunsecker and the other cops were still upstairs, as was the lord of the manor, Littlefield.

That left me. As I approached the door I could see the wavy image of a group of people huddled together, close, but not touching.

I opened the door. A man, a woman, and a teenage girl stood quietly, their faces set in a frozen grimace. They stared at me for a moment. "Are you with the police?" the man finally asked. "I'm Lyle Dougherty, this is my wife Emily and our daughter Jocelyn. Someone called . . . our daughter, Bridget."

The woman gripped her husband's arm tightly with both hands. A large diamond solitaire winked from a simple gold band on her ring finger. She was what dress-shop clerks call petite, maybe five foot two, and pretty; early forties, with dark brown hair cut in a shining page boy. The silver strands that ran through the hair looked like they'd been placed there for contrast, unlike the unruly gray wires that stuck out from my own short mop. She wore an elegant beige linen pantsuit, and those little flats with the linen bow and the gold buckle, Ferragamo, I think they are, the ones that cost more than the monthly house payment on my bungalow. Lyle Dougherty was taller than his wife by nearly a foot, with dark hair, wavy and gone gray around the temple in an attractive kind of way. His eyes behind the tortoiseshell glasses were red rimmed. He wore a camel-colored V-necked cashmere sweater and cream-colored pleated slacks, and his sockless feet were tucked into soft buckskin loafers. The Doughertys were a regular riot of neutrals. The daughter towered over her mother by a good five inches. She was painfully thin, with frizzy brown shoulder-length hair pushed off her face with an African-looking beaded headband. Jocelyn's eyes were her mother's—big and brown and sorrowful—and her lips were the kind all the young actresses wanted, with that swollen bee-stung look. She wore a shapeless gray T-shirt and baggy, faded black shorts that hung low on her bony hips. Her feet were shoved into scuffed leather sandals. She gazed at me steadily, saying nothing.

"Come in," I said, gesturing toward the hallway and ignoring their question about whether I was with the police. I guided them toward the armchairs where Linda Nickells and I had sat earlier.

Lyle Dougherty sank gratefully into the chair, and his daughter perched on the edge of the facing chair, but Emily stood behind Lyle, her hands placed precisely on the chair back, her fingers pinching at the soft brocade upholstery. "Is she really dead?" she asked quietly, her eyes unblinking. "Are they sure it's Bridget? Couldn't it be some other girl?"

"I'm sorry," I said, helplessly. "I'll get Captain Hunsecker. He's the one you need to talk to."

I fled up the stairs, away from the Doughertys, but I felt their anxious eyes following my ascent. This was one aspect of police work that made me glad I'd gotten out and started a cleaning business. I'd never gotten used to notifying next of kin that a loved one was no more. Not many cops do, I don't guess.

On the second-floor landing I paused, listening for voices. At the end of the hallway, I heard voices coming from an open doorway.

"Captain Hunsecker?" I said, speaking up to let him know I was approaching. I poked my head around the door. Hunsecker was seated on a small navy blue suede love seat in what looked like a seldom-used sitting room. Littlefield sat across from him on a matching sofa, hunched over, his head in his hands.

Hunsecker looked annoyed at the interruption. "What?" he snapped. "Callahan, I thought I asked you to stay downstairs."

"I know, Captain," I said. "But there's a Mr. and Mrs. Dougherty and their daughter downstairs. They're asking questions about Bridget. And Detective Nickells is still interviewing my girls. I thought you might want to talk to them."

Littlefield raised his head from his hands. "God. The Doughertys. Bridget's loving parents. Who the hell called them?"

"I asked one of the uniformed officers to give them a call," Hunsecker said evenly. "They're the girl's parents. Got a problem with that?"

Littlefield shook his head, but he sat up straight. "Just keep them away from me," he ordered.

Hunsecker's face stiffened, but he followed me out of the room without saying anything. At the head of the stairs, he pulled my arm to stop me from going down. "You tell the parents anything?" he said in a low voice.

"I'm the cleaning lady—remember?"

He offered me an apologetic smile. "Sorry. That guy

in there"—he jerked his head toward the room where Littlefield was still seated—"he gets to me, you know? Him and his pickaninny bed."

"He got an alibi?" I said, trying to sound casual.

"He's got one," Hunsecker said grimly. "All God's children got an alibi."

Hunsecker headed down the stairs, treading with surprising lightness for a man of his bulk. He glanced back at me. "Where you think you going, Garrity?"

"Downstairs," I said. "You got the crime scene guys on the top floor. Littlefield's on the second. The parents and the girls are on the first floor. I'm running out of places to park myself, unless you want me to go down in the cellar with the spiders and snakes."

"Go home," he said, not unkindly.

"Love to," I told him. "But the girls all came in the van with me. And Nickells apparently isn't done with them yet."

"All right," he sighed. "You can stay. Sit in the dining room until Nickells is finished. Keep your mouth shut, though. Anything you accidentally overhear, you don't hear at all. Understood?"

"Understood," I said meekly.

The Doughertys looked like a couple of stone statues. They'd changed places though. Now Emily Dougherty sat in the chair and Lyle stood behind her, kneading her shoulders with his hands. Mrs. Dougherty sat, twisting the large diamond ring around and around on her finger. At least they weren't hysterical. The daughter sat back in the chair, her eyes closed. I couldn't tell if she was napping or meditating.

I could see the unfolding tableau from my seat in the dining room, but the high ceilings and the densely carpeted floors seemed to swallow the polite conversation going on in the parlor across the hall.

Hunsecker offered his hand to Mr. Dougherty and to his wife. They shook gravely, offering polite but weak smiles. I could tell he was breaking the news of their daughter's death. Hunsecker's gleaming mahogany face was etched with sadness, his jowls seemed to deepen before my eyes. But the Doughertys seemed to take the news tolerably well. Lyle knelt beside the chair and hugged Emily. They clung to each other momentarily, then parted, each wiping away tears. Then both enveloped the other daughter in a hug.

The interview went on for ten minutes or so, with Dougherty answering most of Hunsecker's questions and his wife occasionally glancing about the room, as if to search for some glimpse of her dead daughter's presence.

Since I couldn't hear anything, I'd started my own visual inventory of the dining room, out of boredom mostly.

I'm an antiques buff myself, but not a collector of the caliber of stuff Littlefield deals in. From the decor of the house, it appeared he was heavily into Victoriana, with some meanderings into Biedermeier, Empire, and even a vaguely Gothic piece or two.

I was minding my own business, for once, staring at the wall-to-ceiling walnut china cabinet, trying to count the number of different china patterns on display, when something soft swatted at my ankle.

"Christ," I shrieked, leaping from the chair. The Siamese cat streaked out from under the table and disappeared up the stairs. On the Oriental rug, which I'd already judged to be an Aubusson, lay a bloody half-chewed mouse. A gift, from kitty to Callahan.

In the parlor, the Doughertys and Hunsecker joined in a disapproving stare. "Sorry," I said. "I fuckin' hate cats," I muttered, between gritted teeth, moving around the table to avoid the mouse corpse.

Hunsecker brought out a business card, offered it to

Lyle Dougherty, then slowly steered the family toward the front door. "I'll be in touch," I heard him say.

"I'll be in touch," Linda Nickells was telling Neva Jean as she shepherded the girls through the swinging door of the kitchen.

Neva Jean tried on a lopsided smile, but it didn't take. Pink sponge rollers dangled from various lank locks of her blond hair, and the dry cleaner's bag she clutched to her bosom showed the green satin ball gown had been badly crushed.

Edna held onto Neva Jean's arm, aiming for the front door. "Let's go home, Jules," she said tiredly. "The girls and I are beat."

"Let me get the cleaning cart," I said, "and I need to speak to Mr. Littlefield about whether he wants us to finish cleaning."

But Edna gave me the look. "Home. We're finished all right. You can come back tomorrow for the cart and to talk to Littlefield."

Hunsecker stepped up, took Neva Jean's other arm and guided the group out the door. He touched me on the arm and nodded, almost imperceptibly.

"Ya'll go on and get in the van," I told Edna, handing her the car keys. "I'll be out in a minute."

"One minute," Edna warned. "Then we leave without you."

The door swung shut behind them. I folded my arms across my chest, waiting for the inevitable lecture about keeping my nose out of police business.

Hunsecker sighed loudly. "Got no business tellin' you this. But shit, Callahan, you gonna know anyways.

"Girl's name was Bridget Dougherty. Just turned seventeen. Folks live out in Dunwoody. The parents say she dropped out of All Saints, that fancy prep school, ran away from home, ended up here. They knew where she was and all, but hadn't been talking to her. Littlefield says the girl worked for him and that's it. He says the parents kicked her out when she told them she might be pregnant. He says he don't know who the boyfriend was."

"Might be?"

"It was a false alarm. But she left home two months ago, stayed around with friends and such. Called the parents a month ago to tell them where she was and that she wasn't pregnant, but wasn't coming back."

"And Littlefield has an alibi?"

He nodded. "Says he left here at four to go to Morningside to look at some antiques in some old lady's estate. According to him, Bridget was on the phone with somebody when he left. That's the last he saw her. It does look like the place was burglarized, by the way. Littlefield's all worked up about some missing Civil War shit. Says it's priceless. He's making a list of what's missing."

"And the girl?" I prompted. "How was she killed?"

"About what you thought," he said. "Beaten on the head with something heavy. We don't know what. Stabbed in the chest. Littlefield says there's an old dagger missing from the library."

"And you think Littlefield killed her?"

He sighed again, running blunt fingers through the close-cropped hair. "I'm inclined to think it for now. We'll see."

"If it wasn't Littlefield, how'd the murderer get in?" I asked. "I saw a security system sticker right here on the front door and there are wrought-iron bars on all the ground floor windows. This door doesn't look like it's been messed with."

Hunsecker turned and traced the security sticker pasted on the inside of the fanlight. "Littlefield says Bridget might have turned the system off herself. The cat had set it off the night before and armed alert guards showed up, damn near arrested her until she persuaded them she lived here."

He slapped the sticker with the palm of his hand. "Seventeen. Shit. They're gettin' younger, you know, Garrity? Younger all the time. I got a kid sitting over at the Youth Detention Center now, fourteen, took out his best buddy over a rock of crack. The friend was thirteen."

I patted Hunsecker on the shoulder, awkwardly. "I know, C. W., I know. Thanks for filling me in, anyhow. Talk to you."

Edna gunned the Chevy's engine at me as I stepped onto the front steps of Eagle's Keep. The resulting backfire echoed through the quiet Inman Park streets like a gunshot.

I climbed stiffly into the front seat and barely had the door shut before the van lurched away from the curb.

"Keep it up, old woman," I warned. "This street is crawling with cops. One more traffic ticket and the insurance company won't let you drive so much as a three-wheeler."

She snorted, but slowed down to forty as we careened down DeKalb Avenue toward the midtown senior citizens' high-rise where the Easterbrooks sisters lived.

When we got home I ran the hottest bath I could stand and soaked until I looked like one of those golden raisins. It took thirty minutes to get the smell of that house out of my nostrils.

I went right to bed but after half an hour of wrestling with sheets, pillows, and blankets, I gave up and padded bare-footed into the darkened den.

Edna sat bolt upright in the big red plaid armchair, staring intently at the Sony twenty-seven-inch color set she'd been given for a birthday present that fall.

"Shh," she cautioned, turning briefly my way.

"They're talking about our murder. Team coverage. That must mean it's a big story."

"Team coverage means it's either a slow news night or this rocket scientist here," I said, gesturing toward the television, "is such a dim bulb that they don't trust him to handle the story by himself."

She shot me the look then, so I sat down on the sofa and wrapped an afghan around my feet.

On television, Eagle's Keep looked like something out of a Charles Addams cartoon. All the lights glowed an eerie yellow, and the glare of television cameras picked out a set of evil-looking gargoyles on the front porch that I'd overlooked earlier in the day. A series of blue swirls played across the front of the house from the revolving lights of the police cars parked at the curb, and they'd roped off the front of the house with yellow crime-scene tape.

A tall, slim, olive-skinned man in a tightly belted trench coat stood at the steps to the mansion, just outside the tape, holding a hand mike to his lips. "Ricardo Hill for News Center Six," he was saying. "And so," he added, in the hushed tones of a golf match announcer, "once again tragedy stalks the historic halls of Eagle's Keep."

Edna leaned forward, the better to absorb every nanosecond of the unfolding television drama.

Ricardo Hill tilted his head up slightly, to give the audience a better look at his adorable $200,000-a-year dimpled chin. His black eyes snapped with excitement. "Sources tell us that a maid, employed by the owner of the mansion, prominent Atlanta antiques dealer Elliot Littlefield, found the nude body of . . . "

"It's a cleaning service, you twit," I commented to the television. "You could at least give the House Mouse a plug." I lurched across toward my mother. "Give me that remote control, Ma, let's check the other channels."

"Shut up, dammit," Edna hissed. "I'm trying to watch

this. You can go in the kitchen to watch if you can't be quiet in here."

While the two of us argued over the remote control, the camera switched to a scene that appeared to be a teenage party that had spilled onto the lawn of a typical suburban ranch house. A toothy blonde in a sedate black suit stood in the midst of a ring of weeping teenage girls and obviously embarrassed boys.

"Heather Hathaway live from Dunwoody," the blonde was saying, adjusting her face to properly reflect the tragedy of the moment. "All Saints Prep School students attending a birthday party of a classmate at the exclusive preparatory school were shocked and stunned tonight to hear of the senseless death of their former classmate, sixteen-year-old Bridget Marie Dougherty."

"She was seventeen," I started, but I shut up when it looked as though Edna might bludgeon me with the ashtray she held in her lap.

The two of us watched silently then as the earnest young newscaster interviewed teary-eyed girls who recited the predictable elegy to a fallen classmate.

"Really a sweet girl . . . loved animals . . . never had a bad word to say about anyone."

With difficulty, I pushed myself off the couch. "I can't stand any more of this, Ma. I'm going back to bed," I said, stretching and yawning. But I stayed standing, staring at the TV.

The news didn't get any cheerier. A bag boy at a supermarket on Covington Highway had been shot in the head trying to stop a shoplifter from leaving the store with six dollars' worth of frozen perch and the Dodgers had blanked the Braves, six-nothing.

"If you're done watching the news now, how about switching it to The Movie Channel? I think *The Thin Man* festival is still going on."

Reluctantly, she handed the remote control over to me. "I thought you were going to bed."

"I was, but it's a waste of time with this headache. I think I'll stay up and watch Nick and Nora for a while."

Edna got to her feet and moved toward the hall. "I'll get you some aspirin, then I'm going to bed. Myrna Loy depresses me. She never got old."

"Thanks," I told her departing form. "There's a new bottle of Tylenol in the medicine cabinet in my bathroom."

I let my head sink into the sofa cushions and tried to remember the relaxation exercises I'd learned to try to help with my headaches.

My toenails and kneecaps were loosened and I was working my way toward the bellybutton when I heard a clicking noise in front of my nose. I opened my eyes and focused on a large brown plastic pill bottle, which my mother was rattling in rage.

"And just what are these?" Edna said, her speech clipped.

"You know what they are," I said, closing my eyes in the hopes of avoiding an argument.

"Yes, I know it's the pills your oncologist prescribed on your last visit," Edna said. "What I want to know is why are there so many pills in this bottle? It's nearly full, Jules, and it says on the label that you're supposed to take three a day."

I opened my eyes again and returned my mother's hostile glare.

"Look, Ma. I'm a big girl now. Nearly thirty-five. I don't need my mama to make me take my medicine. Just leave me alone, all right?"

"Just tell me why, that's all I ask. Why do you refuse to listen to your doctors? Do you want to have your breasts hacked off like mine were? Is that what you want?" She was in tears now, but she wouldn't back away.

I rubbed my eyes tiredly. "The pills make me sick. I mean really sick, Edna. I was having hot flashes, my mouth was dry, I was nauseated and dizzy all the time. I can't run a business that way."

"Did you talk to Dr. Kappler about it?" she demanded. "What did he say?"

I laughed bitterly. "'Some mildly unpleasant side effects,' he said. Mildly unpleasant, my ass. I'd like to have someone give him a monster dose of hormones and God knows what all and see him function. I told him the pills make me sick; he told me the pills are necessary to keep my blood count right and that lots of women take them. End of story."

She folded her arms across her chest and started to say something, but I cut her off. "I don't need the pills, anyway. My last blood test was fine. Perfectly normal."

"Fine," Edna snarled. "You're such a smart girl. You know more than doctors with what, twenty years of education and training? You, Miss four years of University of Georgia, know more than doctors from Emory and Duke and Vanderbilt. I don't know why we ever bothered to send you to college. Should have made you stay home and learn a trade."

I tossed the remote control onto the coffee table and eased my way out of my armchair, off toward the hall, away from my mother's insistent voice. "I changed my mind again, I think I will go to bed after all. Guess I'll get my own Tylenol."

Halfway down the hallway I felt something strike my shoulder, then I heard a rattling sound as the plastic pill bottle fell and rolled down the wooden floor.

In the doorway of the den, Edna was silhouetted in the blue light of the television set. "Night night," she called. "Don't let the cancer bugs bite."

6

THE WELCOMING SCENT of bacon grease and hot biscuits wafted out the steamed-up door of the Korner Kafe. I pushed open the door, grabbed a Sunday paper from a wire rack near the door and plopped myself down in a wobbly wooden chair at a table by the window.

On most weekends, the KK, as it's known in the neighborhood, is jam-packed for breakfast, with the waiting overflow spilling out onto the curb outside. For some reason, the Kafe's stained linoleum floors, chipped Formica dinette sets and grease-and-cholesterol-laden menu seems to exert some kind of reverse snob appeal charm on the Volvo and BMW set.

Fortunately, it was raining out, a fine chilly mist, and the yupsters had apparently decided to fire up their espresso machines at home. Two or three other tables were taken and the counter was occupied with a handful of silent types seated with empty seats on either side. Everybody was quiet, slurping his or her runny eggs, sipping coffee, minding his or her own business.

Which suited me fine today. Ever since the doctors had diagnosed the small lump on my right breast as malignant a year ago, my mother has nagged at me like a canker sore that won't go away. My surgeon had done a lumpectomy and the diagnosis had been very early ductal carcinoma. The cancer hadn't spread, hadn't touched my lymph nodes at all; and my doctor and I were optimistic that things were going well. I'd been getting radiation therapy; no picnic, but then it wasn't chemo either. The only cloud on the horizon was the drug he'd recently prescribed: cyclo-something. I'd told him how awful the stuff made me feel, but my complaints were getting me nowhere.

"It's a highly effective drug," Dr. Kappler had assured me. "Thousands of women take it with no problems at all." But I was having problems. The pills were playing hell with my hormones. I was having hot flashes, the works. And the drug was starting to affect my sex life. Dr. Kappler, my oncologist, is in his early sixties. Rich Drescher, my family doctor and an old friend, had recommended him as a medical genius, an authority on breast cancer. Kappler's medicine might have been up to date, but he didn't have a clue about how women live in the 1990s. Since I was unmarried, he didn't see why it was a problem that sex had become painful. But Mac and I thought it was a big problem. He'd been understanding and patient, but voluntary chastity isn't Andrew McAuliffe's idea of a good time. Nor is it mine.

After weeks of my bitching and moaning, Dr. Kappler had finally admitted that since my most recent blood test had been normal, I could forgo the hated cyclo-whatever. I'd felt much better since then, and things were back to normal between Mac and me. Now Edna was the problem.

She was on my case all the time. Clipping articles from women's magazines about breast cancer, asking whether I was still doing daily breast self-exams, and always second-guessing the choices I'd made about living with my disease. It's understandable, in a way. My grandmother had died of breast cancer when Edna was just a teenager; she herself had undergone a mastectomy before she was forty. So when the lump was found to be malignant, she'd begged me to go ahead and have a mastectomy. "Let 'em take it," she'd urged. "It's just a boob. You don't want to be worrying about the cancer coming back for the rest of your life."

But my breast surgeon, Rich Drescher, and Dr. Kappler had all agreed: the cancer was early, microinvasive, and the lump was small. The best course was the most conservative; even if it did make my mother crazy with concern.

Edna was already gone when I woke up that morning, probably to one of my brothers' or sisters' houses. She does that when she's ticked off at me—takes off and doesn't come back till she's ready.

"Coffee, hon?" The voice startled me. Karol, the Kafe's owner-manager-chef-waitress, flashed me something close to a smile.

"Yeah, thanks," I said, pushing the newspaper aside so she could fill my thick china mug.

"You eatin'?" she asked.

I flicked my eyes over the wall-mounted menu, even though I always end up ordering the same thing. "Two eggs with cheese, scrambled, bacon, home fries, biscuits. You got any orange juice?"

She rolled her eyes in exasperation. "I'll see," she said, but her voice promised nothing.

The scalding coffee burned the tip of my tongue. I let it cool while I worked my way through the newspaper, only half-paying attention to the Saturday rundown of the previous day's mayhem.

And then the headline caught my eye. CONTRO-VERSIAL BREAST CANCER DRUG TO BE OFFERED IN EXPERIMENTAL STUDY.

I scanned the story quickly, my excitement mounting. The story said that the National Cancer Institute was launching a massive drug trial to see if a drug called tamoxifen could prevent breast cancer in women at high risk.

The story sounded too good to be true. Here was a drug already being used for women over sixty who'd had cancer, and now researchers thought it might also pre-vent at least one-third of expected breast cancers from ever developing.

Unconsciously, my hand went to my right breast, to the tiny line of scar tissue.

I'd been lucky. My kind of cancer had a 95 percent five-year survival rate, good news since I still had another twenty-five years to run on my mortgage. I'd gone through six weeks of radiation therapy immedi-ately after the surgery, and I'd suffered little or no side effects. I'd been ecstatic when my doctor told me I could skip chemotherapy. My hair, thick, black, and curly like my father's, is one of my few vanities. Privately, I dreaded losing my hair almost as much as I did a breast. Silly, stupid woman.

Somewhere along the way, Karol brought my food. I guess I ate it because when I'd finished reading the paper, all that was left of my breakfast was a greasy egg-colored smear on the heavy china plate.

I went back over the newspaper story, slowly this time, reading aloud the important parts. The study would involve sixteen thousand women, some of whom would be premenopausal women ages thirty-five and older. I'd be thirty-five in July. And I was damn sure premenopausal, the last time I'd checked. They wanted women who'd already had breast cancer or a family history of the disease. I was a double-dipper. Lucky, lucky me.

Tamoxifen. I folded the paper against the edge of the table and tore the article out. According to the newspaper, this drug did everything for women except take out their garbage and rotate their tires. It was an estrogen-blocker and was also effective for developing stronger bones and in helping reduce cholesterol levels.

When I stepped outside the café, the rain had stopped and the sun was making a weak attempt to poke through a gray-edged cloud cover. On the walk home I tried to pick up the pace, striding briskly and swinging my arms in a half-hearted attempt at physical fitness. Tomorrow, I told myself. I'll think about that tomorrow.

Back at home, a boat-size white Chrysler LeBaron was parked in the driveway behind my van. The prodigal mother had returned.

She didn't look up when I walked into the kitchen; just bent her head and acted like she was fascinated with the Dentu-Creme coupon she was clipping out of the paper.

"You not talking to me?"

"That's right," she said evenly.

"Okay. Just checking." If she wanted to be that way, I wouldn't tell her about the wonder drug I'd just discovered.

I felt at loose ends. Mac was gone, Edna was pissed at me, and Paula, my best friend, had gone down to St. Simon's Island with another friend to lay in the sun and slurp margaritas.

"You wanna catch a show with me?" I asked Edna, who was lighting up a cigarette and studiously avoiding my eyes. "The new Michael Douglas flick is on at the

Plaza. Two bucks if we go before two P.M., senior citizens get a fifty-cent discount."

"You forget I'm not speaking to you," she said.

"Perfect," I said, trying to stay pleasant. "It's a movie. You're not supposed to talk. I'll buy the popcorn."

The phone rang before she could reconsider my offer.

"Miss Garrity?"

I recognized the voice at the other end of the line as the master of Eagle's Keep.

"Mr. Littlefield?"

"Very good," he said dryly. "I'm impressed. I'm calling for two reasons. First, I'd like to apologize for last night. It was a horrible shock for me, and I'm certain for your girls, too. But if you're not violently opposed to the idea, I'd like to have you come back and finish the work. I'll pay extra, of course, for your inconvenience."

"What about your party?" I asked.

"Naturally, I had to cancel," he said, permitting himself a small sigh. "But one of the other women in the neighborhood, whose house is also on tour, agreed to move the whole thing over to her house. I just finished taking the last of the petit fours over there."

"How nice," I said. "But I'm afraid we've got a full schedule booked this week. I really don't see how we can fit you in. . . ."

Edna pushed the appointment book across the table toward me, and jabbed a finger at Monday. She'd penciled through Neva Jean's standing Monday morning job at the Cataldos'. "They're in Florida," she mouthed.

"Wait," I said reluctantly. "Actually, my office manager just pointed out that Neva Jean has a cancellation tomorrow. I suppose if we called in one of our part-time girls to help her we could manage to finish up."

"Fine," he said, interrupting. "Now about the other matter. Captain Hunsecker mentioned in passing last night that you're also a private investigator. And it looks as though I'm going to be needing some help."

"I'm sorry," I said, taking my own turn at interrupting. "I can't get involved in an active homicide investigation. If the cops found out I was messing around in their case, I could lose my state certification. Besides, I'm not really taking any new cases right now."

Actually, I wasn't really being offered any new cases. My most recent foray into the wonderful world of private detecting had been helping an old friend gather evidence against her ex-husband, who'd been welshing on his child-support agreement all the time he was building a lake home with his twenty-two-year-old second wife. I'd been trying to get out of investigating and back to grime fighting for the past year, but shit kept happening.

"I'll pay you very, very well," Littlefield said, appealing to my baser nature. "And anyway, it's not the homicide I'm worried about." He paused for a second. "That sounds terrible, doesn't it? As though I don't care who killed poor Bridget. What I meant to say was that I understand how these things work. I've been through this before, you know. What I meant to say was, I'd like your assistance regarding the burglary."

"That's still a matter for the police, not me," I said.

"Miss Garrity, you were a detective in the burglary squad. I checked you out," Littlefield said. "You know from your own experience that the detectives will have nothing to go on to look for my property. These are Civil War–era antiques. Weapons, military artifacts, and an incredibly rare and valuable diary. I believe I mentioned it to you before. The homicide detectives are going to be concentrating on finding Bridget's murderer. Fine. Nobody wants this animal caught more than I. But it is imperative that I recover my property.

The diary; it's the most important piece I've ever handled. It could change the way historians look at the social history of the war . . . "

"Yes," Edna was saying in a loud stage whisper. "Tell him yes."

"I'd like to meet with you, as soon as possible, to discuss this," Littlefield was saying.

"All right," I said, caving in. "When?"

"This afternoon," he said. "Would four o'clock work for you? We've got the final skirmish of the Battle of Kennesaw. I'm the general so it's not something I can get out of, not that I want to. We've been looking forward to this for months now. Why don't you meet me over here then?"

7

"W HAT?" EDNA DEMANDED, as I put the receiver back on the hook.

"Are you on speaking terms with me?" I inquired, as I headed back down the hallway to change out of my drizzle-dampened jeans.

"Shove it," she said sweetly. "What's Littlefield want besides his house cleaned? Are we gonna do a little detecting?"

"Me. Julia Callahan Garrity. Not you," I said. "Not House Mouse. He wants me to find the stuff stolen during last night's burglary."

"Such as?" She lit up a cigarette and managed one deep, unhealthy drag before I crossed the room in a single stride, yanked the cigarette out of her fingers and stubbed it out in an empty coffee cup on my bedside table. "For Christ's sake, Ma," I said. "I can't keep you from smoking in the rest of the house, but you know I hate smoke in my bedroom."

"Don't get your panties in a wad. So what kind of stuff is missing? Jewelry, antiques, bonds, what?"

"I'm supposed to go over there this afternoon, around four, after he gets done playing Civil War games with the other boys," I told her. "As soon as I know, you'll know," I promised, running my fingers through my hair in an attempt to tame the tangle.

"Now what about the movie? Are we on or not? The show starts in fifteen minutes, and Paula says if you miss the beginning you might as well not go. It's a suspense thing."

She looked down at her watch. "Why not?" she said, shrugging. "I'm still not talking to you, though."

"Good," I said, picking my purse up from the dresser where I'd tossed it the night before. "For once maybe I'll be able to follow the story line without you jabbering in my ear."

"I'm not even sitting in the same row with you," she retorted, following me down the hall toward the front door.

As I was turning the lock in the key, she dug furiously in her purse. "Hey," she said, a trace more friendly than she had been. "You got any cash? I'm short."

I handed her a crumpled bill. "Here. That's five dollars. And don't be running to me for more when your popcorn runs out."

She snatched the five out of my fingers and crammed it in the pocket of her slacks. "Ungrateful little snot. I shoulda put you up for adoption when I had a chance."

For a Sunday matinee, the fare was long on naked romping and short on suspense. Edna was standing in the lobby finishing off a cigarette when I came out of the darkened theater.

A wave of humid heat greeted us once we left the air-conditioned lobby.

"Whew," Edna said, fanning herself. "It must be about a hundred degrees out here. Let's get in the car and get that air-conditioning cranked up."

"Sorry," I said. She grimaced. "I can't wait till we

make some real money and you can trade in that piece of crap van."

She bitched and moaned about the heat the whole way home, fanning herself furiously with a folded-up newspaper.

"We'll have something cold for dinner," she said, as I unlocked the back door. "It's too hot to turn on the oven."

I left her in the kitchen, debating to herself about chicken salad versus a nice fruit plate.

It was 3:45. Just enough time to dab a cold wet washcloth on my face and the back of my neck before time to head over to Littlefield's.

Inman Park was eerily quiet for a Sunday afternoon. The unseasonable heat had driven the lawn mowers, flower planters, and garden putterers back inside their homes. Two young kids rode by me on their bicycles, but they were the only ones out on the street.

I got out of the car and rang the doorbell at Eagle's Keep. No answer. I'd been punctual, but maybe Littlefield's period war games were running late. Maybe he'd rewritten the script and the Rebels were whipping Yankee butt clear back to Lookout Mountain in Tennessee.

I sat back in the van to wait. The kids rode by again, and then again a third time. It finally dawned on me that Eagle's Keep had become a murder scene, making it instantly fascinating to any kid over the age of six. I looked around in the van for something to read, but I'd cleaned it the previous week in an uncharacteristic fit of tidiness.

I was hot. My blouse was sticking to my back and the backs of my legs were sticking to the seat. Bored, I shut my eyes and decided to take a short nap.

Right at the gates to dreamland, I heard a car's

engine, followed by the sound of slamming doors. I opened my eyes and saw a knot of gray-uniformed men emerging from a beat-up gray pickup truck parked in Littlefield's driveway.

Two of the men went around to the bed of the truck where two more were lifting something up. "Careful," one of them roared. "If you drop this sumbitch we'll all have hell to pay."

"Get his legs, Ray," ordered one of the men in the truck bed. Grunting, the men lifted the slackened body of Elliot Longstreet Littlefield out of the truck, and began carrying it around to the back of the house.

"What happened?" I asked when I caught up to them at the back door.

"Heat stroke," said the Johnny Reb who was rifling through one of Littlefield's uniform pockets. The man was short and squat, with a full grizzled gray beard and frizzy gray hair that hung down to his shoulders. His uniform was grease-spattered and sweat-drenched, and he smelled like the loser at a day-long goat-roping. "Sumbitch passed out cold right in the middle of our charge up the mountain."

I looked down at Littlefield. The laird of Eagle's Keep wore a splendid blue wool frock coat with double rows of brass buttons and three gold stars on the cream-colored stand-up collar. His tight-fitting trousers were wool too and he wore soft black-leather knee boots. His face was pale and damp and his breathing shallow. In the fierce midday heat, he'd simmered in his own juices just like a Sunday pot roast.

The grizzled Reb looked at me with interest. "Say, lady, are you a neighbor? We need to get the general here in the house, where it's cool, but I can't seem to find his house key."

I shook my head. "Sorry, no. I'm an, uh, business

associate. I had an appointment with Mr. Littlefield. Did you check the pockets of his coat?"

The Reb patted Littlefield's waist until he felt a slight bulge. He smiled triumphantly as he dug out a small ring of keys. A large brass key glittered from the smaller, more modern ones. "Try that one," I suggested.

As the door swung open, I remembered the burglar alarm. Looking quickly around the kitchen, I spotted a nondescript white control panel beside the refrigerator and turned the key that had been left in it to disarm the system.

The men stood dumbly in the center of the kitchen, their patient's bottom sagging on the floor. "What'll we do with him?" the group's spokesman wanted to know.

I looked around helplessly. A white-painted door near the butler's pantry was slightly ajar. I pushed it open. The room was small, with faded floral wallpaper and a quilt-covered iron bed. The former maid's room, no doubt.

"In here," I gestured.

The men filled the small room quickly, unceremoniously dumping their general on top of the quilt.

"Gotta get back," the grizzled veteran said. "We'll call later to see how he's doing. Tell him Billy Dobbs was the one brought him home. Ought to be good for a citation or something."

The men left as quickly as they'd come.

Back in the kitchen, I bit my lip and called my younger sister Maureen.

Maureen is a registered nurse. She works in the emergency room at Grady Memorial Hospital, the city's biggest charity hospital, and she's married to a jerk of an ambulance driver.

Our relationship is not what you could call close. Still, she is a nurse.

Fortunately she answered the phone. "Quick," I demanded. "What do I do for somebody who has heat stroke?"

"Hello, dear sister," she drawled. "I'm fine thanks. Steve sends his love too. Who's got heat stroke? That old man boyfriend of yours? Were you two doing the nasty out in the back of your van?"

"Cute," I said. "You're too cute for words. But it's too complicated to get into right now. Just tell me what to do."

She sighed. "I should charge you for this, you know. How's his color?"

I glanced into the bedroom. "He looks like something out of Madame Tussaud's museum. Is that bad?"

"Not good," she said. "Breathing steady?"

"Shallow and jerky," I said.

"Okay," she said briskly. "Get some cold wet cloths and put them on all his pulse points; forehead, neck, inside of his elbows and his wrists. Keep the cloths cool and wet and get him out of his clothes if possible."

"That's it?" I said. "I thought you were supposed to put people in a tub of ice or something."

"Do something that drastic and you can put them into shock," Maureen snapped.

"How about something to drink? Should I pour some Coke or something down his gullet?"

She laughed. "Only if you want it barfed right back up in your face. See if you can put some ice chips in his mouth. Chips, not cubes. And call a doctor. You're no Clara Barton. Gotta go now."

I followed orders. Maureen may be a sniveler and a whiner, but she knows her stuff as far as emergency medicine. I was trying to pry Littlefield's lips open for the ice chips when his eyes fluttered open.

"What happened?" he asked, looking down at his nearly naked, washcloth-draped form. I'd managed to remove the sweat-soaked frock coat and the boots, but the trousers were a tight fit.

I'd had to settle for just unbuttoning the fly.

"Heat stroke," I said, getting up from the bed. "Your men said you passed out cold during the charge up the hill. They brought you back here and dumped you. I'm supposed to call a doctor for you. Got any suggestions?"

The old iron bedsprings creaked loudly as Littlefield eased himself under the quilt. "Ow, goddamn," he said.

"What?" I asked in alarm. I'd come to Eagle's Keep for a business meeting, not sick call.

"I must have done something to my back," he said. "I had a ruptured disc a few years ago. It hurts like hell again."

"Who should I call?" I asked.

"In the night stand in my bedroom, there's a bottle of pills, some painkillers from the last time I had this thing. Bring me the bottle and a glass of water. While you're upstairs, look in the Rolodex, it's on the desk in my office, and get the number for my doctor. George Koteras, with a K. Call and tell him what happened and ask him if he can come over."

"It's Sunday," I reminded him. "I'll only get his answering service."

"His home number is on the card," Littlefield said. "He's an old friend. He'll come. While you're at my desk, you'll see a manila file folder on top of a stack of papers. Bring it downstairs. It's what I wanted to talk to you about in the first place."

"Please," I muttered, as I picked my way past the clothes and papers strewn in the stairway. "And thank you." Apparently Littlefield's imitation of a Southern gentleman extended only to appearances, and not petty matters of etiquette.

I tried to avoid touching the smears of fingerprint powder on the stair banister and the walls, which meant walking in the middle of the staircase, an odd feeling.

On the second floor, things had been tidied a little bit. The quilted maroon satin comforter on the bed had even been pulled over the sheets in a quick attempt at neatness.

The pill bottle was where Littlefield had promised it would be. My fingers itched to go through the rest of the stuff in the drawer; envelopes, a couple other pill bottles, and a slim book that looked like some kind of appointment diary, but I forced myself to pay attention to the job at hand.

The mess in the office hadn't been touched. It took me five minutes of digging to unearth the Rolodex.

George Koteras was home, fortunately. "Passed out on Kennesaw Mountain?" he bellowed into the phone. I could hear laughter and the clatter of dishes in the background. He'd been having Sunday dinner.

I repeated the details of Littlefield's problems and described the first aid treatment I'd supplied.

"Now he's saying his back hurts. He wants me to give him some of the painkillers he had after his back injury."

Koteras didn't seem terribly concerned that his patient might perish from heat stroke. "Elliot Littlefield is the luckiest bastard in Atlanta," he boomed. "All right. Give him a couple of those pocket rockets. Tell him to sip some fluids. Slowly. The pills should numb up his back for a while. I'll be over as soon as the birthday candles are blown out. It's my grandson's fourth birthday. Give me an hour. You gonna hang around until I get there?"

I looked at the brass ship's clock on Littlefield's desk;

it was nearly five. But someone would have to be around to let the doctor in, and after last night, I felt uneasy about leaving Littlefield there, drugged and suffering the effect of heat stroke, with the door unlocked.

"I'll be here."

Littlefield took the pills gratefully, along with a glass of water, and nodded his approval when I told him I would stay to let Koteras in.

"You bring that folder?"

I showed it to him.

"Good. There's a list of the things taken in the burglary, along with a description and an appraisal value."

I opened the folder. The typed list was short, but full of expensive goodies.

I read aloud. "One Cofer revolver, brass trigger guard, percussion pistol, twenty thousand dollars." I raised my eyebrows in disbelief. "Twenty thousand? This isn't a typo?"

"An extremely rare piece," he said calmly. "Museum quality. But then, most of what I handle is."

I read on. "One Cook and Brother carbine long arm. Value seven thousand five hundred. One W. J. McElroy Confederate cavalry officer's saber with etched blade and scabbard, made in Macon, Georgia, twelve thousand. One presentation shooting trophy, coin silver, inscribed to Captain Frederick Reaber, CSA, bearing the seal of the state of Georgia, twelve thousand. One Oglethorpe Light Infantry cartridge box plate, five thousand.

"That's over fifty-six thousand dollars' worth of stuff, right there. You mentioned a document was taken also, but I don't see it on the list."

"Look at the next sheet of paper," he said, sipping from the water glass.

It was a letter, from the curator of the special collections at the University of Georgia library. It appeared to be a written bid, offering Littlefield $150,000 for the following:

One diary; black leather binding, some wear but otherwise good condition, being the wartime journal of Lula Belle Bird, of Richmond, Va. containing journal entries dating from Sept. 1862 to March 1865. Bid subject to authentication of document.

"A diary? A woman's Civil War diary is worth one hundred and fifty thousand dollars? Who was this woman, Robert E. Lee's love slave?"

"Not quite," he said. "And one fifty is just one bid. I'm still waiting for bids to come in from two other universities as well as some private collectors. This diary is the talk of every collector in the country. You see, Lula Belle Boynton Bird was an educated young woman, a member of an aristocratic South Carolina cotton planting family. She married early and was widowed before the war started. She was not your typical Southern belle. Sometime in the late 1850s, she moved to Richmond and bought a house on Marshall Street, in quite a respectable neighborhood. The first time we find her name on the tax rolls is 1859. To make the story short, by the time the war was under way, she was running what was, by some accounts, one of the more prosperous bawdy houses in Richmond."

"A prostitute," I said wonderingly. "Is that why the diary is so valuable; because she was a prostitute? The diary is sort of a Civil War–era *Happy Hooker*?"

"Not just a prostitute," Littlefield said sharply. "As you may know, Richmond and other large Southern cities near Confederate encampments were hotbeds of prostitution. In some places, they were a real wartime menace.

Some units were decimated by the number of men out on sick call from venereal disease. Nashville was so plagued by prostitutes during the three years it was occupied by Union troops that two hospitals treated nothing but patients with venereal disease. But Lula Belle Bird was a madam; not some illiterate country street strut. Researchers today are dying to get their hands on a diary like this. Historians know plenty about Robert E. Lee and Jefferson Davis. A diary like this sheds a whole new light on the social history of the Confederate capital, and it's written from the point of view of an educated, liberated woman. It's a Holy Grail–quality find."

"Speaking of find," I said, trying to make my voice sound casual. "How'd you come across such a treasure?"

"Proprietary information," he said. "The buyer will be given the diary's full provenance. I can assure you, it was acquired through perfectly legal channels."

"Hey," I said, changing what was obviously a sensitive subject. "Do the diaries mention any of Lula Belle's clients? Like any famous generals or anything?"

Littlefield smiled wanly. "You thought of that, did you? Actually, the few pages I was able to read gave only initials for her regular clients. But the diary is written in such a cramped, spidery script, it's nearly unreadable. As the war went on, paper became scarcer and scarcer, so she wrote in between lines and up the margins. Before the burglary, I was in the process of finding a researcher to prepare a typescript so that prospective buyers could read the thing."

I smoothed the folds of the two pieces of paper. "Can I keep these for my file?"

"Of course," he said, his voice sounding a bit woozy.

I pulled out my notepad and started scribbling notes to myself. "Were all the stolen items taken from the same place?"

He furrowed his brow in an effort to concentrate. "No. As you saw, the whole house had been ransacked. It was a bit of a mess before yesterday, but nothing like what you saw. Let me see. The weapons were all kept in a glass-fronted display case in the third floor library. I kept the silver presentation cup and the saber on the mantel in my bedroom. The cartridge box plate, let me think now, I believe it might have been in a display case in the guest room where Bridget was . . . found."

"And the diary?"

"The diary should have been in a safe in the shop," Littlefield said. "But I'd brought it in the house. Since I bought it I haven't been able to keep my hands off it. It's the most fascinating thing I've ever read. What with the preparations for the tour and battle reenactment coming up, I never put it back in the safe. It was in a wooden document box, on top of my desk in the library."

"So everything that was taken was out in plain view?" I asked.

He nodded yes.

"But the burglars turned the place upside down. Interesting. Was there something more valuable that they might have been looking for?"

"I thought of that," Littlefield admitted. "There are other more valuable things in the house, but they were out in plain sight too. It doesn't make any sense. Take the silver for instance. It's in the sideboard in the dining room, made in Savannah in the early nineteenth century. It's worth tens of thousands. And in the library, there were several other weapons they didn't touch, not to mention my collection of Confederate imprints."

"What are those?"

"Remember I told you, paper was scarce in the South during the later war years? The Yankees had burned the paper mills and rags were needed for bandages. Books, pamphlets, even sheet music published in the Confederacy were extremely scarce and today they're quite collectible and valuable. None of mine were touched. And, of course, nothing in the carriage house, where the shop is, was touched. The police checked, the alarm system was on and nothing was tampered with. The most valuable pieces I have are kept there."

I glanced back over the list. "Can you make out any rhyme or reason for what was taken? Any idea who might have done it?"

"As I told your friend Captain Hunsecker, I have no idea who could have done this. There's quite a black market for Civil War antiques, but I find it hard to believe anyone would murder an innocent young girl to get their hands on the things that were taken; particularly since they left behind so much else that was of value."

I studied Littlefield's profile. He was disturbed, obviously, about what had happened at Eagle's Keep. I found it hard to believe he was responsible for the murder or the burglary.

"You realize that you're the cops' primary suspect, don't you?"

His eyelids fluttered as he tried to fight off the effect of the pain pills. "I know. As I told you last night, I didn't do it. And I won't allow myself to be arrested and tried a second time."

"You won't allow it," I repeated.

"No," he said simply. "I won't."

"Before I forget," I said. "I was supposed to tell you that Billy Dobbs and his men were the ones who brought you back here from Kennesaw Mountain. Dobbs seemed highly pleased with himself, but they were slinging you around in that truck like a fifty-pound sack of yams. They actually had you lying in the truck bed the whole way back from Kennesaw. I'm not surprised your back is hurting."

"Dobbs," he said drowsily, "I should have known."

"Who is he?" I asked.

"The dishonorable and disreputable Major Billy Dobbs, spiritual and de facto leader of the Ninety-sixth Georgia Infantry, better known as the Lost Mountain Volunteers."

"That's another reenactment unit?"

"You could say that," he said. "My unit is the Gate City Old Guard. A group of MOSB members started our outfit a few years ago. We like to think of ourselves as a fairly elite outfit. Not like the Lost Mountain boys."

"MOSB," I repeated. "What's that?"

"Military Order of the Stars and Bars," he said, tripping the words from his tongue with obvious pleasure. "To be a member you have to have a relative who was a Confederate commissioned officer."

"That's like the UDC?" I asked innocently. I'd won a medal for patriotism in junior high school from the local chapter of the United Daughters of the Confederacy and had spent my high school years trying to live down the fact that I'd won the biggest dweeb award of all.

Littlefield rolled his eyes in disdain. He must have met the UDC ladies who'd given me my medal. "No. The MOSB likes to think of its membership as a little more upscale. The UDC is more the female equivalent of the SCV. Sons of Confederate Veterans," he added quickly.

"And the Lost Mountain Boys are sort of riffraff?"

"They're a joke," he said quickly. "A ragtag bunch of yahoos. They put on blue jeans, work boots, and butternut jackets and consider themselves historically attired.

They camp in those tuna-can campers, play loud country music all night, and shoot off their weapons at the slightest provocation. They are, to be exact, a bunch of ill-kempt, bad-mannered ignorant lowlifes, who only come out here to wave the Rebel flag, smoke dope, get drunk, and raise hell."

I suppressed the urge to ask if that wasn't the general idea for Civil War reenactors, who I'd always thought of as pathetic champions of a brutal, but thankfully lost, cause.

"If they're such pigs, why let 'em in?" I asked. "Why not tell them to take their toys and go home?"

"Because," he said grimly, "Billy Dobbs's granddaddy owns the farmland where we reenact. The National Park Service won't allow us on the actual battlefield. It is, to borrow your metaphor, Dobbs's ball and Dobbs's yard."

Littlefield's eyes closed and I thought he'd gone to sleep. I got up quietly to leave the room.

"You don't approve of reenacting," he said.

I turned around. He'd propped himself up on one elbow. "No offense, but I think it's a pretty damn childish way for grown men to spend their days, but like the man said, different strokes for different folks."

"Reenactment groups do tend to attract some odd types," he admitted. "But we're not all like Billy Dobbs. Most of us are in it because we have a lifelong fascination with history. In fact, the majority of my men have ancestors who fought for the Confederacy, even died for it. I'd say most of us just want to preserve the memory of southerners who died for a cause they believed in. Is that so wrong?"

I shook my head in disbelief. "Wasn't that noble cause our ancestors fought for a shameful little institution called slavery?"

Littlefield yawned loudly. "The war was about much more than slavery. Anyone with even a cursory knowledge of Civil War history knows that. But for people like you it always comes down to slavery, doesn't it? I suppose you're one of those types who want to ban the display of the Stars and Bars, or the playing of 'Dixie.' Don't you have any pride at all in your Southern heritage?"

"It's not the flag I mind, and actually, I have a sentimental spot in my heart for Dixie," I said evenly. "It's just the race-baiting unreconstructed Rebels that I object to," I said. "Seems to me they've wrapped themselves in the Rebel flag as a substitute for Klan robes. Symbolism's the same, but the flag's just a little more socially acceptable. And no, I don't particularly like the glorification of a war fought largely by poor, ignorant dirt farmers who died a long way from home for a cause they never understood."

I'd expected my speechifying to throw Littlefield into a tantrum, but apparently, I'd underestimated him. I tend to do that with men.

He put his head back down on the pillow. "I disagree," he said tiredly. "These pills must be kicking in. Want you to bill me for all this time, too," he said.

"I intend to," I said quickly. "Can you answer a few questions about Bridget Dougherty before you go to sleep?"

"I'm really exhausted," he said sharply.

"What was she like?" I asked, ignoring his pout.

"She was a little girl," he said sadly. "Seventeen. But so, so bright and so eager to learn. I was teaching her about history. Real history, not that fairy tale stuff they teach in schools these days. And antiques. I'll say this about the Doughertys, they surrounded themselves with the best. And Bridget was developing a great eye."

"Did you sleep with her?"

There was a sharpness to my tone that I couldn't understand, but instantly regretted.

A smile flitted across Littlefield's face, annoying me further.

"I see you're familiar with my bad press. That was twenty years ago, you know. A different time and a different sensibility. I doubt you'd understand, even if I was inclined to go into the matter. I can assure you I don't have to sleep with children. I've told the police that too."

"They don't believe you."

"That's their privilege," Littlefield said. Raising one eyebrow, his eyes met mine in the mirror. "What about you?"

"Doesn't matter to me," I lied. "As long as you didn't kill her. And no, for what it's worth, I don't think you did. She wasn't any little innocent though," I offered. "I understand she thought she was pregnant when she ran away from home."

He looked surprised. "You know about that?"

I nodded.

"She wouldn't say who he was," Littlefield said. "We didn't have that kind of relationship. I was her employer. I'm sure she thought I was too ancient to be able to perform sexually. When she told me she thought she was pregnant, she was clearly embarrassed. I offered to loan her the money for an abortion. She was shocked. She'd been raised Catholic, and I don't think abortion had ever even occurred to her."

"Don't be too sure," I said dryly.

"Whatever," he said, with a hint of a shrug. "The day after we talked, she came into the shop, singing and dancing around. She'd told her boyfriend and he was going to take care of her, she said. He'd get a job, and they'd get an apartment together, and everything would be cool."

"Then what?"

"Two days later, she was all teary-eyed again. The pregnancy had been a false alarm. She'd started her period. I couldn't understand why that upset her, but it did. I told her, 'You should be glad, you're too young and smart to be saddled with a baby.'"

"And when did all this happen?"

He considered for a moment. "I guess it was last month."

"Did she tell the boyfriend it was a false alarm?"

"Come to think of it, I don't know. I've been so busy with the tour and the battle reenactment, I don't think I asked. And she didn't volunteer."

"And you have no idea who her boyfriend was?" I repeated.

"No," he said. "I told you. She kept her social life to herself."

"No phone calls or visitors?" I asked incredulously. I have a fourteen-year-old niece myself, and my brother's house seems to have a revolving front door and a telephone that never stops ringing.

"She'd only been here about six weeks," Littlefield said testily. "There was a phone in her room, so I don't know who she talked to. And I made it clear from the beginning that I was operating a business here, so I couldn't have some pimply faced heavy-metal head bangers hanging around all the time."

"How'd she get around?" I asked. "You said she went to estate sales every weekend."

He laughed. "She had a car, if you can call it that. One of those ridiculous Korean hunks of junk. Cherry red."

"A Hyundai?" Obviously a man whose idea of a

clunker was a Range Rover couldn't be bothered to learn the name of every silly little import that hit the streets.

"That's it."

"Where is it now?"

"I haven't given it a thought," Littlefield admitted. "I use the garage for my cars, and the van I use for business takes up the driveway. The parking lot in the back of the carriage house is reserved for customers. She usually parked on the street, wherever she could find a spot. Sometimes she had to park a block or two away, especially on weekends."

"I wonder if the cops impounded it? I don't remember seeing a car like that the other night."

"Does it matter?" he asked. "What's Bridget's car got to do with her murder and my burglary?"

"I don't know," I admitted. "I guess I'm just trying to put the pieces together."

"It seems to me that you should be wondering who took my belongings and where they are now," he said peevishly.

"Leave me alone now, will you?"

"Don't worry, I plan to," I said.

8

GEORGE KOTERAS WAS SHORT and stocky, with a shiny bald head and a pair of hornrimmed glasses that kept sliding down his nose. He wore baggy khaki slacks and a green-and-white awning-striped dress shirt. I'd put him in his late forties or early fifties, but it was hard to tell without seeing his car. Doctors over fifty always drive Mercedes or Lincolns, younger than that and it's usually a Beemer, unless they're a surgeon. Surgeons like the jazzy stuff: Jaguars, Ferraris, like that.

"How's the patient?" he asked, looking around the foyer for a trail of blood or some other evidence of the recent violence that had befallen the House of Littlefield. He wrinkled his nose in distaste at the state of Eagle's Keep.

"He's out like a light," I said. "Sorry about the mess. Mr. Littlefield's between housekeepers right now, and then the house was ransacked during the burglary and all . . . "

"No problem," Koteras said. "Where'd you stash the SOB?"

"Back here," I said, leading the way through the dining room and into Littlefield's improvised sickroom.

The patient's eyelids fluttered heavily when Koteras greeted him. "Those Dilaudids pack a punch," Koteras said. "He won't feel any pain for another three hours or so."

As he spoke, Koteras slipped into the kitchen, washed his hands at the sink, and moved back into the bedroom.

He poked a white plastic probe in Littlefield's ear and waited. A few seconds later it beeped and some numbers appeared on a digital readout screen. "Temperature's back down to normal," he said, glancing at me. "What'd you do?"

"Put some cold wet cloths on his pulse points, gave him some ice to suck on, and stripped him," I said. "My sister's an emergency room nurse, she told me what to do."

Koteras had his fingers on Littlefield's wrist, taking his pulse. "Pulse is all right," he said, not looking up. He reached in the bag he'd carried in, brought out a blood pressure cuff, and proceeded to take the rest of the patient's vital signs.

"So what's the story?" I asked. I was getting itchy to get out of Eagle's Keep.

"He'll probably be fine," Koteras said. "He needs to keep drinking fluids, and to stay quiet for the next twenty-four hours."

"What about scotch?" we heard a weak voice asking. "There's a new bottle of Chivas in the kitchen. I'd like three fingers. You two help yourselves, of course."

Elliot Littlefield was struggling to sit up. Koteras helped.

"No booze," Koteras said. "Come on, I want you to try to stand while I take your blood pressure."

"You already did that," Littlefield protested. "I felt it."

"Now we take it standing to see if there's a difference that we should worry about," Koteras said. "Swing your legs over the side of the bed here, can you?"

Littlefield gathered the sheet around his middle and slid his feet to the floor, wincing. "Goddamn, my back hurts," he complained. "I feel nauseous too."

"Don't be such a fucking baby," Koteras said. "This'll just take a minute. You've probably pulled something playing those ridiculous games of yours," he added.

Littlefield shot me a quick glance. I wanted to tell him he didn't have any equipment I hadn't seen, but I thought better of it.

"I'll, uh, just be out in the kitchen if you need me," I said, backing out of the room.

I found paper towels, rags, Spic and Span and Windex under the kitchen sink. I was scrubbing away at the fingerprint powder on the kitchen door when Koteras came in a few minutes later.

He washed his hands again and dried them on the paper towel I offered.

"By the way," I said. "I guess you're wondering who I am and what I'm doing here."

"You're not Elliot's girlfriend?" He seemed surprised.

"Not hardly," I said. "I'm Callahan Garrity. I'm a private detective." Given the sorry state of Littlefield's house, it didn't seem prudent to mention I was also his new cleaning lady. "Mr Littlefield hired me to try to recover some of the antiques that were stolen here Saturday. I take it you know about the murder and burglary?"

He nodded. "Saw it on the eleven o'clock news. I couldn't believe Elliot'd gotten himself in another mess."

"Did you know him during the first murder investigation?"

"I knew him," Koteras said, methodically rolling his shirt sleeves down and buttoning the cuffs. He picked up his bag then and got ready to go. He paused, then pulled a small pill bottle out of his breast pocket.

"These are antibiotics," he said. "Along with everything else, Elliot picked up some kind of a puncture wound on his leg, probably while he was playing Robert E. Lee today. I've washed it, but I want him to start on these right away to make sure the wound doesn't get infected. He's gone back to sleep right now. When he wakes up, make sure he takes them after he eats something."

"Wait a minute," I said, startled. "I wasn't planning on hanging around any longer. Like I said, I'm not his girlfriend. And I've got stuff to do tonight."

Koteras looked annoyed. "Well, somebody needs to be here when he wakes up. I'd stay myself, but I'm on call tonight and I'm already late to see a patient at Georgia Baptist."

He started for the door as though matters were all settled. Doctor's orders.

"I can't stay," I said loudly.

He shrugged but kept walking. "Not my problem. Make sure he starts those antibiotics. Two tonight, four tomorrow."

The front door thudded shut.

There was a mewing sound in the vicinity of my ankles. The Siamese again. It rubbed up against me, looked up, and winked with its one good eye, then flopped over on its belly, offering itself up to be scratched.

"Beat it," I hissed. The cat squirmed in a fit of happiness. Cats can always tell a cat hater. And that's the first person they attach themselves to in a crowd. It's positively Freudian. Grudgingly, I rubbed the toe of my shoe against its fur. The resulting mew sounded strangely orgasmic.

"Now what?" I asked it. The cat probably had one of those revoltingly cute Chinese names like Me Lei or Ping-Pong or something.

I poked my head in the door of Littlefield's room. At least Koteras had covered him up. The quilt was pulled around his chin and he was asleep, snoring gently.

It was five o'clock. My client's estimated time of arrival from the ozone was around eight. How to kill three hours in this mausoleum? Hell, it was still light outside, and would be for three more hours. I decided to make them billable hours.

After checking to make sure the front door was locked, I retrieved Littlefield's key ring from the kitchen counter, pocketed it, and headed out to canvass the neighbors.

Ping-Pong followed me to the door, cocking his head as if to question my intentions.

"Don't wait up," I told him.

The house directly across the street from Littlefield's was also Victorian, but on a much smaller scale, and it was gray clapboard instead of rose brick.

A man knelt in a flower bed in the front yard, working the soil with a hand trowel. Uninvited, I crossed the lawn to have a chat. He was so engrossed in attacking a clump of weeds he didn't see me standing there.

Which gave me time for a quick assessment. I liked what I saw. A fringe of thick dark hair poked out from beneath an Atlanta Braves hat. So he was a sports lover. He wore baggy white dirt-stained shorts and no shirt. The deep tan looked good, and the muscles in his shoulders moved smoothly as he dug. A man of the earth, too.

"Excuse me," I said finally.

He sat up, startled by the interruption.

"I'm Callahan Garrity," I said. I felt awkward, too tall, too fat, with him sitting on his haunches coolly looking up at me.

"Jake Dahlberg," he said, not unpleasantly. "Whatcha need?"

He had me there. What did I need? "Uh, I'm a private detective," I stammered.

"And?"

"I'm trying to find out if anybody in the neighborhood saw anything unusual Saturday afternoon or early evening."

The beginnings of a smile disappeared. "You mean over there?" he said, pointing with a dirt-encrusted finger at Littlefield's house.

"That's right. Were you home Saturday?"

Dahlberg abruptly threw his trowel in a weed-filled bucket at his side, and got to his feet. He looked good from the front, too. Nicely muscled chest, not too furry.

"You're working for Littlefield?" he said incredulously. "Bastard's getting smarter this time around. Hiring private detectives to help beat a second murder rap."

Call it women's intuition, but I had a feeling Dahlberg and Littlefield weren't the closest of friends.

"The police are investigating the murder," I said. "Mr. Littlefield hired me to try to recover the things taken in the burglary. That's why I was wondering if you saw anything out of the ordinary yesterday."

Dahlberg wiped the sweat from his forehead with his forearm, leaving a dirty streak that reminded me of Indian warpaint. "That's a good one," he said. "A burglary. If you want to recover what was allegedly taken, check around in his shop, or in his safe deposit box. He killed Bridget and then made it look like a burglary to cover his tracks."

"That's an interesting scenario you've come up with," I said. "But where's the motive? Why would Elliot Littlefield kill this girl? Besides, he was way across town at the time of the murder. And the house had been ransacked. I saw it myself. Hell, one of my employees found the body. I doubt that someone who was due to give a big party would deliberately murder somebody and then wreck the house just hours before his guests were due to arrive."

"Littlefield doesn't need a motive. He's killed before. He's done it again," Dahlberg insisted. "You don't know the man."

He picked up his bucket and headed up his driveway toward the backyard, with me following.

"And you do know him."

Dahlberg shrugged and kept walking. "I've put up with his Fascist crap for nine years. He's the neighborhood menace. Stuff has been happening in this community lately. Ugly stuff. A woman and her baby, living only a few blocks from here, died in a fire the same night Bridget was killed. I can't prove anything, but I'm certain Littlefield's behind it."

"If you suspect him of crimes, why not go to the cops?" I asked. "They'd love to pin something on Littlefield."

"If I could prove anything, I would," Dahlberg muttered. He unlocked a wooden gate and stepped into the backyard. I was right behind him.

The garden was pocket-size and perfect. The narrow band of lawn was closely clipped and emerald green, with not a weed or a bare spot. Everything else was flowers, mostly roses. They were dazzling, pale pink, white, yellow, peach, lavender. Roses climbed on the white rail fence at the garden's perimeter, clambered over a small wooden garden shed and nodded from beds on three sides. The air was heavy with their sweet summery perfume.

"Wow," I said in a breath, forgetting the contentious nature of our conversation.

"You like roses?" he asked. He drew a pair of snub-nosed clippers from the pocket of his shorts and clipped a pale pink specimen, then handed it to me.

I buried my nose in the soft pink petals and inhaled.

"Mmm. Love 'em, but my yard doesn't get nearly as much sun as yours. I've got a couple of straggly bushes that were in the yard when I bought the place."

"I don't get what it is with roses," Dahlberg said. "These are my dad's hobby, not mine. He took care of them until he had the stroke. When I put him in the nursing home he made me promise to keep them going. Now I'm a prisoner to the damn things."

"Not a bad prison," I said, glancing around. "Is your father still alive?"

He swatted at a mosquito that had landed on his bare shoulder. "Yeah, if you call that living. No thanks to Littlefield."

"What's that mean?"

Dahlberg slipped the flower clippers back in his pocket. "Follow me," he ordered.

We walked back to the front of the house and around to the front porch. We stopped in front of his door and he pointed, across the street, to Eagle's Keep.

"See those flagpoles? Right now Littlefield's flying the Stars and Bars. But three years ago, there was a movie company in town, shooting a period picture set in the 1890s. They were using a couple blocks here in Inman Park for exteriors, so they shut off traffic on the street for a weekend, got the police to make the residents park over in the MARTA parking lot two blocks away. There were all kinds of inconveniences. Littlefield was annoyed that the movie company wouldn't pay some exorbitant amount for the privilege of shooting here. So on the morning shooting was supposed to start on our block, Littlefield hung two huge Swastika flags from those flagpoles. Blanket-size flags. I'm sure he was terribly pleased with himself for having outfoxed the movie people.

"Pop came out of the house that morning to get the newspaper. He's a Holocaust survivor. His parents, brothers, sisters, aunts, uncles, everybody was gassed at Treblinka. When the Temple was bombed, back in the sixties, he was one of the first ones on the scene, afterward. He saw those flags fluttering in the breeze that morning. I found him right here where we're standing. He'd had a mild stroke. Two days later, another series of strokes. His mind is still keen, but his left side is paralyzed and he has problems speaking and swallowing."

I looked over at Eagle's Keep again. The Confederate flag hung limply now, not a ghost of a breeze was stirring. A house or two away, a lawn mower buzzed in the near-dusk quiet. What do you say to something like that?

"I'm sorry," I said finally. "I agree with you. Totally. Elliot Littlefield is a racist, anti-Semitic jerk. Unfortunately, that doesn't automatically make him a murderer. And also unfortunately, I can't afford to turn down clients because they're jerks. If I did, there'd be nobody to work for."

"Work world's full of assholes," he agreed.

"Sounds like you've had some experiences yourself," I said. "If you don't mind my asking, what do you do for a living?"

"I'm an architect," he said.

I turned around for a closer look at his house, surprised that a contemporary architect would choose such an old relic for a home.

He caught my look. "Oh, I don't do residential," he said. "It's all commercial, mostly government work. County courthouses, hospitals, that kind of thing."

An uneasy silence fell over us. I glanced down at my watch. It was after six.

"I better get going," I said reluctantly. "I want to talk to some of the other neighbors before dark. See if anybody saw anything Saturday evening."

"Like what?" he said. The belligerent tone had crept back into his voice.

"Strange cars, strange faces, noises. Anybody walking around who doesn't belong."

"Are you kidding?" he said. "Yesterday was the preview of the tour of homes. Tour buses loaded down with old ladies from as far away as Alpharetta and Covington, cops, trucks making deliveries, workers finishing up stuff on the houses that are on tour. All kinds of people were coming and going, all over the neighborhood."

"That's right," I said. "I'd forgotten. And you didn't hear or see anything unusual either?"

He shook his head. "I shut myself in my office and worked on a proposal for a new municipal building for the city of Valdosta most of the afternoon. All I saw was the four walls of that room. Then last night I treated myself to dinner out with friends. When I got home, the police were swarming the neighborhood."

I scanned the block while Dahlberg spoke. The lawn mower had quit buzzing. "Is there a resident busybody on the block who might have seen something?"

He grinned and jerked his head to the right, gesturing toward a tiny, dark green bungalow next to his.

"That'd be Mr. Szabo. If he was home, he'd have been right on the front porch, sitting in that glider there. His house doesn't have any air-conditioning. You could try talking to him. Tell him I sent you."

"Thanks." I stroked one of the rose petals with my finger. It made velvet feel like burlap. "And thanks for the flower."

I was cutting through the side yard over to the neighbor's house when Dahlberg called after me.

"I forgot," he said. "It's Sunday. A church bus picks him up in the morning and he spends the day fellowshipping and dodging the advances of horny widow ladies. He usually gets home around nine."

"I'll try some of the others," I said. "There's always an off chance somebody saw something."

"Suit yourself," Dahlberg said, heading back toward his own porch. "But you're wasting your time. Littlefield killed her."

"We'll see about that," I muttered to myself.

The house on the other side of Dahlberg's could probably be described as a handyman's special. Paint peeled from the three wooden columns that leaned across the front porch. The fourth column was actually a pair of two-by-fours braced in place. The front door was laying horizontally across a set of sawhorses, and a tall thin man in overalls was running an electric sander back and forth across the blistered surface of the wood. A pair of plastic safety goggles made him look like a giant dragonfly.

He didn't see me standing there and didn't hear me calling "excuse me," until I tapped him on the shoulder.

Startled, he looked up and shut off the sander.

"Sam Burdette," he said, after I'd introduced myself. "Excuse the mess. We've been in the house a year this month. Seems like we'll never get done."

I repeated my anything-unusual questions.

"Let me think," he said, pushing the goggles into a nest of graying frizzy red hair. "Susie and I were home all day yesterday too, and most of the time we were out here, scraping paint. I remember there was a Federal Express truck parked over there in the morning, but I saw Littlefield come to the door for that. I saw him leave too. You can't miss that Rolls of his. There were lots of people walking around, all day, because of the tour preview, I guess. I went out to Sears sometime around three to get more sandpaper and run some other errands, then I stopped off to pick up a pizza for dinner. Got back around six. I remember seeing a white panel truck with some writing on it, parked at the curb."

"That would have been the florist's truck," I said. "Anything else?"

"Oh yeah," he said, "there was a funky pink-and-gray van parked over there a little while later. It's out there again right now," he said, pointing.

"I know about that," I said. "Nothing else?"

"Nothing specifically," Burdette said. "Like I told the policewoman who came over here to ask questions, there were people all over the block Saturday."

I gave him my business card and asked him to call me if he remembered anything else.

"By the way," I said. "How is Littlefield for a neighbor?"

Burdette glanced around, as though checking for eavesdroppers. "He's a pain in the butt, but don't tell him I said so. He's always loaning his house out for these huge charity parties. People park on lawns, and block our driveways. It's a mess. But the neighborhood association won't do anything about it because he always puts his house on tour every year, and it's a big draw. And I guess you've heard about the Nazi flag incident."

"I just talked to Jake Dahlberg," I said.

"Did Jake tell you Littlefield filed a grievance about the color of Dahlberg's house with the association?"

He hadn't.

"Jake had painted the house this cool shade of purple, mauve, Susie calls it. But mauve wasn't on the approved chart of colors for historic homes in the neighborhood, so the association made him repaint it. Jake hired a lawyer and everything, but he lost."

"What happened next?"

"Jake reported Littlefield to the city zoning board for the parking and fire violations from the parties. I heard they socked Littlefield with a fine, but he's had at least one other party I know of since then. The last time, Jake called a towtruck and they towed every single car on the street. Jesus, was Littlefield mad."

Sam Burdette was getting to be a regular fountain of information. I decided to pump him a little more.

"Did you know Bridget, the girl who was killed?"

Burdette nodded. "Cute kid. She used to come over and play with Emma, that's our baby, sometimes. Susie asked her a couple times about baby-sitting, but Bridget was always busy, so we stopped asking."

"Did you ever see anybody coming to visit her, or did she ever mention anybody who might have been mad at her? Any trouble she was having?"

From inside the house a phone rang once, then twice. I could hear bare feet slapping down a wooden hallway. Then a woman called out, "Sam, phone."

Burdette unplugged the sander and wrapped the electrical cord around it.

"Gotta go," he said. "We didn't really know Bridget all that well. Besides, you can't see the carriage house, where she lived, from here, so we wouldn't know who came or went over there."

"But you could see some of the comings and goings from the main house?"

"Sam," the woman called again.

"I'm coming," he hollered back.

"Yeah, we could see who was coming or going, if we were interested, but we've got a new baby, and a life of our own," Burdette said. "Hell yeah, there were plenty of people in and out over there. But I wouldn't know who any of them are, because we don't travel in the same social circle.

"See ya," he said, then he disappeared inside the house.

9

THE FAINTEST PROMISE of a breeze wafted down the street, and I felt the stream of perspiration trickling down my face cool and dry. While I'd been busy detecting, twilight had descended on Jasmine Way. Fireflies filled the treetops along the darkening street, their lights flickering on and off in some mad, urgent mating call. A chorus of crickets competed with the trill of one die-hard mockingbird who sat and sang his heart out from the highest branch of the crepe myrtle tree in front of Eagle's Keep.

Those so-called sensible shoes I'd slipped into hours ago at home had raised blisters on my feet. I took them off and walked barefoot across Elliot Littlefield's side yard, sinking my burning toes into the dew-soaked grass, breathing in deep lungfuls of the hot, damp honeysuckle-scented air swirling around me.

Time to check on my patient. Regretfully, I shoved my feet back into my shoes and let myself in the back door again, pushing my way past Ping-Pong.

Littlefield was still in outer space, snoring loudly. Ping-Pong, who'd shadowed me into the room, leapt nimbly onto the bed and settled himself across

Littlefield's chest. Maybe he planned to suck the breath out of his drugged master. Maybe Littlefield hated cats too. I checked my watch again and sighed. It was still only seven forty-five. I thought back to that blood-splattered room at the top of the house.

Littlefield's key ring jangled in my skirt pocket. Maybe I'd check Bridget's permanent quarters before calling it a night.

A tasteful pair of brass carriage lamps threw a pool of yellow light onto the front window of the two-story brick carriage house. The front door had a plaque over it: *Eagle's Keep Antiques, Prop. E. L. Littlefield. By Appointment Only.* The window had a deep gray painted backdrop and contained a single piece of furniture, a fancifully grain-painted blanket chest that fairly screamed big bucks. I fiddled with the key ring, trying every key on it before concluding that Littlefield must have had a separate set for the shop.

Just in case, though, I circled around to the back, stopping beside a weatherbeaten wooden door. Pots of marigolds were clustered on the brick stoop, and a purple ten-speed bike leaned against the wall. A bare bulb hung from a rusted fixture, moths batting about it. This time it took only two tries to find the right key, and a few seconds more to switch on the light and deactivate the alarm.

Bridget Dougherty had been an orderly little soul.

The old white iron bed was neatly made, with a faded yellow and white Sunbonnet Sue quilt smoothed up to a pile of pillows covered in scraps of old forties chintz. A battered stuffed monkey, the kind made out of old men's wool socks, nestled among the pillows. I'd had a monkey like that as a child; Pookie, I'd called him, until my baby brother Kevin had gotten revenge for some childish offense by field dressing Pookie with my dad's Swiss army knife.

Most of the other furniture in the room looked like the stuff I'd had in my college/first apartment days: a cast-off painted white dresser, a coffee table made from a cut-down wooden cable spool, and tables and storage cabinets fashioned from plastic milk crates.

One crate was Bridget's kitchen, turned on its side. It was stacked with her groceries: boxes of herbal tea, Cup-A-Soup, crackers, Froot Loops. On top of the crate was a tiny one-slice toaster and a hot plate.

Two more crates held her library. Lots of New Age paperbacks, some schoolbooks, and a pamphlet describing the requirements for a high-school equivalency diploma. There was a *Norton's Anthology of Poetry*. She'd dog-eared the pages with the mushiest poems: Elizabeth Barrett Browning, Byron, Shelley, Keats, all the swoon in moon in June specialists. Someone's love was like a red, red rose. I wondered whose.

The schoolbooks held nothing of interest, until I opened her Geometry textbook and a slip of blue-lined notebook paper fluttered to the floor. The printing was bold and black and masculine looking.

Brig—
Can't meet you today. Practice til 6. Call you tonite.
                                        X X X. Me.

Who was "Me"? And what was he practicing? Band? Baseball? Knife throwing? I toyed with the idea of taking the slip, but decided against it. The note was evidence in a murder case, I reminded myself, and my job was to find a missing diary.

The rest of the room contained basic teenage stuff, but no more notes from Me and certainly no missing

Civil War goodies. There were blue jeans and T-shirts, gym shorts, some foil-wrapped condoms. Bridget had gotten wiser, but she hadn't had a chance to get older. Under her bed I found a suitcase. Folded inside were hunter green jumpers in what I like to call parochial school plaid, a pretty cotton print dress, a pair of high heels, and a framed photo of the Dougherty family. It must have been two or three years old. The older sister, Jocelyn, looked straight into the camera, defying the photographer to make her smile. Her cheeks were fuller in the portrait. Jocelyn had lost a lot of weight. A lot. The younger sister, Bridget, smiled wide, showing a mouthful of braces. A whisper of blue eye shadow made her look like a little girl dressing up in mommy's makeup. Both girls were pretty in a quiet, unspectacular way.

I looked around for a bathroom, and opened the only other door in the room. Instead of a tub and sink, I found a hallway that lead to a series of locked doors; probably storerooms for the shop. The bathroom was at the end of the hall—a claustrophobic closet holding only a shower stall, a sink, and a commode. A wall-hung cabinet held a few toiletries, but nothing of interest.

I sighed. Time to go.

George Koteras had been right on the money about the effectiveness of his pocket rockets. Littlefield was sitting up in bed, shaking his head and rubbing the woozies out of his eyes when I got back to the house.

"What's the time?" he said groggily.

"Little after eight." I dug in my pockets and handed him the pills. "Dr. Koteras left these for you. Antibiotics. Take two now, two more with meals tomorrow. You're to call him in the morning. You okay by yourself tonight?"

"I'm fine," he said, yawning hugely. "Back's stiff.

Guess I'll have to go back to physical therapy. My mouth's dry from those pills, too."

"Shall I get you some water before I leave?" I couldn't believe how solicitous I was being to this pompous asshole.

"Never mind," Littlefield said, swinging his legs slowly to the side of the bed. "I've got to go to the bathroom anyway."

"All right then," I said briskly. "I've been talking to your neighbors, and I've gone over the house again. A couple more questions, then I'll leave. Why was Bridget sleeping in the house instead of her apartment in the carriage house? And who knew she was staying here?"

He gathered the sheets around his waist and gingerly touched both feet to the floor.

"She'd been getting harassing phone calls in the last week or so. A voice, whispering, threatening to kill her; warning her to get out of town. I don't know who she'd told about where she was sleeping."

"Was the voice anybody she recognized?"

"She said not," he said, standing now, with the sheet wrapped around him toga-style. "I figured it was just kids, you know how they are. But the threats scared her. She asked if she could move into the house and I agreed to it. I guess she'd been staying here since last Tuesday or Wednesday."

"Did you tell the police about the calls?"

He looked sheepish. "No. In all the confusion I completely forgot about it. Should I have mentioned it?"

"Yeah," I said. "The cops might not have believed you, but at least it might provide motive for somebody else to have killed her. If I were you I'd call my lawyer tomorrow and let him know about the calls. Now I've got to go if you really are okay."

"I appreciate your staying this long," Littlefield said.

"I'll let you see yourself out, and I'll be in touch tomorrow."

Out in the moonlight, I took another gulp of night air as an antidote to the stale smell of Eagle's Keep. Once in the van I resolutely mashed the door lock and headed toward McLendon Avenue, and home.

I'd been mugged walking home on a dark street not far from here a little over a year ago and had the living shit kicked out of me courtesy of a trio of paid sociopaths. It hadn't been a random act of violence, but since then I'm especially wary when I'm alone at night.

Lights blazed in my little bungalow. Welcome home. Mac's Blazer was parked in the driveway. I let myself in the front door, dropped my bag, and headed for the kitchen, where I heard voices and the sound of fat sizzling in a skillet.

Mac stood at the stove, dropping flour-covered fillets into the black iron frying pan. Edna was seated at the table, a long-neck beer in one hand, a lit cigarette in the other. They stopped talking when I walked in.

The room was heavy with the scent of fish and a guilty silence.

"You've got that fire turned up too high," Edna pointed out. "You'll burn that trout."

"Well look what the cat dragged in," Mac said, a little too heartily. I kissed him lightly on the lips and took a swig of the beer he held out to me. It was ice cold and I drank half the bottle before handing it back, burping delicately to show my appreciation.

"You were talking about me," I said. "Fill me in."

"Don't flatter yourself," Edna drawled. "But it's about damn time you got home. We were fixin' to call out the National Guard to hunt you down."

I was too worn out to argue. While Mac fried the trout and hush puppies, Edna mixed up a bowl of her coleslaw. Watching her grate the cabbage on a worn metal grater, then knead sugar into the slaw, was comforting after the long day I'd had. She poured vinegar over it, stirred the stuff with a fork, then added some grated carrot and a little purple cabbage for color. I filled the cooks in while they prepared supper.

"This Littlefield character sounds like a prime asshole," Mac said, mopping up the last of the coleslaw on his plate with a hush puppy. "How come you keep hiring yourself out to do investigative work for clowns like Littlefield and Bo Beemish?"

"Maybe I'm a glutton for punishment," I said wearily. "All I know is their money spends real good. And I've got it figured that with what I'll make off Littlefield I might be able to buy a second van, secondhand. In a nice boring shade like silver or beige, or anything but pink and gray."

"That reminds me," Edna said, rising and starting to clear away the plates. "I saw the funeral notice for Bridget Dougherty in today's paper. Services at ten tomorrow at Christ the King."

"I thought her folks looked like high church," I said. "I wouldn't mind checking out the crowd at that funeral, but I've got a full day tomorrow."

"You don't know the half of what you've got to do tomorrow," Edna said. "C. W. Hunsecker called. He wants to meet you for lunch. Call him in the morning to set a time. And don't forget, it's your turn to pick up supplies at the wholesale house. I've made a list, it's in the appointment book."

"All right," I said. "We'll give the funeral a miss."

"Nothing doing," Edna said. "I'll get the girls going first thing then hop over to Christ the King."

I'd have objected to her pushing her way into the investigation side of the business, but to tell the truth, I was just plain tired. And it wouldn't hurt anything to let Edna enjoy a little funeralizing.

Mac stood up, cleared off both our plates and put them in the dishwasher. "I'm gonna hit the road my own self," he said. "Thanks for dinner, Edna." He kissed me again, a proper good night kiss this time, adding an affectionate squeeze to the fanny, since Edna's back was turned to us. "Walk me to the car?"

I waited until we were outside, leaning our backs against the Blazer. "So what were you and Edna talking about before I came in?"

"Stuff," he said, swatting at a mosquito. "Nothing important."

"You were talking about me," I said flatly. "You're a terrible liar, MacAuliffe."

He sighed. "Only when I'm lying to you. Okay. We were talking about us."

"As in you and Edna? I'm sorry I missed that."

"As in you and me," he said, reaching for my hand and giving it a squeeze. "Your mother can't understand why we don't get married or something."

I turned to face him, amazed. He grinned crookedly. "What?"

"Did it ever occur to you that I might want to take part in this debate before my mother settles the matter?"

"Wait," he said. "Hold on. It wasn't like that. We were shooting the breeze, and somehow we got to talking about how comfortable we are together, and I guess I said something about wishing we were old married folks. And your mother said she didn't know why we didn't just do it. You know, get married or something."

"Unbelievable," I said, wrenching my hand away from his. "It's not bad enough Edna meddles in my business life. Now she's running my love life too. And you encourage her."

"She wasn't meddling," Mac said. "Just offering an opinion. You're blowing this way out of proportion, Callahan, really. It was just a chance remark, is all."

"What other chance remarks did she make?" I asked, fuming.

He put his hand on my chin and turned my head to face him, then stroked my cheek softly.

"She's really worried about your decision not to take the cancer drugs," he said. "She just knows the cancer will come back unless you do."

"We've been over this, Mac," I said. "I thought you agreed with my decision. Now the two of you are ganging up on me, when I really believe I've made the choice that's right for me."

I'd meant to show Mac the newspaper clipping about tamoxifen, but now I'd be damned if I'd bring it up.

"I'm not ganging up on you," he said, his voice getting louder. "And if you'd stop flying off the handle every time the subject came up, maybe you could make your mother understand."

"I've got to go," I said. "If I stay out here and talk about this any more, we'll end up having a fight, and I don't have the energy right now. I'll talk to you later."

I turned and walked back to the house. He stood by the car for a few seconds, then got in and started the engine. I let the front door slam behind me when I went back in the house.

10

INSTEAD OF SLEEPING THE SLEEP of the righteous, I tossed and turned a good part of the night, worrying about my argument with Mac. It was useless to fret about Edna's meddling. And I'd been unfair to accuse him of conspiring with her. But I'd had a long day, and on the best of days I have a short fuse. In between worrying about my love life, I assembled and reassembled what I knew about the burglary and murder at Eagle's Keep, turning facts and snippets of conversation that way and this, trying to make the pieces into something whole.

Problem was, I didn't have enough pieces. It was too early.

By six, I was exhausted with the effort of trying to sleep. I pulled on a robe, went into the kitchen, and made a pot of coffee.

The House Mouse appointment book was lying out on the table where Edna had left it for me. This would be a typical Monday, jammed with more jobs than we could handle with everybody, including myself and Edna, pitching in to clean. Plus I'd agreed we would finish up the cleaning at Eagle's Keep.

I left a message on C. W. Hunsecker's answering machine, telling him I'd meet him at Harold's Barbecue at eleven thirty A.M. If you don't get to Harold's early on Civitans day, you don't get a table.

I was still muttering to myself when Edna dragged herself into the kitchen.

"What's with you?" she asked.

"I've juggled jobs around so we can send Neva Jean and Ruby back to Littlefield's house today," I told her. "Everything's written down. I'll be back by early afternoon—I hope."

She was reading the front page of the paper, and gave me a silent good-bye wave.

For once things went smoothly at the wholesale house and I was right on time when I pulled into the restaurant parking lot.

Like all great barbecue joints, Harold's looks like a potential health hazard. The place sits in the shadow of the Atlanta Federal Penitentiary, so at any one time there are enough cops inside to put down a good-size riot or a small-size revolution. Hunsecker was holding down a booth by the window.

As soon as I was seated a waitress appeared with a pitcher of sweet tea and a menu. I took a sip of tea and waved the menu away. "Just bring me a pork plate. And if you could, an outside cut of the crackling cornbread."

Hunsecker sipped his own tea. I waited.

"So you're working for Elliot Littlefield," he said finally.

I'd figured this might be the reason for the invitation to lunch.

"Yeah."

He took another sip. "You sure you wanna do this?"

"Look, C. W.," I said, feeling my face get hot. "I'm

just trying to help him trace and recover his stolen property. That's all. You know me. I wouldn't get involved in an active murder investigation."

"I know you, all right," he said. "That's why we're having lunch today. So I can tell you to stay clear of this guy. He's a murderer, Callahan. Why you want to take money from a scumbag like him?"

Sometimes it's a struggle to keep my temper under control. Especially when somebody tries to tell me who I should or should not work for. I took a deep breath and reminded myself of how far back C. W. Hunsecker and I go.

"He didn't kill her, C. W." I said.

"Oh, you already solved a murder only two days old," he said, mockingly. "Give this girl a gold badge."

The waitress was back then, setting two green plastic plates of barbecue in front of us. She fussed over Hunsecker for a moment, then hurried away.

"All right, smart ass," I said, squirting a stream of barbecue sauce, the mild kind, on my sliced pork. "Where's the motive? Even for the burglary? The most valuable thing taken, a diary, wasn't insured. Littlefield stood to make a shitload of money on that diary, not to mention the prestige of discovering such a big deal historical document. You know Littlefield's ego, he probably liked the idea of the Elliot Littlefield diary more than he did the money he was going to earn. Besides, he genuinely liked this kid."

Hunsecker stopped chewing on a rib for a minute. "Liked to get in her pants is more like it."

"I think it was a nonsexual relationship. She was involved with somebody else. Tell you what. You find out who her lover was, I'll bet that's the killer."

He mopped his mouth with a paper napkin. "Thanks for the advice. You're wrong."

I pushed a piece of pork around in the sauce. "Give me the Sunny Girl case file."

"That case is over and done with. Why you wanna mess in a twenty-year-old murder?"

"I just do," I said stubbornly. "Are you going to give me the files or not?"

"I don't have them."

"Who does?"

"Beats me," he said. "Few years ago we cleaned out all the old homicide files and shipped them to some warehouse space the city made out of an old elementary school over near Cabbagetown. Haven't seen any of those old files since."

"Damn." I sighed, absentmindedly dipping a piece of crackling cornbread in my bowl of Brunswick stew. Maybe I should let up on Hunsecker about the Littlefield thing. We clearly weren't going to agree on my client's guilt or innocence.

"So how are Vonette and the kids?"

Hunsecker squirmed in his chair. "Not too good. Vonette and I are, uh, separated. Things are pretty bad right now. She and the kids moved out. Ain't none of 'em speaking to me. Before she left, she took a knife and slashed holes in the crotch of every single pair of pants I own. Had to get a credit union loan just to buy clothes to wear to work."

Hunsecker's eyes stayed glued to his plate, which he'd wiped clean of the last vestiges of barbecue. I could see a quarter-size bald spot on the top of his head.

He still wouldn't look me in the eyes. I smelled guilt.

"Sounds like Vonette had herself a royal hissy fit," I observed. "Would all of this have anything to do with your new partner, Linda Nickells? Just how old is she, anyway? About the same age as your daughter Kenyatta?"

He was still examining his plate for any further traces of food. "You're too goddamn smart, you know that? Know too damn much for your own damn good."

"She's what, twenty-two?" I persisted.

"Twenty-six," he admitted defiantly. "Kenyatta's not but nineteen, not that it's any of your business."

I raised my hands to signal a truce. "You're right. What you do with your marriage and your life is none of my business. Just like who I choose to work for is none of your business. Now. What I need is some information about fences, people who deal in stolen historic documents. Can you help me or not?"

Hunsecker pushed his chair back, stood, and pulled a silver money clip from his pocket, peeling off a five and a ten and dropping it on the table.

He was embarrassed and he was mad. I'd done it again. Pushed things too far. Stupid. Stupid. Stupid. "Go to hell, Garrity," he said. "Your client's a murderer. He's going to prison, and this time, he's gonna stay."

11

THE HIGH-PITCHED WHINE of our heavy-duty Electrolux coming from inside Eagle's Keep put a smile on my face. If the girls were at the point of vacuuming, they must be close to being finished. Which meant we were close to being paid.

I knew the vacuum would drown out the sound of the doorbell, so I walked around to the carriage house to see if Littlefield might be working in his shop.

He was seated at a desk with his back to me when I knocked on the door. Littlefield swiveled around in his chair. He was on the phone, but gestured for me to come in.

The antiques shop smelled of lemon and beeswax. There was none of the mustiness of the house.

"Fax me that catalog, will you?" Littlefield was saying. "Good. I'll talk to you soon."

He hung up the phone and motioned for me to be seated in a leather armchair facing the desk.

"How's the back?" I asked. He had some kind of wedge-shaped pillow he was sitting on. There were large bags under his eyes and his color was still pale.

"Dandy," he said sarcastically. "I've had it x-rayed this

morning, and they tell me it's nothing surgery and six months flat on my back won't take care of. But what about you? Have you any ideas on how to track down my diary?"

"I thought you might be at Bridget's funeral," I blurted out.

He frowned. "Under the circumstances I decided it would be best to stay away. I've made a donation to the Humane Society in her name. That damned Siamese was hers. I had forbidden her to bring it into the house, but she sneaked it in anyway while she was sleeping on the third floor. She said the cat couldn't sleep without her. Now. About the diary?"

"Right," I said briskly. "I'd like to have the names of the people who'd expressed an interest in buying it. In fact, I need the names of everyone you'd approached to sell the diary."

He opened a drawer in the desk and pulled out a manila file folder. Extracting a piece of paper from it, he handed it over to me. There were three names typed neatly with addresses and phone numbers below.

"These were the only three I approached directly," he said. "But news of a find like this travels rapidly through the marketplace. There were probably dozens of people, all over the country, who'd heard about the diary and were drooling over the possibility of acquiring it."

"So you're telling me you have no way of knowing how many people might have known about the diary's existence?"

"Correct."

I read over the list. There were two institutions, Emory University and the University of Georgia, listed. And one individual, someone named Stephen Blakeford. "Who's this guy?"

"Speedy Blakeford? He's in oil and gas in Houston. I'd never heard of him until his lawyer called and asked me to send a photograph and description of the diary. It turns out that Mr. Blakeford is something of a speculator. He buys things, the rarer the better, holds onto them for a short while, then sells them again, usually to the Japanese. At an enormous profit."

"And Emory University and UGA were competing for the diary too?" I was surprised that a state institution, especially one more noted for football than its library, had the means or the interest to buy something as rare as Lula Belle Bird's diary, and I said so.

"You're wrong," Littlefield said. "The university actually has a decent special collection. They have the Margaret Mitchell papers, of course, and quite a few other things."

"And they can compete with all that Coke money at Emory?"

"Probably not." There was that smile again. "That bid you saw was the first one I'd received. I will say that Peter Thornton, Georgia's new director, is young and ambitious for the collection. And he's well connected."

"So that leaves us Emory University," I said. "I find it hard to believe anyone there would have to resort to murder and theft just to pick up some moldy old diary."

The smile disappeared. "I hope you're being facetious. That diary is in excellent condition. As for someone at Emory being capable of this kind of crime, I'd have to agree."

I traced the names on the list with my finger. "Did it look like Emory might be able to compete with Blakeford?"

"The last conversation I had with Shane Dunstan at Emory led me to believe that they were definitely in the running."

"Did he mention a price?"

"She," Littlefield said. "Shane is a woman. We discussed the fact that she'd been in contact with a donor who was considering putting up the funding to buy the diary. We haven't talked since before Bridget, uh, the other night. As you can understand, I'd prefer for people not to know about the burglary. Discretion is a very large part of what I do here."

My eyes traveled around the shop. It had a burglar alarm and looked secure, but I was still surprised there hadn't been an attempt to break in here, too. "Have any of these people ever been here in the shop, or in your home?"

He frowned. "Peter Thornton and Shane Dunstan have been in the shop. I showed them the diary here. And they've been in the house, too, for parties and other functions for the Society for Southern Historians. Speedy Blakeford, I've never met."

Littlefield seemed irritated by my questions about the diary's prospective buyers. Fine. I was getting irritated by his answers.

"Let me ask you something, Mr. Littlefield. Who do you think did this? And why?"

He was fidgeting with something on his desktop. It was a small beautifully formed silver dagger with engraving on the handle. He turned it over and over, running long slender fingers over the blade. At this rate he'd wear the silver plate right off the thing.

Littlefield looked up angrily. "Obviously it's someone who knows me. Who wants to ruin my business and implicate me in another murder. Someone who knows enough about my business to know what an incredible find the diary is, and how important it is to me."

So. Littlefield had paranoid tendencies.

"Well," I said patiently. "Who might that be?"

He crossed his arms over his chest. "It's crazy, yet, he hates me so passionately I believe he just might have done it. He just might have."

"Who?" I asked.

Littlefield got up from his chair awkwardly, holding himself stiffly. He walked haltingly to the shop window and stood there, looking out. When he turned to face me his face was contorted in rage.

"It's that fucking Jew," he spat. "Dahlberg."

I listened silently while Littlefield recited chapter and verse of Dahlberg's campaign to run him, Elliot Littlefield, the man who'd rescued Inman Park, out of his own neighborhood. Dahlberg was always running to the city, complaining about parking violations at Eagle's Keep. Lately he'd complained about code violations at several small rental properties Littlefield owned at the edge of Inman Park. "He wants to harass me so much that I'll sell my houses to his little nigger-lovers' club," he raged.

"What?" I said. I'd only been half-listening to Littlefield's tirade.

"It's true," he insisted. "Dahlberg and his liberal pals want to turn Inman Park back into a slum again. Those houses of mine, I picked them up for back taxes. When I'm done renovating them, they'll sell for one hundred fifty to two hundred thousand each. But Dahlberg wants to buy them now, for nothing, through his phony foundation. Then he'll turn around and give them to homeless bums and winos on the condition that they fix them up themselves. It'd be the death of this neighborhood."

Sounded to me like a great solution to the city's homeless problem, but I didn't share that opinion with my client.

"And you believe Dahlberg murdered Bridget and burglarized your house because of that?" I said, trying to keep the disbelief out of my voice.

"You've got to prove it," he said, turning toward me. "Dahlberg's behind this. He's got my diary over there."

He clumped back to his chair and sank down slowly.

I was at a loss for words.

"I'll do what I can," I mumbled.

After writing me a check for $1,000 for the cleaning and another $750 as an advance for my investigative work, Littlefield picked up a file folder on his desk. "Let me know when you find something, will you?" he said politely. The rage had disappeared as quickly as it had come.

Neva Jean and Ruby were slumped against the side of the van when I got to the street. They'd loaded their cleaning gear in the van already, but were avoiding getting into the ovenlike interior.

Neva Jean started to complain about how hard she and Ruby had to work to clean up Eagle's Keep, but I shut her down fast.

"You got us into this deal, Neva Jean," I said. "Right into the middle of a homicide. So I don't want to hear one damn word out of your mouth. Understand?"

She rolled her eyes, but after that she sipped her Mountain Dew in silence. Ruby hummed gospel songs on the way back home.

12

THE COLD BOTTLES OF BEER made a welcome clinking noise as I opened the refrigerator door. In the summertime Edna and I drink our beer and our Cokes out of bottles. Somehow they taste colder that way. The kitchen smelled like pot roast. A colander of string beans stood on the kitchen counter next to a cooling pound cake.

The troops had obviously escaped to the patio. I let the screen door bang to announce my arrival home. Edna looked up from the week-old issue of *People* magazine she was reading. The girls always bring in all the latest magazines from their jobs—a week late.

She got up, as if on cue, and walked into the kitchen. "Let me put my green beans on and check this roast," she said.

"So what did you find out today?" she called from inside.

I had to raise my voice so she could hear me in the kitchen. The details didn't take long to tell.

The smile she wore when she came out of the kitchen could only be called smug. "I was able to do a little detecting of my own on your behalf."

"Oh no," I said wearily. "What did you do?"

"Don't take that tone with me," she warned. "After Bridget's funeral I noticed a bunch of teenage girls standing around in the parking lot boo-hooing. So I stopped and walked over to them and struck up a conversation, acting like I was a family friend at first. I asked them if Bridget had any enemies at school, any new boyfriends, that kind of thing. From the giggles I got, when I asked about the boyfriend, I gathered they knew about him, but they wouldn't say anything. Closemouthed little twits. The one thing I did find out was that she and the mother fought like cats and dogs. Had a big blowup right before she dropped out of school and ran away from home. I was about to ask what the fight was about when the mother showed up. The girls acted real nervous around her and they took off as soon as it was politely possible."

"Ma," I said, a thought occurring to me. "How did you get those girls to talk to you? Most of the teenage girls I've had experience with wouldn't give you or me the time of day."

"Easy," she said, leaning her head back and blowing a puff of smoke skyward. "Right before the mother came I told them I was a private detective. Passed around a couple of cards and told them to call if they think of anything. They were impressed as hell."

"You didn't."

"Sure did," she assured me. "Why not?"

"No." I moaned. "We're not having this conversation again." I got up and went over and kneeled in front of her chair, taking her face between my two hands, the way you do to a small child when you want to emphasize a point. "Listen. You are not a detective. You are not licensed to do this stuff. And you are going to get us both in a world of trouble if you keep butting in on my cases. And in my life," I added meaningfully.

I'd just gotten launched on my usual lecture about the possible results of Edna's meddling when the doorbell rang.

She set her jaw stubbornly. "Get that, will you, Miss Big Deal Detective? I've got to go check on my pot roast."

Jocelyn Dougherty was standing by the front door, wearing an ill-fitting dress that looked four sizes too big. Her arms and legs, matchstick thin, hung from her clothing, the veins beneath the skin gleaming blue through the pale white skin. She'd scraped her hair back into a ponytail, and her feet were stuck into a pair of wornout rubber flip-flops. Her face wore an expression that said she was mightily pissed. In her hand she held one of my business cards.

"Mrs. Garrity?" she demanded.

"Miss Garrity. Or Ms. You're Jocelyn, right? Come on in."

Reluctantly, she edged her way into the living room, finally coming to light on the floral chintz sofa that matched the armchair I sat in. She was so small, so thin, she didn't even make a dent in the thick down sofa cushion.

"Look," she blurted, before I could say anything. "That old lady, is she your mother? She was at my sister's funeral today. One of my sister's friends gave me this. She was asking a lot of nosy questions. You people have a lot of damn nerve, you know that? You go to work for that pig Elliot Littlefield, the guy who killed Bridget, then you have the nerve to crash her funeral and ask a lot of questions and get everybody upset. My sister's dead, goddamnit. And my mother and father don't give a shit. The cops don't give a shit. Nobody cares. Except me. And I'm not gonna let this sonofabitch get away with killing my little sister."

The girl's voice barely rose above a whisper as she spat out her diatribe against me. But the thin muscles in her neck stuck out, and her eyes were narrowed into furious slits.

When she paused to gather more steam, I had time to ask more nosy questions. "How old are you, anyway?"

She frowned. "I'm nineteen. What's that got to do with it?"

For a nineteen-year-old, the chick was pretty ballsy.

"Look, Jocelyn," I said. "I'm not trying to cover up your sister's murder. Honest. I was at the house where she was found. I saw what the killer did to her. I'll never forget it. Believe me, I want to know who killed her, too. And if I thought Elliot Littlefield did it, I'd be all over him like white on rice. But he didn't do it."

Her lips were pressed so firmly together that they formed a thin white slash in her pale, bony face. She obviously didn't believe me. "Who did kill her then?"

I sighed. This kid wasn't going to let me off the hook. "That's not my job. I've been hired to help Littlefield track down some very valuable antiques that were stolen during the burglary. That's all. It's the cops' job to find out who murdered Bridget, not mine. There's a good possibility, of course, that the same person who took the antiques killed Bridget. There were thousands of dollars' worth of very rare Civil War artifacts taken from that house. Whoever killed Bridget probably did it because she caught them breaking into the house."

She wasn't really listening.

"How much do you charge?" she said abruptly.

"Forget it. I've got a client."

"You just said he hired you to find his stuff. Fine. I'm hiring you to find who killed my sister. If Littlefield didn't do it, there shouldn't be any conflict of interest—right?"

Such a pushy kid. I was never this pushy when I was nineteen. A little brassy maybe. But not pushy.

"It's not just a matter of conflict, Jocelyn. For one thing, I don't investigate homicides. That's a good way to step on the cops' toes. And for another thing, you can't afford me. I charge seventy-five dollars an hour, plus expenses."

She was thinking, adding up her life savings probably. "I've got money," she said firmly. "And I'm not changing my mind."

"It's none of my business, but where does a nineteen-year-old get enough money to hire a private investigator?" I asked. "What are you, an heiress or something?"

She shook her head vigorously. "Nothing like that. I've got my college money. My grandparents set up a special account for me. There's like twelve thousand in there. That ought to be plenty."

"Don't they expect you to use that for college?"

She crossed her legs and the fabric of her dress fell away in folds. It was one of those forties cotton housedresses, they sell them in the vintage clothes stores at Little Five Points. "I'm sitting out a quarter or two.

"So what about it?" she repeated. "Are you gonna work for me, or do I go to the yellow pages and find somebody else?"

I considered her proposition. I had no doubt this kid would do exactly as she threatened and end up forking over her college money to some cheesy ripoff artist. Or she could just get herself killed by whoever had murdered her baby sister.

"Let's compromise," I said. "I can't take your money. But I could use your help. And maybe, but only maybe, we can be of some use to each other."

She looked at me dubiously. It was a look I'd perfected

at her age. "Right," she said, curling her lip. "You're going to let me help you. How?"

"By doing exactly what I say. And not one thing more. Understood?"

"Understood," she said reluctantly. "Can we start now?"

My stomach was crying out for the dinner Edna was putting on the table in the other room, but my mind told me there was no time like the present.

"I guess so," I told her.

"The main thing I could use your help with is your sister's friends and teachers at All Saints. We know Bridget had a boyfriend, and we know she had a pregnancy scare. But we don't know who the boyfriend was. Do you?"

"No," she said sadly. "Bridge wouldn't tell me. I didn't even know she had run away and dropped out until she called me a couple weeks ago and told me where she was staying."

"Didn't your folks mention it?" I said incredulously.

"Let's just say my folks and I aren't exactly close," Jocelyn said tersely. "I'm house-sitting for one of my college friend's parents this summer."

"Oh. Well, do you think she told any of her friends who the guy was?"

Jocelyn thought about it. "Maybe. Maybe not. Bridge totally changed this year. She'd dropped most of her old friends. And she was so moody. She and my mom had terrible fights. Her grades dropped, too, and Bridge has always been on the honor roll. She quit all her outside activities, drill team, drama club, everything except soccer. She was always such a jockette."

"Could she have been doing drugs?"

Jocelyn laughed. "Little Miss Just Say No? Not hardly. She had this thing about her body being a temple. She'd quit eating red meat and drinking Cokes. She wouldn't even take a Midol when she was in her period. No way she was into drugs."

Teenagers had definitely changed since the 1970s, when my girlfriends and I had sat in the parking lot of our high school and washed down half a bottle of Pamprin with cheap wine in hopes of getting a buzz. "What about enemies? Littlefield told me Bridget said she'd had some scary phone calls."

"She mentioned it, but she said she had no idea who it could be."

Jocelyn sunk her head down to her knees, covering her face with her hands. Her voice broke. "I don't get it. Up until this year, Bridget was the good one in the family. The cutest, the smartest. The nicest. I was the screw-up, not her. Then bam. She drops out of school, runs away, thinks she's pregnant."

She looked up at me and there were tears running down her face. "I was pissed when she told me that. Here I am, in college, still a virgin and she's having sex and she's only a junior. And now this. I don't get it."

A sob caught in her throat, but she choked it back, rubbed the tears away and stood and straightened her shoulders. I walked over and put my arm around her shoulder but she shook me off. "I'm okay. So where do we start?"

"Let's start with her best friend."

"Sara Parrish," Jocelyn said quickly. "They were best friends since parochial school at St. Thomas More. But she and Bridge had a fight. They weren't speaking. You want her phone number?"

"No," I said, looking around for my purse. "I want you to go with me to her house. It's an investigative technique we call ambushing."

13

A BEAT-UP RED HYUNDAI was parked at the curb in front of our house, sticking a good eight inches out into the street. My heart gave a small skip. "Is that Bridget's car? The cops have been looking all over for it."

The car door creaked as she opened it and slid into the driver's seat. My door made the same sound. I moved a pile of sneakers and books, and got in. "It was our car," Jocelyn corrected me. "We shared it. But when I went to college in Athens my Dad made me leave it behind for Miss Perfect. When I came home we agreed to take turns using it. I picked it up Friday morning."

"Damn," I said, looking around. The car was an archaeological dig of contemporary teenage culture. It smelled a lot like french fries, a smell I normally enjoy. There were empty fast-food wrappers, wads of dirty clothes, a box of cassette tapes, two more pairs of shoes, a Judith Krantz paperback novel, a hairbrush, and a pair of neon purple-and-green in-line skates.

"What?" she said. "So it's messy. Big deal."

"That's not it," I said, poking at the glove box until it opened. There was an empty box of Tampax, half a package of moldy-looking cheese crackers, and a rolled-up pair of pantyhose. "It would have been helpful if whoever killed Bridget had had the car in his possession. We might have found something to link him to it."

"Sorry," she said. "See anything in there that looks like a clue?"

"Not really," I said, shutting the glove box. "So where we going?"

"Dunwoody," she said absentmindedly. "Beautiful Downtown Dunwoody."

Jocelyn drove fast but expertly through the vestiges of rush hour traffic. Although it was after six, heat shimmered off the blacktop Interstate and the car's tinny little air-conditioner rattled powerlessly against the oppressive summer temperature.

"Jocelyn," I said tentatively.

"Yeah?" She was absorbed in some rap song on the radio, something about killin' and chillin' and illin'.

"Have you been sick? I saw an old family photo in Bridget's things and it's obvious you've lost a good bit of weight."

The rapsters' ranting took over the car for a minute, the heavy bass beat thumping so hard and so loud it seemed to vibrate my seat cushion. I reached over and turned the volume down to ear-bleeding level.

"No big deal," she said lightly. "I've had sort of an eating disorder. I lost about forty or fifty pounds while I was away at school, and my parents put me in the hospital."

"Forty or fifty pounds," I repeated. Personally, I would have given my right and left arm to lose that kind of weight. But this kid was only nineteen, and she couldn't have weighed much more than one twenty in the photo I'd seen of her. "That can't be healthy."

She giggled. "That's what my doctors said. See, I

gained some weight when I first went to school. Freshman fifteen, they call it. I was really bummed out, until this girl in my dorm hall told me about eating Correctol. It was great. I could eat all I wanted in the cafeteria, chocolate donuts, double mashed potatoes, really scarf out. Then I could take my Correctol. I lost the fifteen and kept going. It felt great to be thinner than anybody I knew. My mom was bitching about it, but there wasn't anything she could do to make me stop."

"And then you got sick?" I suggested.

She nodded. "Guess it got out of hand. I'd skip classes so I could lock myself in my room, pig out, then take the Correctol. When my parents got my grades, they freaked. My mom put me in one of those private hospitals they have for kids."

"Adolescent treatment centers," I prompted. "I've always wondered what they treat at those places. Snottiness? Bad attitudes? Poor study habits?"

"The usual," Jocelyn said. "Drugs. Alcohol. Psychosis. Neurosis. Bulimia. Anorexia."

"And the program works?" I said. "What exactly do they do?"

The rap song had ended, so Jocelyn fiddled with the radio dial, trying to find some more mood music. "Well, you've got daily sessions with a shrink. Then weekly group sessions. And you meet with this dietitian and they work up a food plan. You're supposed to write down everything you eat. And they have these really lame exercise classes. Oh, yeah, and because I was a binger and purger, while I was in the hospital I had a staff person baby-sitting me at mealtime and afterward. They wouldn't even let me go to the bathroom by myself."

"Gross," I said faintly.

"No shit," she agreed. "When I was discharged even the shrink, who is a total jerk, agreed that I shouldn't be around my mom. She's got this control thing. She wanted to run me and Bridge's lives. So I'm staying at a friend's house, while she and her family are down at their beach house in St. Simon's. And I have to see the shrink every week.

"Here it is," she said, taking a sharp right turn into a driveway in front of a large two-story redbrick house that looked exactly like every other house on the street.

"Run up and see if she's home," I suggested. "We don't want to talk to her in front of her parents, and we definitely don't want mom and dad to know I'm a private investigator."

"Wow," Jocelyn said. "You've really got this ambushing gig down."

"It's my job," I said modestly. "Go."

In a moment she was back in the car. "Good news. Sara's over at the swim and tennis club. It's just two streets away."

The "Club" turned out to be a fenced-in slab of concrete with a dinky kidney-shaped pool set in the middle. Hordes of small children swarmed in and around the water, with a bored-looking lifeguard sitting high above the crowd. Beside the pool was a single fenced-in tennis court where a pair of tennis-togged women swatted a ball desultorily over the net.

We parked and got out. Jocelyn stood at the gate, hands shading her eyes as she looked for her sister's friend.

"There she is," she said, pointing to a girl stretched out on a beach chair near the bend of the kidney.

Sara Parrish was a cute little number, with pixie-cut short brown hair, a sunburned nose, and a bright orange bikini that could have been a Cracker Jack prize. Her hazel eyes brimmed over with tears at the sight of her dead friend's sister. "Oh Jos," she said, her voice breaking.

Jocelyn sat down beside Sara, put her arm around the younger girl, and looked up at me. "Sara, this is Ms. Garrity. She's, uh, a friend of mine. We're trying to find out who killed Bridget."

Sara's eyes widened. "For real? Are you a cop?"

"Used to be," I said.

Sara shrugged herself out of Jocelyn's embrace. "The real cops came to the house this morning. My dad came home from work to be there while they talked to me. My mom's really upset, Jocelyn. She's talking about sending me to stay with my aunt up north until they find whoever killed Bridget. What a bummer. I told the cops I don't know anything. Bridget and I broke up as best friends. She wouldn't even look at me in the hall at school."

Jocelyn interrupted gently. "We know, Sara. I'm sorry. But we really need to know who Bridget's boyfriend was. She told you everything."

Sara examined her toenails carefully, brushing a red ant off her ankle. "I don't know who it was."

"Sara," Jocelyn said. "I bet that fight you had was about her boyfriend, wasn't it?"

She looked up angrily. "This was the first year we were allowed to go on car dates," she burst out. "We were gonna double date, pick up guys at the mall. We had it all planned. Then one day at lunch, I go in Bridget's purse to look for some Life Savers, and what do I find? A package of Trojans!"

"Oh man," Jocelyn said in a breath.

"I know," Sara said. "We were supposed to be best friends, but here she doesn't even tell me she's not a virgin anymore.

"That's when we had the fight. Bridget said I didn't

have the right to judge her. She said I was worse than a nun. So I called her a slut."

"That must have been hard for you," Jocelyn said. She'd obviously picked up a lot from all her therapy sessions.

"It was," Sara agreed. "I've been bummed ever since I heard about her being killed."

"Who was the guy, Sara?" Jocelyn persisted. "I know she told you. Bridget could never keep a secret. She always used to tell me what she was giving me for Christmas and birthdays days ahead of time."

Sara's lower lip pooched out stubbornly. "I promised I wouldn't tell. I swore on the Blessed Virgin Mother's eyes."

"Come on, Sara," Jocelyn coaxed. "Bridget is dead. It doesn't count now."

"No kidding?"

"No kidding."

"Swear you won't tell anybody else?" Sara said, glancing around to make sure she wouldn't be overheard.

"Swear." I only hoped Jocelyn had her toes crossed.

"It was Coach J," Sara whispered.

"Who?" I said, loudly.

"Shh," Sara said. "He'll know I told."

"Shit," Jocelyn said. "Coach J. I should have known. He's a major stud. There were rumors about him and Ashley Gates my senior year. Sara, are you sure? Cross your heart?"

Wordlessly, Sara crossed her teeny bikini top.

"Okay, thanks a lot," Jocelyn said. "I mean it. See ya around, Sara."

I had to break into a near run to keep up with Jocelyn as she sprinted back to the car.

"Shitfuckdamnhellpiss," Jocelyn said, pounding the Hyundai's plastic-wrapped steering wheel. "Coach

Jordan. Her stinking soccer coach." She pounded the steering wheel some more, this time with her forehead.

"Calm down," I said, lifting her head up. "And tell me who this Coach Jordan is."

"He's old," she said, her voice dripping scorn. "He's old, and he's married, and he has about a million kids and he spits when he says his *T*'s."

"He sounds revolting," I said. "Now tell me something else. Does he live around here? Do you feel up to another ambush?"

We zipped over to a nearby Burger King for a strategy session. I had a Whopper with cheese and fries, Jocelyn had a diet Coke. "Aren't you supposed to eat?" I asked.

"You sound like my mother," she snarled. "I'm on a strict plan. I'll eat dinner when I get back to my house. Don't worry. No more laxatives. I'm cured. I couldn't stand another second in that nuthouse."

I tore open a package of Sweet'n Low and poured it into my iced tea. "Good. I don't want you back in the nuthouse either. You're too good an interrogator."

It took a while to find the right Coach Jordan, but after some calling around, Jocelyn recalled the coach's first name. Kyle. Kyle Jordan. I called the house, and when a masculine voice answered, asked to speak to Mrs. Jordan. "She's not home," her husband said. "Call back around eight."

I hung up and flashed Jocelyn the victory sign. "Let's go for a visit."

Mr. Jordan's neighborhood was a mile or so from Sara Parrish's house, and several rungs down the Atlanta social ladder.

The houses here were smaller, set on tiny lots, with aluminum siding instead of brick, and economy compacts parked in driveways instead of Dunwoody's maxivans and Volvo wagons. Yards were littered with children's riding toys, plastic wading pools, and snarls of bicycles.

We rang the bell four times. From inside the house, we could hear a television and the sound of an extremely cranky baby. "Hold on, I'm coming," said the same voice I had just talked to on the phone.

Kyle Jordan had golden brown hair nearly the same shade as his tan. There was a dangerous-looking cleft in his chin. He wore a YMCA T-shirt, black soccer shorts, and a wailing diaper-clad baby on his hip. He flashed an apologetic smile. "Trevor here is just waking up from his nap. What can I do for you?"

Jocelyn and I exchanged uncertain glances. In the meantime, Jordan had a chance to study her and to recognize the family resemblance.

"Jocelyn, isn't it? Jocelyn Dougherty? I saw you at Bridget's funeral today. I'd like you and your family to know how sorry I am. Bridget was a great girl, a really valuable member of our team. Such a sweet kid."

"You're a pig," Jocelyn said bitterly. "You slept with my sister. She dropped out of school and ran away from home because of you. Because of you, she's dead. I'm reporting you to All Saints. I'm reporting you to them, and to the archbishop of Atlanta and to my parents and the cops . . . " Her voice became shriller by the second.

Baby Trevor screamed, louder, at the sound of the angry voice. Jordan reached in his pocket, brought out a pacifier, and stuck it in his son's mouth. Instantly the child calmed down. Kyle Jordan looked as though he could use something to suck on too.

"Hey," he said. "Hey, that's not right. Come in. Okay? Just come inside so the neighbors don't get the wrong idea."

The Jordans' living room was smaller than mine,

crammed with a big-screen television, a black leather sofa and matching recliner, a weight bench, and a brightly colored playpen overflowing with children's toys and stuffed animals.

Jordan sat briefly in the recliner, balancing the sucking baby on his knee. He got up, paced the room, and stopped to place the baby in a wheeled walker. Then he stood in front of Jocelyn and me, who were seated on the sofa. He stood there, hands clasped behind his back, legs slightly apart, ready for team roll call.

"You've got it all wrong," he said.

Jocelyn snorted and rolled her eyes.

"Do you deny you slept with Bridget?" I asked.

He looked at me angrily. "Who are you? What business is this of yours?"

"She's a private detective I've hired to find out who killed my sister," Jocelyn volunteered.

"I didn't do it," he said. "I swear to God I didn't do it."

"You slept with her," I said. "She thought she was pregnant. She told you she planned to keep the baby and you told her you'd marry her."

"Never," Jordan said hoarsely. "She made all that up. These girls, you don't know how they are. They imagine things. Blow things all out of proportion. I'm a married man. I've got three kids. Why would I risk that on a silly little high school kid?"

"You're a fucking child molester," Jocelyn cried, leaping up from the sofa. "How dare you talk about my sister that way?"

Jordan's blasé manner pissed me off so royally I wanted to see how much of my fist would fit inside that cleft chin of his, but I suppressed the urge.

"Why don't you explain to me why you'd risk sleeping with your students," I said calmly. "It shouldn't take much for the cops to prove you had a relationship with Bridget. I found one of your notes to her. They can probably find more. She told her best friend about the affair, and her boss."

"It was not an affair," he said, nearly shouting. The baby's face crinkled in unhappiness, his pacifier dropped to the tray of the walker, and he gave a single sharp, warning cry of distress. Quickly, Jordan popped the pacifier back into his son's face. He lowered his voice. "It wasn't an affair. I slept with her once. No more, and it was all her idea. She came on to me. She showed up here at spring break, when she knew my wife and kids would be in Florida with my in-laws. She showed up late, with a bottle of wine and a pizza. All the kids at school hang out at our house. But this time Bridget was alone, and she had big ideas."

"You're telling us she seduced you," I said sarcastically. "Save it for somebody who cares."

"She thought she was pregnant," Jocelyn said, breaking in. "That's when she had the big fight with my mom."

"Impossible," Jordan said. "I used a condom. In fact, she brought them with her. She planned the whole thing. Look. I'm sorry your sister is dead," he said, turning to Jocelyn. "But she was no innocent little kid. Bridget had been around the block. I wasn't her first."

"Liar," Jocelyn said, fighting back a sob in her fury at hearing her little sister's character being maligned. "Lying pig. Let's go, Callahan. Let's call the cops. I don't think Littlefield killed Bridget. I think Coach J did it."

I shrugged but got up. Jordan followed us to the door.

"I didn't kill her," he insisted again. "It was that pervert she was living with, not me. I'd never have hurt Bridget."

"Hope you've got an alibi," I told him, my hand on the doorknob.

Jordan seized the idea of an alibi instantly. "That was Saturday, right? I was at soccer camp. I run a soccer camp for the Rockdale Y. You can check. I was there."

Headlights shone in through the living room drapes, and a horn beeped once, then twice.

"Oh Jesus," Jordan whispered. "It's Lissa and the kids."

Jocelyn and I exchanged looks again. I shook my head as a warning, but she chose to ignore it.

"How nice," she said, sitting back down on the sofa again. "I'd like to meet your wife. I bet she'd like to meet your girlfriend's sister."

She crossed her legs at the ankle and folded her hands neatly in her lap like a good little Catholic schoolgirl and smiled sweetly at both of us.

"Let's go, Jocelyn," I said. She continued to smile but shook her head no.

"Please," Jordan said, going to the window and peering out. "Oh God. You don't know Lissa. This would kill her. Please . . . "

We heard voices on the front walk, a woman's voice. "Come on, Jessica, tell Daddy to open the door. Kyle," she called. "Open up quick. I've got Megan asleep in my arms."

Jordan turned back to us, his golden face etched with panic.

I crossed over to Jocelyn, grabbed her, and effortlessly jerked her to her feet. She tried to pull away, but I held on to her arm and moved her toward the door, with Jordan right at our heels. "I don't give a rat's ass about your marriage," I hissed. "I'm not going to be the one to tell your wife you were screwing around. But I can't promise she won't find out from the cops. Let's go, Jocelyn."

Scowling, Jocelyn removed my hand from her arm and followed me to the front door. Jordan opened it and Lissa Jordan stumbled across the threshold, holding a sleeping toddler in her arms. In a white knit mini skirt and matching halter top, Lissa looked like a career aerobics instructor. She had streaked blond hair cut short and moussed straight up into mega-mall bangs. Big brown eyes washed over the two of us. Rose-bud lipsticked mouth and a sharp little chin. What the hell was Kyle Jordan doing screwing teenagers when he had this hot number at home, I wondered. Close on Lissa's heels followed a three-year-old version of the mother, wearing a smudged playsuit and sucking on a Popsicle.

"Hello," Lissa Jordan said, her narrowed eyes making the word a question. Her husband stood there, frozen in terror, like a frog about to be gigged.

"Mutual of Minnesota Life and Casualty," I said smoothly. "My assistant and I were just giving your husband a complimentary estate planning needs assessment. With all these beautiful children you folks have, it's time you . . . "

"Kyle gets insurance through the school. You told them that, didn't you, honey?" she said sweetly. "Maybe you could call some other time. I really need to get these kids in bed now." She lowered the sleeping child onto the sofa and walked quickly back to the door, holding it open wide to let us know her needs no longer needed assessing.

"Thanks for coming," she said firmly.

I caught Jordan's eye just before the door shut. "We'll be in touch," I promised.

"Jeez," Jocelyn exploded, once we were in the car, with the motor started. "What a weenie. What a lying, pussy-whipped weenie. You know, I used to think

Coach J was a stud. Now I can't believe Bridget let him get in her pants."

I made a halfhearted attempt to look shocked at the crudeness of her language.

"Well, Jocelyn," I said, "it's like those great rock philosophers Mickey and Sylvia used to say."

"What?" she asked, accelerating so quickly that the car fairly jumped away from the curb.

"Mickey and Sylvia," I said, appalled at her ignorance of rock history. "You know. 'Love Is Strange.'"

14

SHANE DUNSTAN, THE HEAD of Emory University's special collections, returned my phone call on the fourth try. I guess she was busy spending the school's money. Ever since 1987, when two of Atlanta's Coca-Cola billionaires had given Emory a $110 million endowment, Emory has been rolling in dough.

"This is about the Lula Belle Bird diary?" she asked, when she came on the line. Elliot Littlefield must have told her to expect my call.

"That's right," I said. "The other items taken in the burglary were valuable too, but it's the diary that Mr. Littlefield is particularly anxious to recover."

"We've withdrawn our bid," she said abruptly. "I've just been drafting a letter to notify Mr. Littlefield. The chairman of the library board called me this morning."

That, I thought, would jar my client's preserves. I had a feeling he'd hoped some of Emory's prestige would rub off on him if he helped the university acquire such a prized find.

"Any particular reason?"

"One very particular reason. Our board is unhappy with the source of the funding for the acquisition, and the terms. I disagreed, but the board members were unanimous, and very adamant."

"Who was the source?"

"I'm not certain I'm at liberty to say."

"Go ahead," I urged. "I'm very good at what I do, so I'll probably find out anyway. You could save me some time by just telling me now."

She hesitated. "I'm assuming you'll consider this as confidential information. Two weeks ago, P. G. T. Vickers came to my office and told me he'd been contacted about buying the diary. We'd also been contacted, but of course, our purchase fund could never cover what Elliot Littlefield was asking for a floor bid. Mr. Vickers said he wanted to bid on it. You know him, don't you?"

The name seemed to ring a bell, but I didn't know why and admitted it.

"Pierre Gustave Toutant Vickers III. He's named after the great Civil War general who directed the attack on Fort Sumter and commanded at First Manassas, of course. He runs a very successful publishing company, and is involved in some rather extremist political activities."

"P. G. T. Vickers, now I know the name," I said. "He's not extreme. He's a certified lunatic. He lives in that fortress at the base of Stone Mountain and he publishes that states' rights newspaper, *Rebel Yell.* And didn't he run for Congress for the American Eagle party?"

"I'm afraid so," she said, sighing. "It was the newspaper and Mr. Vickers's politics that made the board decide to decline his offer to provide the money to buy the diary for our collection. The board felt it was not in our best interest to have a P. G. T. Vickers collection here at the library."

"I can see why," I said. "He's always campaigning for

a return to the gold standard and writing letters to the editor about keeping Georgia's Confederate flag intact. He's also got some kind of half-cocked Kennedy assassination conspiracy involving a lost tribe of Seminole Indians and an albino hit man. The man is a nut, Ms. Dunstan."

"A rich nut, Ms. Garrity. The arrangement he proposed would have given us physical possession of the diary and a grant to research the life of Lula Belle Bird. Mr. Vickers's Rebel Yell Press would subsequently publish a trade version of the diary. And he would have retained rights to develop a screenplay of the diary."

"A profitable arrangement for both sides," I remarked.

"There's nothing wrong with profit," she snapped. "It was Coca-Cola profits that built this school. But that's a moot point now. The diary is missing, and our board is adamant about keeping P. G. T. Vickers's name from being associated with Emory."

"Tell me something, will you?" I asked. "Is this thing really as big a deal as Mr. Littlefield is leading me to believe?"

"The Lula Belle Bird diary is the single most exciting acquisition I've pursued in my career," she said.

"Oh," I said. "I'm sorry."

"I'm sorry it's been stolen," she said softly. "Your client let me hold it, and open it, but I never had a chance to really examine it. What a loss."

I couldn't find a home listing for P. G. T. Vickers in the Atlanta telephone directory, but I did find one for Rebel Yell Press.

"Vickers here," barked the voice at the other end. I was momentarily taken aback. I'd expected layers of secretaries and assistants. Not the head man himself.

When I told him I'd been hired by Littlefield to

recover the diary, he readily agreed to see me, and gave me directions to his office. "Come on out. We'll have lunch," he said.

Stone Mountain is a sleepy little hamlet, aspiring to nothing more than selling a few trinkets to the tourists who come to see what's billed as the World's Largest Granite Outcropping. Most of them are actually more interested in the carving on the north side of the mountain, a two-thousand-foot-long sculpture combining the likenesses of the South's three most enduring icons: Robert E. Lee, Stonewall Jackson, and Jefferson Davis. (The carving was designed in the 1920s, which explains why Elvis Aaron Presley, who wasn't born until 1935, was left off.)

Stone Mountain's main street looks like the main street in one of those cowboy movies of my youth, with flat storefronts, gingerbread trim, and window boxes full of red geraniums.

Cute as it is though, Stone Mountain has a darker side. For years the mountain served as a staging area for the Georgia chapters of the Ku Klux Klan and other radical white-power groups, drawing hundreds of robed and hooded Klansmen for festive cross burnings and race-baiting rallies.

The new Stone Mountain has almost lived down its nasty old image. But the headquarters of Rebel Yell Press is a handy reminder that bad times there are not entirely forgotten.

I found Rebel Yell tucked between an ice cream parlor and a country collectibles boutique. It would have been hard to miss; a three-story-high cross between a Chevy dealership and an exact replica of Tara, with a wrought-iron fence keeping undesirables off a skinny sliver of lawn that separated the building from the outside world.

Inside, the receptionist, a frail-looking lady who looked nearly as old as the mountain, looked surprised to see a visitor. "I'm Callahan Garrity," I said, shouting so she could hear me. "I have an appointment." While she frantically punched buttons on the office intercom, I glanced around the two-story lobby. The walls were covered with a colorful mural of a Civil War battle, with a battalion of mounted gray-coated Rebs victorious over a sea of fallen federal soldiers. The carpets were the same shade of gray, and in the middle of the room, a grand staircase swept the eye up toward the second floor.

The old lady pushed every button in front of her. "Hello. Come in, hello," she shouted.

"Send her on up, Miss Kate," called a voice from above. A boyish-looking man with chestnut-colored hair hung over the second-floor balcony.

At the top of the stairway, the man stuck out his hand. He wore a taupe-colored double-breasted Italian-looking suit, with a brightly flowered tie and modish pointy-toed shoes. Right-wing zanies dress a lot better than they used to. They're a lot younger, too. I was expecting a geezer in a string tie and red suspenders, not this thirty-something dandy. "Pete Vickers," he said. "Excuse Miss Kate. She was my father's secretary, and she likes to totter in now and then to help out. We've got lunch ready in my office. All right if we eat and talk? I've got a meeting outside the office at one."

I followed him through a short hallway whose walls were actually glass bookcases full of the collected works of Rebel Yell Press. More books lined the walls of Vickers's office. The walls were crowded with leather-bound volumes, and where there weren't books there were busts and paintings of Civil War battles and generals. A display case directly behind Vickers's desk bristled with a nice selection of semiautomatic weapons, carbines, and martial arts weapons. An *Impeach Earl Warren* sign, the kind that had once been tacked to every tree in the rural South, was prominently displayed on top of the case.

He caught me staring at the sign. "That was my daddy's legacy," he said, smiling at the memory. "Rebel Yell printed thousands of those signs. Did it for cost, too. Those babies are collectors' items these days."

I gestured toward the semiautomatic weapons. "Aren't those babies illegal in Georgia?"

"Hell no," he said. "We still got our Second Amendment to the Constitution, don't we?"

He moved over to the case, took a small key from his pocket, and opened it. He took one off the rack and cradled it in his arms like a newborn baby. "Colt Industries M-sixteen," he said, looking down fondly. "This one," he said, pointing to another, "is a Colt AR-fifteen, and of course, I've got my Heckler and Koch model ninety-one semiautomatic. You can see the Galil there, that's from Israel, and then I've got a seventy-four hundred, thirty oh six Remington automatic too. These are my little play toys. Don't get enough time to play with 'em though. Business, business, business." He put the M-16 back, gave it a final loving pat, then closed and locked the cabinet door. A shiver went from the base of my spine to the top of my neck. I've been around guns since I was a kid hunting with my dad, and later, of course, as a cop, but people who think of guns as toys scare the hell out of me.

The top of the large mahogany desk had been cleared off and a silver tray held two steaming plates of food and two tall crystal glasses of iced tea.

"Set right down," Vickers said, motioning to an armchair facing the desk.

He handed me a plate and a packet of silverware rolled up inside a linen napkin.

The food smelled and looked divine. I had a fried chicken breast, fresh-cut corn off the cob, green beans floating in a puddle of bacon-scented juice, and a fat red slice of tomato. A corn muffin balanced precariously on the edge of the plate.

I looked up expectantly. "You always feed visiting private investigators this well?"

Vickers stopped chewing on his drumstick. "I treat everybody except liberals, the IRS, and the ATF like this. The Olde South Cafeteria next door caters for us, when we have visitors around lunchtime. We feed them too, just like my mama used to do. It's kinda a Rebel Yell tradition."

"Nice," I said, between a bite of muffin and a sip of tea.

"So you want to know what I know about the Lula Belle Bird diary," he said. "Damn shame about the burglary. And the girl too, of course. I've already told Littlefield, when and if the thing is recovered, I want my bid automatically reinstated. I mean to have that diary."

I wiped the chicken crumbs off my fingers. "Shane Dunstan says you planned to publish the diary."

"Planned to make a killing out of it," he said. "No pun intended. Our Civil War titles always do well, but a book like this, 'The Diary of a Confederate Madam,' that'll be the title, should be a blockbuster. And by the way, we're looking at either a PBS miniseries or a theatrical feature. We think this thing could be bigger than *Gone with the Wind*."

"If you can recover the diary."

"Exactly," he said, squeezing a slice of lemon into his tea.

"But Emory University is declining to accept the

money to buy the diary, even if it is found," I pointed out.

He frowned slightly. His cheeks were round and full and freckled, and he had a thin ginger-colored mustache, which he probably thought made him look like Clark Gable.

"They don't want Emory's hallowed halls besmirched by the villainous Vickers name," he said, chuckling. "Everybody in Atlanta knows that P. G. T. Vickers stands for states' rights, a strong national defense, an end to the welfare state, and the preservation of our white, southern heritage. I don't apologize for any of that. Emory doesn't approve of my ideology. All right. I don't approve of theirs either. They're the people who hired that professor who said 'God is dead' in the sixties. A religion professor, can you imagine? After Ms. Dunstan called today and gave me the news, I called the University of Georgia. Their special collection curator accepted my offer in a New York second."

"Why give it away at all?" I asked. "You're clearly a Civil War collector yourself. Why not just keep it?"

"Love to," he said. "But I get a nice little old tax write-off and the kind of favorable publicity from making such a generous gift that money can't buy."

"Did you want the diary bad enough to steal it?" I asked.

"Why sure," he said. "I didn't though. I thought there was no way anyone could outbid me, until I heard through the grapevine that Speedy Blakeford was making a run at it."

"You hated that idea," I guessed.

"Are the Kennedys gun-shy? Yes, ma'am. I don't mind saying I wouldn't want to see that precious piece of southern heritage sold off to some slant-eyed Japanese bankers."

"Would Blakeford have stolen it?"

"Ask him," Vickers suggested. "I kind of doubt it, though. I understand he's one of them Bible-thumping committed Christian kind of fellas. Don't believe in cheatin', stealin', killin', or committing adultery."

"Do you?" I asked.

"Don't believe in getting caught at it," he grinned.

I pushed a green bean around my plate until I cornered it up against a chunk of bacon. "Did the police ask you about your whereabouts on Saturday afternoon?"

"Sure did. You wanna hear what I told 'em?"

I did.

"Told 'em I was at the dedication and ribbon-cutting ceremony for the P. G. T. Vickers Memorial Branch of the Stone Mountain Community Library." He picked up a folded-up newspaper from the credenza in back of his desk and handed it to me. "See there," he pointed. "Made the front page of *The Stone Mountain Courier-Express.*"

He had indeed. The photo was in color and showed a smiling hard-hatted Vickers wielding a huge pair of scissors in front of a new-looking brick building.

"Memorial Library?"

"After my father," he said quickly. "P. G. T. Junior. I'm P. G. T. the third; 'Pete' to my friends. Daddy gave part of his personal library to start the first Stone Mountain library, and then he left them money in his will to provide for a new building."

"Philanthropy seems to be a family tradition for the Vickerses," I said. "How nice."

He snorted. "Shrewdness is what runs in my family, as I'm sure you're aware. We're in the book business here. Just makes good sense to have our name connected with a library."

I looked down at the newspaper photo again. Vickers

and the others in the crowd appeared to be squinting in the face of strong sunlight. "Looks like the ribbon-cutting took place in the morning," I said. "Bridget was killed sometime in late afternoon. And Mr. Littlefield mentioned that you'd been in his home before for social functions. Did the police ask you about that?"

He snatched the newspaper away. "I been trying to treat you like a lady, like my mama brought me up, but you keep on asking a bunch of snotty, smart-alecky questions. You remind me of my first wife. She had an attitude just like yours."

"Does that mean you're not going to answer my questions?" I asked innocently.

He pushed his chair back from the desk, bumping into the gun case. "That means I've given you all the time you're getting," he said. "I got a meeting to go to."

With great deliberation I dabbed daintily at the corners of my mouth and set my plate and glass of tea squarely on the newspaper, deliberately spilling a little in the process. "Good-bye, Mr. Vickers," I said, holding out my hand to shake. He grasped it, shook once, and dropped it. "Thank you for the lovely lunch," I added. "I'm sorry you find uppity women so intimidating, but I'm afraid that's often the case with men who have unresolved questions about their own virility. I understand your hero, Robert E. Lee, had the same problem."

I might have flounced an imaginary hoopskirt as I swept out. He deserved it.

15

I SAT IN THE VAN OUTSIDE the Rebel Yell
offices and fumed. There was no real satisfaction in
sniping at somebody like Pete Vickers, and I felt unset-
tled and confused.

If the diary wasn't in the hands of a serious collector,
what then? I ticked off the possibilities in my head: that
the burglary and murder had been a random act of violence by a crack-crazed junkie; that Littlefield had killed
Bridget, just as he'd killed before; that Kyle Jordan had
killed his lover to keep his family together; and the scenario that Littlefield was pushing, that the crimes had
been committed as part of a plot to destroy him.

None of the choices pleased me. To be honest, I'd
have to admit that my enthusiasm for finding Lula Belle
Bird's diary was waning fast. The real crime at Eagle's
Keep had been the murder of Bridget Dougherty.
Despite my protests to the contrary, that was the case I
was itching to solve.

I was still sitting there cogitating when Pete Vickers
walked out the front door of his office and got into a big
black Oldsmobile parked three spaces down from me. I
waited until his car had turned the corner, then hopped

out of the van and walked back into the Rebel Yell lobby.

Miss Kate had propped a tiny portable television on the edge of the reception desk and she was addressing two on-screen actors who appeared to be indulging in some afternoon delight. "Oh my," she said, looking away, her hand to her mouth. "And here that little April is just back from her honeymoon, climbing into bed with that no-good Dack."

"Miss Kate," I said, loudly.

She jumped, and looked around guiltily.

"I'm Callahan Garrity," I reminded her. "I was just here to see Mr. Vickers. I'm, uh, with the Stone Mountain Historical Association and he, uh, mentioned you might know whether anyone photographed the library dedication last Saturday."

She turned down the volume on the set. "What's that?"

I repeated my question.

She scrabbled around on the desktop, opened some drawers and briefly ducked under the desk to look there.

"No'm," she said. "I seen some photo fellas snapping pictures that day, but young Pete never gave none of 'em to me."

"You were at the dedication?" I asked casually.

"Sure was," she said proudly. "Young Pete picked me up himself, brought me an orchid corsage to wear too."

"He's quite a guy that Pete," I said. "Tell me, was the ceremony a long one? Sometimes these things drag on and on."

"No, not too long," she said, glancing toward the television. "Mr. Pete took us to a nice reception at the Magnolia Plantation afterward. Then he had Miss Vicki, that's the youngest sister, take me home."

"He didn't take you himself?"

"No'm. He had to be in Atlanta that afternoon for his study group. War Between the States, you know. Young Pete's always studying on that. He's a real scholar."

"I could tell," I lied. "Say, you know, I believe I must have left my notebook in Mr. Vickers's office when I was here just now. I'll just run up and get it if you don't mind."

She reached over and turned the volume back up. The soap opera lovers were rolling around on satin sheets. She didn't look back at me. "Can't get up those stairs my own self any more. You go on ahead."

I took the stairs two at a time. Vickers's office door was open, but his desktop was disappointingly clear, holding only a telephone. I peeked out into the hallway. Nobody there. His appointment calendar was in the top right-hand desk drawer. Pete Vickers was a thorough kind of guy. Each page of the calendar was marked off in hour increments, with appointments and reminders neatly inked in. I leafed backward to Saturday. He'd marked the library dedication time, eleven A.M., and the reception time at one P.M. If he'd left after an hour, he'd have had plenty of time for a trip to Eagle's Keep. There was no notation about a Civil War study group. I turned the page to Sunday. There were no notations, but he'd stuck a yellow Post-It note to the page. *Darryl, 555-2303*, it said. I took a pen out of the drawer, helped myself to a piece of paper and jotted the information down. Then I slid the drawer shut and sauntered down the stairs.

Miss Kate was so involved with April and Dack she barely gave me a nod when I got back to the lobby.

There was a Starvin' Marvin down the street from Rebel Yell. I decided to pull over and make a phone call. I dialed the *Constitution* newsroom and asked for Brownie Brownell. After five minutes of being switched from phone to phone, the veteran crime reporter came on the line.

"Brownell," he said. Brownie sounded old and slightly feeble, but I knew he couldn't have been sixty yet. He said he remembered me from the cop shop, but I could tell he didn't have a clue who I was. He did, however, remember the Sunny Girl murder case.

"Big story," he said, relishing the memory. "I got pulled off the James Earl Ray murder trial to cover Sunny Girl. Never did find out who that little gal was, or where she was from. My own little girl was a teenager at the time, and I'll never forget how bad I felt for that girl's folks, whoever they were, that their daughter ran away from home and never came back. That's a terrible thought, isn't it, not knowing what's happened to your kid?"

"It is," I agreed. "I know Littlefield's conviction was overturned, but what happened to the retrial?"

"There never was a retrial," Brownell said. "Jim Barchie, the district attorney, stalled and stalled, then finally announced that there wasn't enough evidence to guarantee a conviction. Barchie was up for re-election that year, and there was no way he wanted people to remember how badly he'd screwed up that case. He let a rookie cop take the blame for fouling up the evidence, but I always maintained it was Barchie's own fault for not having tighter control of the investigation."

"What happened to the rookie?" I asked. "Who was he?"

"Calvin Shakespeare," Brownell said promptly. "Funny kind of name for a cop. He got put on administrative leave and was fired later. He appealed it, but nothing ever came of it."

"You sure remember a lot about this story," I remarked.

"It always bothered me," Brownell said. "Back in seventy-nine, on the tenth anniversary of the murder, I did a big investigation. Best story I ever wrote. I went back and talked to everybody. Hell, I even turned up a witness who was in the next bedroom at the time, heard screams and later saw Littlefield coming out of the bedroom alone."

"You're kidding," I said. "Why didn't the cops reopen the case then?"

He laughed bitterly. "The story never ran. We had a hotshot young city editor who thought nobody cared about a ten-year-old murder. The story got canned. I nearly quit over it."

"That sucks," I said, mostly to myself.

"It was a long time ago," he said quietly.

A series of short beeps interrupted Brownell's train of thought. "Whoops," he said, "call holding. Gotta go."

"Wait a minute," I said, "who was the witness?"

"I don't guess it matters now. At the time it was a big secret. It was a young doctor named Koteras," Brownell said. "He and some stewardess were screwing in the next bedroom. They never came forward because the stew was in the middle of a divorce and was afraid she'd lose custody of her kid if it came out in court. Bye."

Koteras. The doctor who made house calls. No wonder he didn't like to socialize with Littlefield. He'd covered up a murder for the sake of convenience all those years ago, and now it looked like his old buddy had pulled it off again.

I got back in the van, but I wasn't going anywhere in a hurry. Traffic had gotten worse while I was on the phone. The street was clogged with MARTA buses, overheating cars, and darting in and out of traffic, bicyclists. There was no way I would voluntarily wade into that mess. I felt in my pocket for more money for a phone call, but all I found was a crumpled five-dollar bill.

Inside the Starvin' Marvin I treated myself to a kiwi-lime wine cooler and got a handful of change for the phone.

Hunsecker was away from his desk at a meeting, but his new partner, Linda Nickells, said she expected him back soon. She acted friendly on the phone, a somewhat encouraging sign. "Ask him to call me at home tomorrow, will you?" I said. "And tell him I'm sorry I ran off at the mouth."

Nickells had a nice laugh. "He's used to mouthy women," she said. "Don't worry. I'll make him call."

I dropped another quarter in the slot. "House Mouse—ask about our summer savings super special," drawled a female voice.

"Neva Jean," I said, "let me talk to Edna."

"Hey," I said, when my mother came on the phone.

"Hey your own self," Edna said tartly. "Where are you?"

The wail of a police siren drowned out my reply.

"Where are you?" she repeated. "A drunk tank?"

The police cruiser was trying to inch its way through the clogged traffic, but with traffic blocked both ways, it was slow going. I could feel the sweat dripping down my back. With the heat coming off the asphalt and the fumes from overheating engines it must have been over a hundred degrees.

"I'm on Ponce," I said patiently. "Traffic's all snarled up, so I stopped to use a pay phone and while I was on the phone it's gotten worse. Now it's not moving at all. Either way."

"Too bad," she said. "The air-conditioner blew a compressor right after you left this morning and the repairman says he can't get the parts till tomorrow, if then. It's a hundred and ten degrees in this kitchen right now and Ruby's blood pressure is up again so I spent two hours sitting with her at the clinic at Grady today before they'd see her."

"She okay?" I asked anxiously.

"She's home sleeping, but now my own blood pressure's sky high, thanks for asking."

"Other than that, how's it going? Any messages?"

"Nothing urgent," she snapped. "I'll talk to you later."

I was almost home when I remembered the blown air compressor, so I decided to take a detour to Inman Park. I took a left on Dolan Avenue, and from there I could see the redbrick turrets of Eagle's Keep. Might as well give my client an update, I reasoned.

The Rolls was parked in Littlefield's open garage, but his van was missing. I parked on the street and walked up to the front and rang the doorbell, just in case. On the other side of the door I heard loud mewing and scratching. "It's me, Ping-Pong," I called. "Where's the boss?"

The cat mewed pathetically again. "Surprised you haven't been packed off for a permanent catnap," I muttered to the door. I'm no cat lover, but I felt sorry, even proprietary toward Bridget's abandoned pet.

"I'm surprised he hasn't drowned her," said a voice from behind me.

Jake Dahlberg looked as good in a dress shirt and unknotted tie as he had in shorts and no shirt.

"Actually, I hate cats," I said apologetically. "Or I'd take her home with me."

"Allergies," Dahlberg said, pointing to his eyes. "Only pet I can keep is a goldfish."

We smiled at each other in a goofy kind of silence, fresh out of meaningful things to say to each other.

"Littlefield left an hour ago," he volunteered. "Want to come over and have a cold beer?"

I hesitated. I was hot and cranky. But Dahlberg intrigued me. "Make it something nonalcoholic and you've got a deal," I said finally. "If I have any more liquor in this heat, I'll positively swoon."

"I like the sound of that," he teased. "How does iced tea sound?"

"Nice."

I sank gratefully into a dark green painted rocker on Dahlberg's porch. It was cool there in the shade, and it felt like the first time that day that I'd had a minute of peace. I sank my head back and closed my eyes. I sat like that for five minutes or so, not sleeping really, but not really alert, either.

When I opened my eyes again, he was standing over me, a frosty glass of tea in his hand. He'd changed back into shorts and a T-shirt.

"You've got nice skin," he said casually. "Creamy. It reminds me of the women I saw in Ireland. Not like women here who stay out in the sun until they look like a hunk of Slim Jim."

I yawned to cover my embarrassment. For some reason I felt silly and slightly giddy around Dahlberg.

The tea was cold and scented with mint and lemon. I smacked my lips appreciatively. "Good," I said. "I feel better already."

He sat down beside me and opened his Kronenberg. "How's the investigation?"

"So-so," I said. "Lots of possibilities, very few real leads."

Then he wanted to know how a nice girl like me got into something as seedy as private investigation. He wanted to know all the stuff other people always ask when they meet a woman whose work they consider unusual.

Normally I hate talking about that stuff. Like anybody else, I do what I'm trained to do—what I'm good at. Besides, for the most part what I do is run a cleaning business, a distinctly unglamorous career.

"The House Mouse?" he said when I told him about my business. "You're a maid?"

I bristled at his tone of voice. "I run a business," I said testily. "We employ six people full-time. I own my own home, pay taxes, and we make a small but respectable profit. I myself am college educated and I even watch 'Masterpiece Theatre' occasionally."

"Okay," he laughed. "Sorry if I acted like a snob. Actually, after you mentioned the cleaning business it occurred to me that you might be able to give some work to some of our tenants."

"Tenants?" I said innocently. "Are you running a rooming house here?"

"Not exactly. I'm the founder and president of the board of Home for Hope. Maybe you've heard about us. We're a nonprofit outfit. We buy abandoned houses in in-town neighborhoods, rehab them, and sell them for a very low price, with no down payment to the working poor."

"Did I read something about your winning an award from the state?" I asked.

"Better," he beamed. "We were one of President Bush's last Thousand Points of Light. We've got five houses in Cabbagetown, over near the old Fulton Bag plant, and three houses here in Inman Park. We've applied for a grant to expand the program this year and buy four more houses."

"That's wonderful," I said sincerely. "In my own neighborhood, homeless women and men wander the streets all the time. And Edna and I cook for a family shelter run by an Episcopalian church in Decatur."

"You see," Dahlberg said, his dark eyes shining with enthusiasm, "we do much more than a shelter ever could. By buying and rehabbing these houses we take derelict housing stock and make it a viable, attractive part of the community. Plus we make homeowners of the working poor."

"How do your neighbors feel about your moving homeless people into Inman Park?" I asked. "These are some pretty pricey houses around here."

He twirled his empty beer bottle between the palms of his hands. "Most people applaud what we're doing," he said, choosing his words carefully. "But yes, you're always going to hit the NIMBY effect."

"NIMBY?" I said. "What's that?"

"It's an acronym for 'not in my backyard,'" he said. "There are certain people around here who believe that only white, middle-class, heterosexual Protestants deserve to have a home in a nice neighborhood."

"People like Elliot Littlefield?"

"What have you heard?" he said tensely. "What did he tell you?"

The ice was melting in my tea, leaving a pool of clear liquid on top of the amber tea.

"I've heard that he's organized the neighbors to try to stop you buying any more houses here. That he actually bought one vacant house for substantially more than it was worth just to keep your group from getting it. I also heard that you got your revenge by reporting him to the city zoning board over parking and fire regulations. I heard the feud between you has been going on for some time."

"He told you that?"

"Some of it. I'm a detective, remember?"

Dahlberg got up and leaned against the porch railing. "This whole feud deal has been blown way out of proportion. Littlefield may have some hard feelings against me, and yes, I was upset about the flag thing, but I'm personally too busy to spend much time mounting a conspiracy against Elliot Littlefield."

He turned and smiled, flashing beautiful, even white teeth. The Dahlbergs had spent lots of money on orthodontia.

"As long as you're in the neighborhood, why not stay and have dinner with me? I've got a couple salmon steaks in the fridge and a nice bottle of wine. What do you say? When Littlefield gets home, you can pop over there and see him, as you intended. Just don't tell him you had dinner with me."

The offer was tempting. Lunch had been a long time ago, and it sounded like Edna wasn't planning to do any cooking with the air-conditioning on the fritz. Besides, this leafy front porch had a nice feel to it.

"Thanks, but no," I said reluctantly. "I've been out all day and I've still got more work to do at home tonight."

"You sure?"

I nodded yes. "Maybe another time?"

"For sure," he said. "But would you have time to look at our Inman Park houses? I'm really proud of them. They're just right over on Gormley. It's only a five minute walk."

I glanced at my watch. It was getting late. "Just a quick look."

Even with ancient oaks shading the sidewalks as we walked, the heat was daunting. I was wilting fast, but Dahlberg, in his shorts and sandals, didn't seem to mind the heat. He was fresh as a daisy and talking a mile a minute about his project.

"We buy the houses with a revolving loan fund," he was saying. "We're able to pay the small down payment ourselves, and with volunteer lawyers and brokers, the other fees are minimal. On the first house we let the tenants do the work themselves, but the quality of their work wasn't too good, so now we hire everything out."

"How do you choose who gets a house?" I asked.

"We have three or four social service agencies who make recommendations. Then the tenants go through a rigorous screening process before we accept them into the program. They have to be working, of course, or at least in an approved job-training program. We don't take substance abusers, or anyone with a recent felony arrest record. Family size is limited because of the size of the houses, and of course, we try to promote a good racial mix."

I raised an eyebrow at that.

"It sounds trivial," Dahlberg said, "but we want our neighborhoods to be a real mix of rich and poor; black, white, and brown; single, married, what have you. If people like Littlefield had their way, only certified yup-sters would live in Inman Park."

"Yeah, yuppies," I said, halfheartedly. I was hot and hungry and my feet hurt.

As we walked south toward Gormley, the lots got smaller and the houses humbler. Brick and stone gave way to asphalt shingles. We passed a somewhat run-down brick apartment building.

That's when I noticed an acrid, smoky smell to the air. Two houses down on my right sat the burned-out skeleton of a small house, the brick chimney poking precariously through what was left of the roof. The fire had happened fairly recently. There was shattered glass on the sidewalk, and on the singed patch of front yard rested a blackened iron bed frame and a half-melted child's plastic riding toy.

Dahlberg kept walking, looking straight ahead. Two houses down, he stopped in his tracks. A skinny brown-skinned woman sat on the brick stoop of a neat little green-painted bungalow. The paint was fresh and gleamed in the late afternoon sun. Two pots of bright red geraniums were set on either side of the door. The woman fanned herself and stared at us.

Dahlberg turned up the walkway to the house. "This is Valeria King, Callahan," he announced. The woman stood, straightening her cotton housedress. She folded her arms over her chest and gave a wary nod of her head as a sort of greeting. "Valeria was our first tenant," he said. "She and her husband Juan are success stories. Juan is a shift supervisor over at the pie bakery, and Valeria works as an aide at a nursing home. Two years ago, they were living in Juan's car and their three children were in foster care."

Valeria King's eyes swept over Dahlberg. "How you doin', Mr. D?" she called. He walked up to the edge of the stoop and sat down beside her.

"I'm just great," he said. "How are you and Juan?"

She hugged herself tighter and I saw that her chin was quivering. "Well, tell the truth, I'm still mighty cut up 'bout Josephina and the baby. Mighty cut up. Can't stop thinkin' about that fire and her and the baby."

Dahlberg put an arm around her shoulders and hugged her fiercely. "We're all upset about Josephina and little Maria," he said soothingly. "I talked to Josephina's aunt on the phone today. Oscar is going to be released from Scottish Rite's burn unit next week. The skin grafts seem to be healing, and she's going to keep him until Josephina's mother can get here from San Antonio."

He looked up at me sadly. "Valeria's best friend, Josephina Rosario, lived in that house we just passed. She was another of our tenants. She and the baby died in a fire Saturday night. It was a terrible, terrible tragedy. But somehow her four-year-old, Oscar, managed to get out alive. Josephina and Maria were asleep in a back bedroom, and they didn't make it out."

"Burned alive," whispered Valeria in a flat voice. "Those two sweet souls burned alive." Her shoulders shuddered slightly with a suppressed sob.

Dahlberg grasped her hand in his. "I know," he said

soothingly. "It is awful. But the fire marshal told me Josephina and the baby died of smoke inhalation before the fire got to them. They never felt the fire, Valeria."

She shook her head and bit her lip. "Burned alive."

He glanced up at me, and I saw anger in his face.

"I know she was your friend, Valeria, but Josephina had no business letting her boyfriend stay over here again. She knew the rules. The marshal said it looked like they'd been drinking, and Josephina might have dropped a cigarette on the couch or something. Either that, or Oscar might have been playing with matches on the couch. Once it started, the fire engulfed the house at an incredible speed. The entire house was in flames before the trucks got here. I could see the light from my house."

Valeria's face was expressionless. "Josephina quit smoking. The doctor down to Grady said the smoke made the baby sick, so she quit."

"Then it was Oscar playing with matches," Dahlberg said firmly. "You've got kids, you know how they are, Valeria. At that age they're fascinated by fire."

"I know," she said slowly. "I just can't get around those precious souls burning up in that house. Her and that sweet baby."

Dahlberg patted her shoulder one last time. "I'm sorry, Valeria," he said. "You're still upset. We'll leave you alone to do your grieving."

I followed him back to the sidewalk and we walked briskly past the house at 212 Gormley. This time there was no talk about the vibrancy of the neighborhood. "Goddamn boyfriend had no business staying in that house," Dahlberg muttered. "She knew the rules."

16

WHEN I GOT HOME MY OWN house was blast-furnace hot and eerily quiet. Too quiet. It wasn't until I missed the reassuring hum of the central air-conditioning unit outside the kitchen window that I remembered Edna's remark about its being out of commission.

We'd fought for months over the decision to install central air, with Edna complaining that air-conditioned air gave her sinus headaches, but since the first August night we've had it, she's been addicted.

She'd clearly flown the coop in the face of the unrelenting heat of the house.

I kicked off my shoes, unbuttoned my sweat-drenched blouse, and opened the refrigerator door for a shot of deliciously chilled air. With my mother gone I felt no guilt about taking half a dozen gulps of cold, sweet iced tea out of the pitcher on the top shelf.

Reluctantly, I closed the refrigerator door and sat down to assess the situation. Even with the front and back doors wide open and the ceiling fans turned on high, the air in the house was depressingly warm and stale. How had we ever lived like this, I wondered.

Edna had left the newspaper on the kitchen table, and I leafed absentmindedly through it, halfway looking to see if there were any more stories about Elliot Littlefield, halfway trying to gather the energy to flee to cooler quarters.

Edna had probably gone over to her best friend Agnes's house. I myself could go to my brother's house, but Kevin and his wife have a new baby, not to mention their five- and six-year-olds, the ones even Edna calls the wombats. I'd get no peace and certainly no bed of my own, at Kevin's.

My friend Paula would have been happy to take me in. Her condo in Virginia Highland is only a couple miles away and I've crashed many a night on her sofa in the past. We could whip up a batch of margaritas and send out for a pizza with sun-dried tomatoes and artichoke hearts. The idea had its merits.

Then I had a better idea. Mac. I rarely spend the night at his house, mostly because he lives so far out in the country. It's nearly forty miles to Alpharetta where he lives, and besides, most of the restaurants we like to eat at, and the friends we socialize with, are closer to town. Besides, I suspect he secretly enjoys the comforts of my bungalow.

Not that his cabin is a shack or anything. He has all the basics, indoor plumbing, running water, heat, and air, but I'm the one with the queen-size orthopedic mattress and the home-baked biscuits on Saturday mornings.

I tried to remember what day it was, to see if Mac would be home. Since I'd started working this crazy case all the days seemed to run together. Mac's work with the Atlanta Regional Commission frequently kept him at city and county zoning meetings that ran late into the night. My eyes caught the date at the top of the *Constitution*. Tuesday. I decided to call and invite myself over for the night. Maybe we could make up for the semifight we'd had. And I'd show him the article about tamoxifen. I'd kept the clipping in my pocket since I'd found it. I dug it out again and reread the article.

Which reminded me. I glanced at the clock on the kitchen stove. Nearly eight o'clock. Still, I grabbed the phone on the table and dialed my doctor's office. The story said only a few hundred women in Georgia would be accepted for the drug trial. I meant to be one of them, even if I got in at gunpoint.

Kappler's answering service girl promised to relay the message in the morning to have him call me. "Tell him it's vital," I urged, knowing she'd do no such thing. That was another thing that pissed me off about Kappler. Sometimes he'd wait two or three days before returning my phone calls.

I held the receiver down and dialed Mac's number.

"Hello, big fella," I said, breathing into the phone. "This is Sugar Cookie of Cookie's 'n' Nookie Escort Service calling to offer you a free in-home demonstration."

"Is there an extra charge for the whipped cream and maraschino cherries?" he asked.

"Not if you supply your own."

"I'll leave the porch light on," he promised.

"Jack up the air-conditioning too," I said, dropping the phony accent. "Ours is on the fritz and it's hotter than blue blazes over here. Edna blew the pop stand before I got home. If you'll invite me to spend the night I'll make it worth your while."

"You got a deal," he said. "I was just getting ready to light the grill. Stop at the store and get yourself a steak and a bottle of red wine. All I've got is that dark beer you hate."

"I'm there," I said.

I threw some clean clothes in an overnight bag, then I

grabbed a cold beer out of the fridge, held it to my neck for a minute, turned out the lights and locked up.

North Fulton County, where Mac lives, used to be considered rural. Now the intersection that used to hold Goolsby's gas station and general store has a strip shopping center with an all-night Kroger, a wine and cheese shop, and a hardware store so chic they do tennis racket restringing.

Local old-timers bitch and moan about creeping suburbanization, but most, like me, welcome the opportunity to shell out $4.99 a pound for a bacon-wrapped filet mignon, $3 for a loaf of fresh-baked French bread, and $11.99 for a decent bottle of wine. It beats the hell out of a can of Vienna sausage and a Yoo-Hoo.

From the shopping center it was still another fifteen minutes to the horse farm where he rents his cabin.

Mac's been there for three years, and he and his black Lab, Rufus, love the place. A caretaker lives in a small modern ranch house and looks after the horses, and Mac and Rufus fish on the small lake nearly every night in good weather.

The van bumped off the paved road and onto the gravel road to the horse farm, kicking up a cloud of fine red dust. Choking, I rolled up the window as fast as I could.

At the end of the road I could see the lights of the cabin, and as I got closer Rufus ran out and barked a happy greeting, running along beside the van and nipping at the tires.

Mac was on the back deck, dropping two foil-wrapped bundles on the glowing coals. I dropped my sack of groceries on the wooden picnic table and gave him a quick, grateful kiss. He grabbed me again and kissed me again, slowlike.

"How was your day?" he asked, when we parted for air.

"So-so," I said. "Felt like a lot of wheel-spinning. I talked to a lot of people who told me a lot of nothing. How was your day?"

"Meetings," he said simply. "Sit." He picked up the bag of groceries and opened the door to the kitchen with his foot. "I thought we'd eat out here, unless you were serious about wanting the air-conditioning."

The back deck was shaded by big oak and hickory trees, and the tree frogs and crickets were trying to outdo one another. Alpharetta may be only forty miles north of Atlanta, but it felt fifteen degrees cooler. "This is fine," I called. "Crack open that wine and feed me a little something and you'll have a happy woman on your hands."

Rufus loped onto the deck and licked my bare toes. I scratched his ear with my foot and he lay down with his head under my chair.

Mac emerged from the house with two water glasses of wine and two bowls of tossed salad cradled in his arms. He set the stuff down on the table then reached around and pulled bundles of napkin-wrapped cutlery from his shorts pocket.

"I'm buying you wine goblets for your birthday," I said pointedly, taking a sip of the wine.

"Goblets, schmoblets," he said, sitting opposite me. "Don't look a gift port in the storm in the mouth."

"This ain't no port, this is Bordeaux," I pointed out.

The wine was nice, the salad was cold, and the French bread was warm and crusty and dripping with real butter. We ate the steaks and potatoes slowly and I piled extra sour cream on my potato to console myself for having endured such a long, difficult day. I hadn't realized just how hungry I was until I pushed the last crust of bread around to mop up the last bit of steak juice.

"God, that was good," I said meaningfully. "Thanks, Mac, I really needed this tonight."

"Then I'm glad you called," he said simply. "Any time."

"Okay."

"No, I mean it," Mac said, suddenly serious. "I've been thinking about this off and on lately. What would you think about us living together?"

"I don't know," I said, trying to choose my words carefully. "I haven't really thought about it. I guess I thought our current arrangement was working all right. Isn't it?"

He got up and started clearing dishes, scraping the plates a little harder than necessary, letting the knives and forks rattle loudly as he stacked the dishes and silver.

"I just thought we might want to come up with something a little more permanent, is all. Instead of all this running back and forth between your house and my house. You really haven't thought about it at all?"

I sighed. "I guess I've toyed with the idea. But I always push it to the back of my mind. The logistics are such a hassle. Do we live in my house or yours, or do we compromise and get a new place in between? And what about Edna? I can't just put her out on the street, Mac."

Mac sat down and pushed his chair closer to mine. "I'm not asking you to. Edna and I get along great. It might look weird to some people, but I got no problem with her living with us. In fact, I always sort of assumed that would be the deal."

He'd vaulted easily over the big obstacle I'd put in front of him. But I wasn't ready to articulate the real reason I kept avoiding a serious discussion of where our relationship was headed.

"Let's think about it, okay?" I said, reaching across

the table and holding his hand. "I do want to be with you, honest. But right now I just don't have the energy to get into this."

"Well, think about it. That's all," he said.

I got up to clear away the dinner plates, but he pulled me down into his lap. "What was that you said about a free in-home demonstration?" he muttered, nibbling my ear and sliding his hand up under my blouse.

I put my arms around his neck and tilted his head back for a long, searching kiss. The tensions of the day slowly ebbed away. Mac lowered his head and started kissing the vee between my breasts, unbuttoning my blouse as he went.

"Why don't we continue this in the house?" I suggested, looking uneasily around. The cabin seems miles from civilization, but in the wintertime, when the leaves are off the trees, you can see the caretaker's house from Mac's back deck. If I could see him, I reasoned, there was a chance he could see me. Mac and I had this discussion frequently. He's one of these macho guys who seem to get turned on by rolling around on pine cones under the stars. Me, I like a nice soft bed.

Mac laughed and kept unbuttoning. "Relax. The guy's at a horse show in Tennessee. Not even the horses are home to see us. What do you say to a little skinny dip?"

The back steps of the porch wind down a steep slope to a rock-covered patio and a swimming pool that looks like it was blasted out of the rock.

We left our clothes on the porch and ran butt-naked, down the steps, with Rufus barking joyously at our heels. He didn't know exactly what was going on, but he seemed to sense it was something fun.

Later on, when things got serious, we had to put Rufus outside. "He's only a puppy," Mac explained. "I don't want him to know I let girls spend the night."

We were both too keyed up to sleep much. When he got up to let Rufus back inside, I switched on the bedside lamp. "Sorry," Mac said, getting back into bed. "I didn't mean to wake you."

"You didn't. I don't know what's wrong with me tonight. Seems like a million things jumping around inside me. Not a very restful state of mind."

"Tell me about the case," he suggested. I propped my head up on my elbow and looked at him with surprise. "Really? I thought you thought I was stupid to take on Elliot Littlefield as a client."

"I still do," he said, wrapping one of my curls around his finger. "But that doesn't mean I'm not interested in how things are progressing."

"It's not going so hot," I admitted. I outlined my conversations with Shane Dunstan and P. G. T. Vickers.

"I hadn't realized Vickers was that crazy," Mac said. "I've got a couple Rebel Yell books in the den. Think I should burn 'em?"

"You're kidding," I said, appalled.

"I'm kidding. Those are expensive books."

"The thing that bugs me," I told him, "is that I can't figure why Vickers would have stolen the diary. He could easily afford to outbid anybody else, from what he says. I just can't picture him stabbing and clubbing somebody like Bridget to death. But he's hiding something. He told me he was at some library dedication all afternoon, but his secretary told me he left early to go to Atlanta. There's something weird going on with him."

"I thought you were only supposed to recover the diary," Mac said.

"Look," I said. "I've tried, but there's no way I can separate the diary and Bridget's murder. Did I tell you she was sleeping with her high school soccer coach?

She ran away from home when she thought she was pregnant with his child, but it was a false alarm."

"Do you think the coach killed her?"

"Maybe," I said. "He claims he was at his summer soccer camp when the house was broken into. But then he also claims he only slept with Bridget once, and I know that's a lie."

"How?"

"I just do," I said stubbornly.

"What about Littlefield?" Mac asked. "Was he sleeping with her?"

"He says not, and about that I think he's telling the truth."

"Why?"

"Not because Littlefield didn't want to," I said. "Those old newspaper clippings said he was notorious for preferring nubile young things. And Littlefield definitely killed Sunny. I know that for a fact. It's just that I think Bridget thought she was in love with Kyle Jordan—that's the coach's name. I've been talking to Bridget's sister, Jocelyn. Bridget was a virgin before Jordan. I think she was too hung up on him to be sleeping around with two different guys. She thought Jordan was going to leave his wife and marry her."

"And he wasn't."

"He's married to one foxy-looking little blonde, he's got three young kids, including one that can't be six months old. Unless he's got an independent source of money, Jordan couldn't afford to live on his coaching salary, pay alimony and child support, and get remarried to a seventeen-year-old kid. Jordan is a shit-heel."

"So this guy and Littlefield are your favorite suspects," Mac said, not bothering to try to stifle a huge yawn.

"Maybe," I said. "It's too early to tell."

"It's late for me," Mac said, raising his arm to look at his watch. "After one. This old boy's got a full day tomorrow."

"I know," I said, leaning over to kiss him good night.

"Wait," I said, suddenly remembering the newspaper clipping in my purse. "I've got something incredible to show you."

Mac read the article slowly, knitting his eyebrows together as he concentrated.

"Well?" I said, when he'd finished and handed it back to me. "Don't you think it sounds great? I called Kappler's office before I came out here tonight. I want him to get me included in the drug trial."

Mac nodded, but he didn't say anything.

"What?" I said, sensing his reservation. "This tamoxifen sounds like it was made for someone like me. What do you think?"

"I think I read some stuff that's very exciting, and some stuff that's scary. They think this drug could cause liver cancer, Callahan. You're healthy right now. Liver cancer's a lot nastier than the cancer you've had. And what about the blood clots and uterine cancer? You want my advice, I say ask your doctor about it, sure. But go slow, okay? Will you?"

I switched the light off. In the dark he couldn't see the set of my jaw. You don't tell a woman to go slow when she's staring cancer in the face. I didn't tell him that. I told him good night.

17

JOCELYN DOUGHERTY AND Edna sat across
the kitchen table from each other, their heads nearly
touching, so deep in conversation they didn't look up
until I deliberately let the screen door bang shut. "Hi,
Mom, I'm home," I called.

A plate of biscuits lay on the table between the two
women and an opened jar of muscadine preserves sent a
warm fruity scent wafting around the room.

The television was turned on, tuned to the "Today"
show, but nobody was paying any attention to Willard
Scott hyping the Iowa City sweet corn festival. It was
stiflingly hot in the kitchen, even at eight A.M.

I pulled out one of the oak ladder-back chairs and
helped myself to a biscuit, popping it whole into my
mouth.

"Nice manners," Edna said pointedly.

I chewed contentedly, then got up and poured myself
a cup of coffee to wash down a second biscuit. "I take it
the compressor's still not fixed," I said, seated again. "I
can't believe you baked biscuits in this heat, Ma. Not
that I'm complaining, mind you."

I looked at Jocelyn closely. A smudge of grape jelly

decorated her chin and there was a light dusting of flour on her navy blue T-shirt. "What brings you over here so early?" I asked.

She ducked her head in embarrassment. "Nothing, really. I was thinking about what you said about helping find the person who took that diary. Maybe you can't investigate my sister's murder, but I sure can."

Edna and I exchanged quick glances. I hadn't told her of my decision to try to find Bridget's killer. Edna's look spoke volumes. She was always a sucker for every misfit kid any of us brought home from school, making us invite the kid to spend the night or go on family outings long after the kid had ceased to be attracted to the Garrity clan.

I reached for the jelly jar and smeared a layer of the thick brown goo on my biscuit. "As it happens," I said, trying to sound casual, "I've got assignments for both of you today, if you don't have anything better to do."

"The mouses have all reported to their assigned houses," Edna said. "What have you got in mind?"

"We might as well start checking these alibis," I said. "Littlefield claims he was appraising an estate Saturday afternoon, around the time of the murder. I'm sure the cops have checked it out, but let's do it for ourselves. The attorney for the estate is a woman named Donna Cosby," I told Edna. "Call her and tell her you work with me. She handled a divorce for a friend of mine. Ask her if she was at the old lady's house the entire time Littlefield was there, and make sure you ask her if he gave her a detailed, written appraisal. In fact, ask her if we can have a copy of it. I want to see if he did an item-by-item list, or if he only gave her an estimate from Donna's description of what was included in the estate."

Edna was writing as I talked. For once, she was listening instead of interrupting.

"If you have time, drive over to Eagle's Keep, then drive over to the old lady's house. Clock it both ways to see how long it takes, but make sure you do it in the middle of the day, when traffic is fairly light, like it would have been Saturday."

"What else?" she asked.

I hesitated. Edna loves to play detective, but she always bitches about doing the endless grunt work that most of us spend the majority of our time dealing with.

"Pete Vickers, he's one of the people who was bidding for that diary, lied to me about where he was Saturday afternoon. He told his secretary he was going to some kind of Civil War study group in Atlanta that afternoon. Call around and see if any such group met that afternoon, and if Vickers was there. You can start with the Atlanta Historical Society, I think they sponsor a bunch of those groups." I handed her the slip of paper from Vickers's office. "Call this number and ask for Darryl. See how he's connected to Vickers."

"What about me?" Jocelyn asked. She'd pulled her hair on top of her head in a waterfall. The hairdo accented the gauntness of her face and frame. She looked about twelve years old. Still, her face fairly crackled with excitement this morning. She absentmindedly picked at the edge of a biscuit, nibbling at the pieces until she'd eaten almost the whole thing.

I eyed her frankly. "Does your shrink know that you're getting involved in this investigation? For that matter, do your parents know?"

Her eyelashes fluttered and she looked me square in the face, her blue eyes suddenly cold and old beyond her years. "Are you afraid I'll flip out over Bridget's being dead? I have an eating disorder, okay? I'm not mental or anything."

"I know," I said. "It's just that I don't want to be responsible."

"You're not responsible. I am. I'm nineteen. I can vote. I can drive. I'm living by myself and eating my Wheaties. My parents don't want to know what happened to Bridget. You know what? I think my parents are glad. That's sick, isn't it? Well, maybe my father isn't glad. Bridge was his pet. It's just that my mother raises all this stink about how disruptive Bridget and I are. I think he lets her get away with all her shit just so he can keep the peace. He's not even home that much anymore. But man, yeah, I think my mom is glad Bridget isn't around to embarrass her anymore. She freaked when she thought Bridget was gonna be an unwed mother."

"Jesus," Edna exclaimed. "Jocelyn honey, you don't really believe your parents don't care, do you? I'm a mother and all four of my kids put me through different kinds of hell, but believe me, no matter what happens, parents love their children. No matter what."

"Maybe," Jocelyn said expressionlessly. "My shrink says we're dysfunctional."

"Dysfunctional," Edna repeated. "I never heard that word before I started watching Sally Jessy Raphael. And I work the *New York Times* crossword with an ink pen."

"Never mind," I said, trying to get the subject off the dysfunctional Doughertys and back on the investigation at hand. "I'm going to run to Athens this morning to see the director of UGA's special collection. Peter Thornton, that's the guy's name, had been trying to raise money to bid on the diary."

"I'll go with you," Jocelyn offered.

"No," I said quickly. "I've got something else for you to do, if you're up for it. How do you feel about doing some, uh, fast talking?"

She grinned. "I'm a teenager. Lying is second nature. What do you want me to do?"

"Remember how Kyle Jordan told us he was at soccer camp Saturday, when Bridget was killed? We need to check that out. I want you to call some of the kids who were at that camp, ask them if Coach J was there, what time he got there, that kind of stuff."

Jocelyn blinked. "How do I find out who the kids were? Who do I tell them I am?"

"All right," I said patiently. "Call All Saints and tell them you're calling to inquire about summer activities for your cousin who is transferring here in the fall. Ask them about soccer camps. If they give you Kyle Jordan's name, tell them you want to talk to some parents to see if their kids have enjoyed the camp. Then call the kids. Easy. But if that doesn't work out, get creative. Call Jordan's wife. Tell her anything you have to, but get the location of the camp. Then drive down there and look around. Be discreet, but talk to as many kids as you can."

She still looked bewildered. "Look," I told her. "You said you want to help out. I'm telling you how. In this business, you have to go with the flow. If one thing doesn't work, try something else. If you want to find something out you have to figure the easiest, least offensive way to get the information you need. See?"

Jocelyn straightened her shoulders. "I guess. Think it would work if I told his wife I wanted to talk to him about coaching an all-star soccer team?"

"Beautiful," I said, rewarding her with a hug. "Just right. She'll fall all over herself telling you about his camp."

But Jocelyn still wasn't sure. "What if Coach J is home? What if he answers the phone?"

These kids today. Microwave popcorn, programmable VCRs. They want everything handed to them. "Hang up and figure out something else," I said.

Just then I glanced idly at the television. "Turn it up," I said. During our strategy session, Willard Scott had been replaced by C. W. Hunsecker, standing awkwardly in front of police headquarters with Ricardo Hill sticking a microphone in his face.

C. W. had obviously had a long night. A thin grayish stubble covered his chin and there were layers of bags under his light-colored eyes.

"Captain," Hill said excitedly. "We understand you've made an arrest in connection with the slaying of Bridget Dougherty. Can you confirm that for us this morning?"

Hunsecker looked annoyed. "No, Ricardo, as I've told all the media people this morning, we've made no arrest for that young lady's murder."

Hill looked confused, glancing down at his little official reporter's notebook, then up at the camera, then back at Hunsecker. "But you have made an arrest for something," he insisted.

"We've made lots of arrests," Hunsecker said wearily. "Which one do you want to know about?"

Hill glared at him, and Hunsecker gave in. "I can tell you we have been questioning a man, a transient, who lived in and around Inman Park, in connection with an assault late last night on a young girl who was walking her dog."

"Was the girl murdered? Were there any signs of sexual activity? Do the police think a serial thrill-killer is loose in Inman Park?" Ricardo Hill's juices were flowing.

"No, no," Hunsecker finally said. "The girl was assaulted, but she's fine. She wasn't even bruised. There was no murder, no rape. The suspect jumped out at her from some bushes, knocked her down and was attempting to get her watch off her wrist when the dog's barking alerted neighbors who called the police. One of our patrol officers apprehended the man about a block away from the crime scene."

Hill was closing in on big stuff now. His voice lowered, confidentially. "Captain, our sources tell us this transient, a man we understand is named Gordon Allan Madison, is also being considered a suspect in the killing of the All Saints coed, Bridget Dougherty. We understand he knew the young woman, and that your officers are even now combing the places Madison stayed, looking for evidence to link him to the slaying. Can you confirm that for us, Captain?"

Hunsecker's lips set in a thin, disapproving line. "I can't comment on an ongoing investigation," he snapped, then he turned and marched away from the cameras and into police headquarters.

"Oh man," Jocelyn whispered. She'd been standing in the kitchen doorway, her eyes fixed on the television. What little color she had in her face had drained away. Once again she was the walking cadaver I'd seen the day of Bridget's funeral.

"Oh man," she repeated, sliding to a lump on the kitchen floor. She scrunched her knees up to her chest and wrapped her arms tightly around her legs, pressing her face into her knees.

I knelt down beside her. "Jocelyn, are you going to be all right?"

She kept her head buried, but the sobs seemed to wrack her body for a long, long time. Then she looked up, turning from Edna to me, searching for answers.

"This is it?" she said tearfully. "Some old wino killed my sister? Why? Bridget didn't have any jewelry. Did he rape her? Did he? My mom won't tell me."

Tears were streaming down her face and she was

rocking to and fro, the tears making dark blue splashes on her T-shirt.

I felt totally ineffective there, kneeling on the kitchen floor, trying to comfort this strange child, stroking her hair and trying to find words that would deaden the pain.

"Is this it?" she demanded. "Is it?"

"I don't know, Jocelyn," I said truthfully. "I'll have to check it out. But I do know one thing. That rape stuff is just television bullshit. Your sister was not raped. She wasn't."

With my finger, I lifted Jocelyn's chin so she could see I was telling the truth. "I promise," I repeated. "Bridget wasn't raped."

"Okay," she said, her voice wobbly. "I believe you. I do. You think I should call my mom? She always does her Jane Fonda exercises about now. I don't want the cops to be the ones to tell her."

Over Jocelyn's head Edna raised her eyebrows in surprise. Maybe Emily Dougherty was a zombie, but her surviving daughter still felt some concern for her mother. It was a good sign, I thought.

I stood up stiffly, then offered her a hand, but Jocelyn scrambled to her feet unaided. "Maybe I better go over there," she said.

"Good idea," Edna said.

"I'm going to make some phone calls and check out this Gordon Allan Madison guy," I said. "These TV clowns get wild hairs sometimes. This whole thing could just be a figment of their imagination."

I patted Jocelyn on the shoulder again. "Go see your folks. Then call me later on and I'll let you know where we stand."

18

"CALLAHAN, GOOD TO HEAR from you," Jake Dahlberg said warmly. "I hope you're calling to firm up our dinner plans."

"Dinner?" I had to think quickly. "Well, yeah. I was hoping we could do it one night this week. Can we say Friday, tentatively? I'll have to call you back to confirm, but it looks like my week should have stabilized by then."

"Friday," Dahlberg said. "Seven thirty at my house." His voice had a note of finality in it.

"Wait," I blurted. "I, uh, was hoping you could help me with something else."

"Sure," he said affably, "what's up?"

"I'm looking for some information about a homeless man who apparently hung around your neighborhood."

"There are at least half a dozen regulars, and then we have seasonal ones too. Most of them I only know by their street names, of course, but give me a description and maybe we can figure who it is."

"All I have is his name: Gordon Allan Madison. Does that ring a bell?"

"Gordo?" Dahlberg said. "Yeah, sure. I know Gordo.

Sort of. I met him a couple years ago when I caught him sleeping in the crawl space under my back porch. What do you need to know about him for?"

"It's in connection with Bridget's murder," I said. "He tried to mug a young girl in the neighborhood last night, and now it looks like he could be a suspect in the thing at Eagle's Keep. The cops haven't charged him yet, but it looks like they're pretty damned interested in him."

"Whoa. Hold the phone," Dahlberg said. "Gordo Madison a murder suspect? Your client Littlefield must be working overtime to shift the blame. Gordo's harmless."

"How do you know?"

"Gordo's a Vietnam Vet," Dahlberg said. "Came home with the usual drug and alcohol problems. Told me he used to live in a rooming house here in the neighborhood, before people like Littlefield started buying up houses and fixing them up. Now he just hangs out, sleeping in cars or porches, or sometimes, if somebody leaves a window open, in an empty house. I'm no psychiatrist or anything, but from what I've seen, Gordo's mentally disturbed. Sometimes he's so shy he won't even look at me. Other days, he stands outside and roars and curses, raising all kind of hell. But really, I'm sure he's harmless."

I wasn't convinced. "The cops say he jumped out of some bushes Tuesday night, knocked a teenage girl to the ground and tried to rob her," I said. "That must be the connection they're looking for, young girls."

"No, no, no," Dahlberg said. "This makes no sense. I tell you what. Talk to Verna Dykes over at the night shelter on Moreland Avenue. I took Gordo over there a couple times in the winter, when it was too cold to sleep outside. I think he stayed there on and off, when he had the two-dollar cover charge and wasn't hitting the booze."

"I will," I said. "And thanks for the help. See you Friday, I hope."

"You bet. Call me if you find the cops are going to charge Gordo, will you? Maybe there's something I could do for the poor guy."

The Praying Hands Night Shelter was housed in an old elementary school. Weeds had grown up in what had once been the playground, and graffiti had been sprayed all over the outside walls.

Verna Dykes's office was in the former principal's office. She was talking on the phone when I pushed open the frosted glass door. A petite, round black woman with cornrowed hair and a pair of horn-rimmed glasses that seemed to cover two-thirds of her face, she was distressed about something.

"He is indigent," she was telling someone on the phone. "Yes. And if you'll call the Veteran's Administration and talk to Graham Keithley, his doctor, you'll know Gordo is not a violent person. Yes. Do that. All right."

She hung up the phone, took off her glasses and polished them with the hem of her T-shirt. That's when she noticed me standing there.

"Are you Detective Nickells?" she asked, standing up to greet me.

"Afraid not. I'm just a private investigator. My name's Callahan Garrity. I've been looking into the burglary at Eagle's Keep for the owner, Elliot Littlefield."

"Sit down, anyway," she invited. "Elliot Littlefield. That's the man lives in the big red house looks like a castle? Got Confederate flags flyin' all over the place?"

"Afraid so."

"Honey, I don't mean to offend, but that man is plain bad. Anytime he sees any of our clients in that ritzy neighborhood of his, he calls the cops and has 'em hauled to jail."

Verna Dykes shook her head vigorously. "So much meanness in the world."

"I know," I said. "Just between the two of us, I'm not real fond of him either. But could we talk about Gordon Allan Madison for a minute? Someone else in the neighborhood told me he doubts Mr. Madison would have killed Bridget Dougherty or even have burglarized Eagle's Keep."

"That's what I been trying to tell the cops," she said. "That was Gordo's public defender on the phone just now. I told him, Gordo wouldn't kill nobody. He talked loud and cursed sometimes, but that's what schizophrenics do. Hell, honey, I talk loud and curse sometimes, but I wouldn't hurt a fly."

"Was he ever violent?"

She took a deep breath. "When he was sober and doin' right, Gordo was so bashful he couldn't hardly talk to a stranger."

"So he was an alcoholic?"

"About eighty percent of our clients are," she said. "Gordo's doctor over at the VA had him on Antabuse. You know what that is, right? If you're taking it and you drink, even a sip, you'll puke your brains out. Now, when he took the Antabuse, and took his seizure medicine, he was just fine."

"But he didn't always take it?"

For an answer she rummaged in the scarred oak teacher's desk drawer and came up with a Ziploc sandwich bag. It was labeled *Gordo Madison* and contained three half-full pill bottles.

"The thing about schizophrenics is, they forget they are schizophrenics," she said, laughing in spite of herself. "When Gordo was here, he brought his medicine in, and we gave it to him, just like clockwork. Then he'd do his share of the chores. We got rules about that. And he was fine."

"You said 'when he was here,'" I said. "He didn't come every day?"

She folded the bag in half and placed it back in the desk drawer. "This is a night shelter. Our clients come at seven P.M., eat a meal, and it's lights out by ten. They gotta be back out on the streets at six A.M. They pay two dollars a night to stay, and we got strict rules about fighting, stealing, drugs, and alcohol. Gordo didn't always feel like following the rules. Like a lot of our clients, if he got a little piece of money, say from working a labor pool or a disability check, he'd stay somewhere else, like at one of the SROs. Gordo liked the Clermont over on Ponce. They got a nudie show in the lounge there, you know."

"I know."

"On the other hand, if he was broke, or drunk, Gordo'd sleep where he could. He liked Inman Park."

"He'd been on the streets a long time, hadn't he?"

Verna nodded. "I been knowing Gordo since we opened up here in 1982, right in the middle of the first Reagan administration. He'd been on the streets long before that, maybe since '78 or so. Most people can't last that long on the streets. Gordo's been lucky."

"Did he have a criminal record?"

"Honey, we don't ask. If they're hungry, we feed 'em. If they need a place to sleep, we give 'em a bed. Got showers if they're dirty. But if they act out, we put 'em out. Next night, mostly, they come back all sorry and apologizin'. And we take 'em in again. That's Christianity."

"Was Gordo here Saturday?"

Her face fell. "No. I checked. Didn't come in Saturday or Sunday."

"What about Monday?"

"He came in, but we wouldn't let him stay. Drunk as a lord. I tried to talk to him about gettin' right, but you can't do nothin' with 'em when they're like that."

"Wait a minute," I said, "He'd been drinking, but he had the money to stay here."

"That's right," she said. "Kept waving around this little change purse, like it woulda made a difference."

"Where would he have gotten money this late in the month? Don't Social Security and disability checks usually come at the beginning of the month?"

She nodded grimly. "First of the month is Christmas, Easter, Father's Day, and birthday for these guys. They drink it, smoke it, eat it, whore it, maybe remember to buy a MARTA card or send some money to their kid or their old lady. Then it's gone. I wondered myself where he coulda gotten money this late in the month."

"Verna, whoever broke into Eagle's Keep took some very valuable stuff. Some of it could have been pawned. Maybe that's where Gordo got the money to drink. Maybe he was in an SRO Saturday and Sunday, too."

She shook her head violently. "No, ma'am. That's not Gordo. He wouldn't kill nobody."

I pointed to the desk drawer where she'd stashed the pills. "There's his medicine right there. He hadn't taken his Antabuse or his seizure pills. And there doesn't seem to be any question that he tried to mug that girl last night."

Verna folded her arms defiantly across her chest. She was a tough cookie, to be able to run a place like this full of used up, burned-out street people. I liked that she still believed in something.

"No, ma'am," she repeated again. "That ain't Gordo. Okay, maybe he did the burglary. I'll give you that much. But not murder. Not Gordo."

I got up to leave. "I hope not," I said.

On the way out of the building, I ran into Linda Nickells.

She flashed me an apologetic smile. "C. W. ever call you back?"

"Nope."

"I tried," she said. "But this case is making him nuts."

"Yeah," I said. "I know. Linda, could I talk to you about Gordo Madison?"

She glanced down the hall. "You've already talked to Ms. Dykes?"

"She's insisting he wasn't violent, but admits he hadn't been taking his medication and hadn't slept here in two nights."

Nickells nodded. "That fits. We know he was at the Clermont Hotel Sunday and Monday nights. The desk clerk ID'd him and so did some of the girls in the lounge. He was hollerin' at them so loud the bouncer threw him out."

"What about Saturday?"

"We're working on that. But it looks like we're gonna be able to charge him with the murder and burglary."

"You must have more than you've already told me."

She frowned. "You know I can't tell you anything else."

"Come on," I pleaded. "My client was the number one suspect up until now. Hell, I halfway believed he did it too. And I know Hunsecker wants Littlefield's hide. Why the change of heart? You ask me, Gordo Madison's just another down and out."

"You baiting me?" she asked. "If C. W. finds out I

told you this, he'll chew my ass raggedy. All right. I think they're gonna try to charge Madison sometime today, so it won't make that much difference if I tell you now. We found a Confederate Army doodad wrapped up with a bunch of Madison's clothes and stuff, in a shed down the block from Littlefield's house. The owners said they've seen Madison sneaking around there, and chased him off before."

"A doodad?" I thought back to the typed list of missing relics Elliot Littlefield had given me. "Could it be a cartridge box plate?"

"Search me," Nickells said. "I just know it matches something on Littlefield's list."

"Good Lord," I said. "Have you or C. W. talked to Littlefield yet?"

"Not yet," she said. "And you keep your mouth shut, too. It's funny. Here we get a guy caught red-handed with stuff from the burglary and C. W. still can't let go of the notion that Littlefield's behind all this. We'll notify Littlefield after we finish talking to Madison and check out his story."

"What is his story?"

"Not much of it makes sense," she said. "He freely admits to having the Civil War thing. Says he found it in the neighborhood."

"Where? Have you searched for the other missing things? There's a diary that's incredibly valuable."

"I know," she said. "We've got teams of uniformed officers with metal detectors working all the vacant lots. All Madison knows is that he saw something shining in some tall grass and he picked it up. He claims he kept it because he thought it might be worth something."

"Linda," I said excitedly. "If he had that cartridge thing, that's what it is, by the way, and it's worth about five thousand bucks. If he had that, he must know where the other stuff is too. He must have pawned something to get the money to stay at the Clermont. Did he have a lot of cash on him?"

Nickells laughed. "He had about four bucks in his pockets and he doesn't even remember being at the Clermont. He says a guy in a gray pickup truck picked him up at the Big Star Shopping Center Saturday afternoon, and had him move some furniture. Guy gave him fifty bucks. We've checked the room he stayed in, nothing. It's early yet, but the pawn shops within staggering distance of Poncey Highland haven't seen any of the other stuff taken in the burglary."

"What's he say about the murder?"

"Can't remember," Nickells said.

"Have you got anything to tie him to Bridget?"

Nickells eyed me up and down. "C. W.'s right. You are a pushy bitch. That's all right though, so am I. The assistant manager at that health food store on Euclid Avenue, what's it called?"

"Sevananda."

"Yeah. Well, the woman says Madison was hanging around there Saturday morning, trying to get people to let him carry their grocery bags for tip money. Bridget came out of the store and apparently he cussed her when she wouldn't let him carry her bags. She ran inside and hid there until Gordo wandered away. But she wouldn't let the manager call the cops on him. Said she'd seen him around the neighborhood and felt sorry for him."

I felt chilled. Bridget's tenderheartedness might have been what got her murdered. "Shit," I said. "Maybe he didn't wander away at all. Maybe he followed her back to Eagle's Keep, broke in, and when she caught him, he stabbed her to death."

"That's what we're thinking," Nickells said. "Say

now, what about a little sisterly sharing, as long as I've let you pick my brains?"

"I'm not looking into the murder, just trying to recover the diary," I told her.

"Keep sayin' it, maybe you'll believe it. What do you know that we don't know?"

"All right. I did find out who Bridget's boyfriend was. Kyle Jordan, her soccer coach at All Saints. Bridget told him she was pregnant, but she forgot to mention it when she found out it was a false alarm. He's married, got kids. I thought he looked good for it. I've got somebody checking his alibi for Saturday."

"Good," she said, writing Jordan's name on a pocket-size notebook she'd fished out of her purse. "What else?"

"Well, Littlefield's theory is that whoever did the murder and burglary was someone out to get him. It's wacky, but he thinks his neighbor, Jake Dahlberg, could be behind it. They had kind of a feud going."

She nodded. "We've talked to Dahlberg. We'll talk to the other neighbors about it too. Anything else?"

"Not really. I've been looking into the people who wanted to buy that diary. They're kind of a spooky crowd, especially this Vickers character, the right-wing nut, maybe you've heard of him? But that's all preliminary, and there's nothing solid to tie them to the diary."

She put the notebook away. "All right, girlfriend," she said. "Let me go talk to this shelter lady. I got miles to go before I sleep tonight."

19

JUST FOR THE HELL OF IT, I decided to cruise over to Inman Park to see what was happening. For a Wednesday afternoon, the joint was jumping. Police cars were parked on every block and uniformed officers and dark-shirted police cadets tramped uneasily through the kudzu-covered vacant lots that dot the area; with one officer swinging a bush hook to ward off snakes and the other wielding a metal detector.

Housewives, kids, and retirees stood around their yards in knots, watching the cops fling hubcaps, beer cans, and other rust-encrusted goodies onto a growing pile. The kids were having a dandy time pawing through the pile looking for souvenirs. An old man stood on the front porch of the house next to Dahlberg's, staring intently at all the activity. Mr. Szabo, the neighborhood busybody. I'd meant to go back and talk to him about the day of Bridget's murder, and I hadn't gotten around to it. I made a mental note to go back and pick his brain.

As I rode slowly past Eagle's Keep I spotted Elliot Littlefield standing on the front step of the house, leaning heavily on a cane with one hand and training a camcorder at the officer who crisscrossed his front yard, poking a beeping metal detector into the hydrangeas and azaleas. He spotted me too, and flagged me to a stop.

Reluctantly, I pulled into his driveway. He may have been paying me for this investigation, but I was in no mood to talk to my client, who'd probably be wanting a report on all my activities.

He walked stiffly over to the side of the van, leaned up against the door and looked in at me. "Did you see the news this morning? I should have known one of those bums was behind this. This Madison fellow, I've seen him around the neighborhood. He always wears green army fatigues. Probably stolen. Dahlberg over there," he said, pointing with his cane to the house across the street, "he encourages these people by giving them handouts all the time. And of course, these types are like rats; you feed one and pretty soon you have an infestation."

"The news report I heard said they haven't charged the man with anything except the mugging," I reminded Littlefield.

He pointed the cane toward the police officer, who'd crossed the street and was working the hedge in Dahlberg's front yard. "Use your head, Callahan. Obviously the police believe this Madison person has hidden some of the loot in the underbrush over here. What else would they be looking for?"

I'd thought about that. "The murder weapon for one thing. The preliminary autopsy said Bridget was stabbed with a short-handled knife. You told the police there was a dagger missing from the house, but there was no dagger on the list of antiques you gave me."

He shrugged. "Oh that. It's a silly little Korean Army thing I got in an estate sale. Not at all in the same category as my Civil War things. It's hardly worth a hundred dollars. The police have a description of it. Maybe they are looking for it, but I still believe they're searching for the rifle and the silver cup and the other things."

Littlefield's ebullient manner irritated me. "Do you really believe they'll find those things in one of these kudzu patches? Besides, we had a hard rain here Monday night. Wouldn't the diary, for one, be ruined? Understand, I'm not trying to be a pessimist, but I do think you should be prepared for the possibility that the diary may be lost. The police think the man is mentally unstable. If he did kill Bridget and steal those things, he may have thrown them away or done who knows what with them."

His face darkened. "I hadn't thought of that. But maybe he sold the things in one of these shoddy pawnshops or so-called antiques shops around here. That's what I want you to do, by the way, check all the pawnshops. And those cutesy little 'grandma's attic' places. This Madison person probably isn't as deranged as he looks. He probably sold the stuff and hid the money somewhere."

Even if Linda Nickells hadn't warned me against confiding in Littlefield about their discovery of the cartridge box plate, I would have kept it to myself, just out of spite.

"All right," I said evenly. "I was planning on typing up a progress report for you by the end of the week. That's my usual procedure, but if you like, I'll fill you in now on what I've learned."

"No, no," he said impatiently. "The end of the week is fine. Shane Dunstan and Pete Vickers both called to say they'd spoken to you, so I know you've been earning your fee. Just slip an invoice in with your report and that'll be fine."

I nodded curtly, and started the car.

"Just a minute," Littlefield said. He walked stiffly to the front door of the house, opened it, reached in, and pulled out a small beige plastic box.

He walked around to the side of the van, opened the door, and tossed the box on the seat. A loud protesting mew came from the box.

"That's the damned cat," Littlefield said. "Drop it off at the pound, will you? The damned thing pissed all over my Heriz."

"Wait a minute," I said, "pet disposal isn't exactly my line of work."

"Do what you want with it," Littlefield said, turning his back on me. "If you don't take it I'll just call animal control to come get it. Either way the cat's not coming back on my property."

I started the van and shot away from the curb. If I stayed within sight of my client for one more second I knew I'd throttle the bastard.

Another loud yowl came from the box, then the lid fell off and Ping-Pong stuck his flea-bitten head out, giving me an inquiring, one-eyed glance.

"We can't let the bad man gas the nice kitty," I told the cat. "Looks like you're in for a change of address, Ping-Pong."

I was so irritated, I ran the red light at the next intersection. Littlefield had that effect on me. Or maybe it was this damned investigation. Only a few hours ago I'd thought I was getting a grip on this case. I'd developed what I thought were decent leads on Bridget's murder and resigned myself to the fact that I'd become involved in that investigation. Now the cops had a schizophrenic homeless man under investigation and I was no closer to the truth.

My mood didn't improve when I saw the cars parked in the driveway at home. All the girls appeared to be sitting around my kitchen when they should have been out working.

"God damn," I said, grabbing the cat's box with one hand and slamming the van door with the other. It never failed; as soon as I took my eyes off the House Mouse to try to conduct some other business, things seemed to crumble to pieces.

I let the cat out in the backyard. No need for Edna to know just yet that we had a house guest.

"All right," I announced, stomping into the kitchen where they were all gathered. "What the hell is going on here?"

"What the hell has gotten into you?" asked Edna, their designated spokesman. "The girls are done for the day."

Neva Jean got up and went over to the refrigerator to help herself to another Mountain Dew. She got the drink and set it on the counter, then continued rooting happily through the fridge.

"Say ya'll," she said, holding up a dish of leftover macaroni and cheese and scooping some of the cheese topping off with her fingernail, "wanna hear what Swannelle told me about his Civil War reenactment unit?"

"What are they gonna do, get hoods and robes and have a bonfire over at the Martin Luther King grave site?" Jackie asked.

Neva Jean flipped her friend the bird. "I told you a hundred times, Jackie, this is not about racism, this is about preserving our Southern heritage. In fact, it might interest you to know that there are several very highly regarded all-black reenactment units in Atlanta."

"Heritage my ass," Jackie muttered. "Black folks got heritage too, but you don't see no George Washington Carver or W. E. B. DuBois carved up there on the side of Stone Mountain."

"Anyway," Neva Jean said, popping the top on her soda can, "Swannelle says the Gate City Old Guard is fixin' to have a Civil War of its own."

"I thought they did that all the time, Neva Jean," I said. "Isn't that their hobby?"

"Nooo," she said, relishing her tale. "This time they're fixing to make their general secede. They're gonna kick his tail right out of the unit."

I looked up in surprise. "What are you talking about? You mean they're going to force Elliot Littlefield to resign?"

"Fire him is more like it," she said smugly, sitting back down at the table with a pint jar of fig preserves and a handful of saltine crackers. I grabbed the preserves away from her and put them on the shelf behind me.

"See," she said, "Tommy Jack Dawson's wife, Marvella, she's the unit historian, does all the research and looking up to make sure everything is authentic? Well, she was down in Savannah for a historical meeting and she went over to the Georgia Historical Society archives, and when she told the librarian there that her husband was with the Gate City Old Guard, the lady mentioned that somebody had just given them a handwritten unit history for the Old Guard that they'd found in a garage sale in Pooler. The lady wouldn't let the book out of her sight, but she did let Marvella sit and read it and make notes and you know what?"

"No, what?" Edna chimed in. She'd gotten up to pour us both a glass of iced tea and had gotten as engrossed as I had in Neva Jean's long-winded story.

"Elliot Littlefield's great-great-granddaddy wasn't no kind of officer at all. Eustis Littlefield, that was his name, he was a private, and he never fought at

Kennesaw Mountain at all because he had been thrown in the brig for stealing from the unit paymaster."

"Son of a bitch," I said.

"Amen to that," Edna said. "I knew all along that man was all hat and no cattle."

"Oh, before I forget, call Dr. Kappler," Edna said. "His office called right after you left this morning. What's he want?"

Now was not the time to discuss experimental cancer drugs with my mother. "Nothing," I said quickly. "I'll tell you later. Now before I forget—what did you find out about Pete Vickers's study group?"

She flipped open the appointment book in front of her and plucked out a pink telephone message slip. "I spent the whole morning on the phone, and nobody knows anything about a study group that met in Atlanta that Saturday. I called and called that phone number too, but nobody ever answered."

"Maybe it's a pay phone," Neva Jean piped up.

Edna glared at her. She hates for anybody to beat her to the punch. "I thought of that already." Deliberately turning her back to Neva Jean, she added, "I put a call in to Alan Jerrolds. He's the boy just bought that cute bungalow up the street. Does something with computers for Southern Bell."

"You don't even know him," I said. "I can't believe you called and asked a favor of a total stranger."

"He's not a total stranger now," Edna said sweetly. "I told him about the House Mouse New Neighbors half-off special. Ruby's going down there in a little bit. He said he'd get right on it this afternoon."

"Well, keep calling the number," I said. "I want to know who Darryl is and what he is to Pete Vickers."

"You don't need to tell me what to do," Edna snapped. "I got the number on redial. Now do you want to hear about Jocelyn, or do you have any other instructions for me?"

Jocelyn. I'd forgotten all about her. "What did she say?"

"She and her mother had a talk. Her folks want her to move back home for the rest of the summer, but Jocelyn wants to stay put, and her shrink is backing her up. Oh yeah, she also said she'd gone ahead and made some phone calls about that soccer camp."

"She's probably wasting her time," I said.

"Why?"

"Linda Nickells told me it looks like they are going to charge the homeless guy with Bridget's murder. They know he saw her Saturday morning. He hung around Inman Park all the time. And get this, they found a Confederate cartridge box plate in a stash of the guy's stuff. The cops are swarming Inman Park right now, looking for the rest of Littlefield's missing antiques."

"So Littlefield's off the hook."

"Looks like it," I said. "It's just as well. He is my client. If he gets thrown in jail, I might not get paid."

Her eyes narrowed. "If you're so convinced this Madison did it, why are you still poking around with Pete Vickers and all that other mess?"

"I'm being paid to recover Lula Belle Bird's diary," I reminded her.

"You don't believe this homeless guy killed Bridget any more than I do," Edna said flatly. "Admit it."

"I don't know what to believe," I said slowly. "But I've got to cover all the bases. That's the only way we'll find out who killed Bridget. That's why I've got you making all these phone calls. Understand?"

She lit a cigarette, inhaled, and let a long thin stream of smoke whistle through her lips. "What do you want me to do next?"

I opened my Eagle's Keep file folder and handed her the list of items taken in the burglary. "Madison told the cops he found the cartridge plate in some tall grass in the neighborhood. I think he's telling the truth. But I want you to check the antiques shops, especially all those ones along Highland Avenue and within walking distance of the shelter and Inman Park. Madison doesn't drive, so if he did sell any of the stuff, he wouldn't have gone far."

I watched idly as Baby and Sister struggled out of their chairs to get ready to leave. Baby had on a pink cotton print dress, thick elastic Supp-Hose, and her favorite black lace-up oxfords with metal cleats on the soles. Sister, as usual, was dressed in layers. Under the black warmup jacket she had on a white Atlanta Braves T-shirt that had been placed over a red cotton turtleneck shirt. She wore baggy green surgical scrub pants with "Property of Grady Hospital" stamped all over them, and white orthopedic nurse's shoes.

Neva Jean had Baby by the arm, guiding her toward the door. Suddenly an idea occurred to me.

"Miss Baby, Miss Sister," I said loudly. Baby turned slowly around to try to see where my voice was coming from. "Do ya'll feel like doing a little snooping for me today?"

Baby beamed. "Hear that, Sister? Callahan done give us an assignment. Yes, ma'am. We're going undercover."

20

WHEN I WENT OUT TO GET in the van, Ping-Pong had stretched herself out across the hood. She raised her head questioningly, but didn't move, not even when I slammed the car door, not even when I started the engine. She didn't move, in fact, until I honked the horn and tapped the gas pedal. Then she leaped off the van and skulked toward the back of the house.

Stupid cat. I'd have to tell Edna about her sooner or later, but right now I thought I'd check on Coach J.

Maybe with all the other cars parked in the driveway and the curb nobody else would notice the red Hyundai parked across the street from the Jordans' house. But I noticed it as soon as I turned onto the street. I parked the van in the cul-de-sac and walked quickly back to the Hyundai, jerking the front door open, and sliding into the passenger seat.

"Just what on earth do you think you're doing?" I demanded.

Jocelyn was slouched down in the driver's seat, nibbling on french fries. She hurriedly stuffed the french fry bag under her seat.

"I'm on a stake-out," she said, showing me a pair of expensive Swiss binoculars she held in her lap. "These are Dad's, he uses them at Falcons games, but I don't think he'll miss them."

I slouched down in my seat as low as I could go, but it's tough for a five-foot-seven woman to slouch in a car built like a Spam can.

"Well, tell me what's going on," I said resignedly.

She picked up a new-looking spiral-bound notebook and began reading from her entries.

"Two P.M. Subject Lissa Jordan and white male teenager return to house in white Camaro. Enter house. Mrs. Jordan carrying grocery sacks in arms.

"Two fourteen P.M. Black Jeep arrives at house, white male driving, two white female passengers. All three enter house. Loud music coming from house. (Bon Jovi)

"Two thirty P.M. Powder blue VW beetle and bronze-colored Toyota arrive at house. Five more teenagers enter house. Music turned up louder. (Metallica)

"Three ten P.M. Domino's pizza delivery boy arrives with three large pizzas, white male with strawberry blond hair in ponytail pays driver.

"Three twenty P.M. Pregnant woman walks across the street, bangs on Jordan door. Lissa Jordan answers door, angry conversation, pregnant woman shakes finger in Mrs. Jordan's face, Mrs. Jordan gives her the finger. Woman leaves. Music gets louder. (Megadeth)

"Three forty-five P.M. Tall, balding older man from house next door crosses lawn, bangs on door. Lissa Jordan answers, angry conversation. Music turned down."

"That's it?" I asked.

"Yeah," Jocelyn said. "How am I doing?"

"Fine, I guess," I said. "I wonder where Lissa's kids are?"

"She didn't have them with her when she got home, and I haven't seen them playing outside, but maybe they're inside having naps," Jocelyn said.

"Or they could be at a sitter's. You recognize any of the partygoers?"

"Well, they all look vaguely familiar. The guy who came in with Mrs. Jordan, I think he drives that rusted-out green Vega. He might be Zak Crawford, but his hair's a lot longer than it was the last time I saw him. A couple of the girls used to play on the soccer team with Bridget: Kelly and Brittni, I think their names are. The other guys, I don't know, they might have graduated the year after me."

"You know anything else about the friends?"

She wrinkled her nose. "I remember having heard something about Zak Crawford getting kicked out of All Saints, but I don't remember why."

"Think about it," I suggested. "Maybe it'll come back to you. What about the soccer camp alibi? Does it check out?"

She flipped to another page and surveyed her notes. Her handwriting was neat and she'd outlined her notes in Roman numerals. I was impressed again. Must have been that Catholic school training. Me, I could never remember anything higher than X.

"Coach J got to camp about nine A.M. Saturday. It was team picture day. They had their picture taken. Then they practiced until eleven. The kids swam until noon, and then had lunch. After lunch the kids had free time for a couple of hours, then at three they scrimmaged again, and at five their parents picked them up."

"And Coach J was there all day?"

"As far as the kids knew. I talked to two different kids. They said he was there."

"What about free time?" I asked. "Was Coach J around for that?"

She reread her notes. "Hmmm. No, they said he was just in his office as far as they knew. Free time is when they can watch soccer videos or swim again or just hang out. Randy Myers, the assistant coach, supervises free time."

"So there was a period of two hours in the afternoon when they weren't sure whether or not he was there?" I asked. "Read your notes carefully, Jocelyn, this is important. Bridget was killed sometime before five o'clock."

Her face fell as she went back over the notes. "Geez. I'm sorry, Callahan. I just don't know if he was there."

"No problem. Sometimes I have to go back and ask questions a second time, too. Don't sweat it. You learn as you go, and you're doing fine."

"Really?" She looked dubious.

"Yeah."

We sat quietly for a while after that, watching the sprinklers whirl and the grass grow. The neighborhood was quiet except for the occasional deep bass thump of Lissa Jordan's heavy-metal platter party. I glanced sideways at Jocelyn. She looked very young and vulnerable.

"You and your mom have a good talk?"

"As good as it can get with her," she said. "She thinks this homeless guy did it. But then my mom thinks anyone who doesn't wear a three-piece suit or drive a BMW is the equivalent of Charles Manson. My shrink says my mom is controlling. Or maybe it was codependent. I can't remember which is which."

"Oh." I wondered to myself how it felt to have an outsider explain your family dynamics. A shrink would have a field day with the Garrity clan.

A thought occurred to me. "You said Bridget and your mom had a big fight before Bridget ran away.

Was that when Bridget told her she thought she was pregnant?"

"Bridget didn't tell her anything," Jocelyn said. "My mom had been sneaking around, going through Bridget's room. She read Bridget's diary. That's how she found out."

"Oh, no."

"Yeah. Bummer, huh? The worst thing is, before she even talked to Bridget, my mom called her gynecologist and told him and they made an appointment for Bridget to have an abortion at this clinic in midtown Atlanta. So one day my mom picks Bridget up after school and she just announces, 'We're going to the abortion clinic now, and you're gonna have an abortion, and then you're gonna be on restriction for the rest of your life.'"

"What did Bridget do?"

"Oh man. It's kind of funny, if you forget how awful it is. See. Bridget was really, really pro-life. They give them all these lectures at All Saints, show them pictures of fetuses sucking their thumbs and stuff. Bridget had already decided she was going to keep the baby no matter what. So she's crying and screaming at my mom, telling her she hates her and she's keeping the baby, and she'll never speak to her again. Then, when they get to the hospital, Bridget hops out of the car and goes running down the street, in her school uniform, with her book bag. And my mom is standing there—you've seen my mom, right? I've never in my whole life heard my mom so much as raise her voice at us. She said yelling shows bad manners. So, my mom is screaming at her, 'Come back, you little bitch, I won't let you ruin your life.' And she's dressed in high heels and a dress and pearls, chasing Bridget down this street, with all the winos laying on the sidewalk."

I'd started laughing in the middle of the story and

now, picturing blond, beige Emily Dougherty chasing her daughter through midtown Atlanta, I laughed so hard tears streamed down my face.

"I'm sorry," I apologized, once I'd gotten a hold of myself. "But the way you tell it, it's really funny. Awful, but funny."

"I know," Jocelyn said. "We're a pretty fucked up family, huh?"

"Wait," I said. "Look. The party's breaking up. Hand me those binoculars."

A boy and girl swaggered out of the house, their arms entwined around each other. The girl took a long drink from a green glass bottle, offered it to her boyfriend, and then tossed the empty into the yard. A few minutes later, the other teenagers Jocelyn had described came straggling out, followed by Lissa Jordan.

I hadn't noticed the other two times just how young Kyle Jordan's wife must have been. In her black Spandex bicycle shorts, and a sexy black lace bustier, with her hair gelled and spiked, and without a kid on each hip, Lissa Jordan looked the same age as the high school kids. She spotted the wine bottle in the yard, frowned and picked it up, then walked over and leaned against the hood of the bronze Toyota, laughing and flirting with the young men who'd gotten into it.

Both the boys were bare-chested and summer-tanned, wearing only knee-length, dark, baggy shorts, the same kind we kids had always begged our dads not to wear to the beach. They wore black high-top sneakers. One had his hair cut in the 1990s version of a buzz, the other wore a bandanna around his head, tied buccaneer-style.

"Is that the latest style for guys?" I asked Jocelyn. She leaned over and looked at the boys I pointed to.

"If you're a skate rat."

After a few more minutes, the other carloads of teens

pulled away from the house, music blasting from their car windows.

"Was that everybody?" I asked.

"Everybody I saw go in, except for Zak Crawford," Jocelyn said. "His car was parked in front of the house when I got here."

She pointed to a green Vega parked at the curb. It had so much rust on it that it looked like the large patches of Bondo were actually holding it together.

"Bad ride," I said.

"What?"

"Nothing," I said. "Must have been another seventies flashback. Happens sometimes."

She sat straight up in her seat, yawned and stretched. "What now? I need to pee."

I looked at my watch. It was after five, and I hadn't had any lunch. But I wasn't ready to give up on Lissa Jordan just yet. I handed Jocelyn the keys to the van.

"Go back to that Burger King we went to the other day," I suggested. "Have yourself a potty break, and call Edna. Find out if she turned up anything at the antiques dealers, and ask if she talked to the lawyer about that estate Littlefield appraised on Saturday. If she's not in too crabby a mood, ask if she's found out anything about our mystery phone number. You might also call one of your friends and ask about those kids we saw leaving the Jordans' today."

"Anything else?" Jocelyn said, looking up from the list she was making.

"Yeah. Double cheeseburger, hold the lettuce and mayo, double pickles. Fries, no ketchup. Diet Coke with extra ice. Money is in the ashtray. And watch you don't pop the clutch on the van."

After Jocelyn left, I settled in for a staring contest at the Jordans' house. The neighborhood was starting to shake itself out of its late-afternoon slumber. Women in office clothes and stockings stepped wearily from cars bearing armloads of dry-cleaning and sacks of groceries. Dads came home, turned on their sprinklers, then reemerged to play catch with children.

Soon a haze of barbecue smoke started rising from backyards up and down the block. I would have killed for a slab of ribs.

I wondered where Kyle Jordan was, but then remembered it could be a long ride home from his soccer camp in Rockdale County.

The sound of a car door closing, and an engine starting, startled me. I looked up in time to see Lissa Jordan back out of her driveway in the white Camaro, a pony-tailed young man in the front seat beside her.

Although tempted to follow, I decided to stay where I was.

Maybe ten minutes later, the Jordans' front door opened again. Two towheaded little girls dressed only in cotton panties scampered out of the house and ran for the sprinklers, where they darted in and out of the spray, screaming with glee each time the cold drops touched their skin. A young girl appeared in the open doorway, nearly dwarfed by the baby she lugged in her arms.

I raised the binoculars to my eyes to get a better look. The sitter Lissa Jordan had left her three babies with was little more than a child herself. Long skinny legs had scraped knees, and there was no sign of breasts. The kid couldn't have been more than ten years old.

I watched for a while longer, wondering if maybe an adult was there supervising the group, but after twenty minutes or so, the children were still playing, and there was no sign of an adult.

The girl disappeared into the house once, briefly, and

when she came back out, the baby was no longer in her arms. "Megan, Jessica," she called. "Come on and eat your pizza."

The two preschoolers screamed again, darted in and out of the spray once more, and then obediently ran for the front door, their soggy drawers drooping from the weight of the water. The baby-sitter waited until they were safely in the house, then closed the door.

I sat and waited and watched and fumed. Somebody should report these people to the child welfare authorities, I thought. Leaving three small children alone in the care of a kid barely out of Pampers herself.

Maybe somebody would.

I dug around in the glove box of Jocelyn's car until I found a hairbrush and a lipstick, then applied both liberally. Straightened my rumpled skirt and blouse and looked ruefully down at my muddy tennis shoes. The kid was young, maybe she wouldn't notice them.

I rang the doorbell purposefully, indignantly even.

"Yes," came the muffled reply from behind the door. At least the kid knew better than to open the door to a stranger.

"Eliza Adams of the Department of Family and Children Services," I boomed. "Someone has reported an underage minor is caring for three preschool children in this home. I'll have to come in and make an inspection."

"I'm not allowed to open the door," the girl said hesitantly. "Mrs. Jordan told me not to."

"Mrs. Jordan is in direct violation of Georgia Code six nine, oh oh seven, eight six," I improvised in my best Jack Webb imitation. "Failure to yield children to an authorized agent of the state. Now open this door immediately before I have this home impounded and these children inoculated."

A latch turned then, and the door opened an inch or two. The little girl stood bravely in the doorway, the baby boy clinging to her neck and the two toddlers cowering behind her.

"Aw you gonna put Twaci in jail?" the older of the two girls lisped. Pizza sauce was smeared over the children's faces, and all three were dressed in their father's oversize cotton T-shirts.

"No no," I reassured them. "I'm just going to make an inspection and report my findings to the proper authorities."

Quickly I turned to the baby-sitter, my pen poised on the open page of the notebook. "Name, age, address?"

The girl's lower lip trembled slightly. "Traci Hancock, age 10, 722 Crestview Court," she whispered.

"And Mr. and Mrs. Jordan," I said, "when do you expect them back?"

"Mr. Jordan went to a Braves game and Mrs. Jordan said she'd be back in a couple hours," Traci stammered. "Am I in trouble? I watch Trevor and Megan and Jessie all the time. I'm real careful. Honest."

My eyes swept around the room. The floor was littered with toys, games, and books, and the coffee table was covered with pizza boxes and empty beer cans. The VCR was on, and Lady and the Tramp were sharing a plate of spaghetti.

I felt bad about scaring this kid, but not so bad I was ready to quit.

"I'll have to inspect the premises before I fill out my report," I said.

Using my notebook to write my "findings," I wandered around the room. Stepping in front of the soccer photos I'd noticed on the television the other night, I picked one up to get a closer look. The kids wore red jerseys with *Riverview Raiders* written on them, and the coach, Coach J, wore the same jersey, topped with an FSU Seminoles baseball cap. There was a framed photo of Kyle and Lissa Jordan on top of the television too, with Lissa looking baby-faced and extremely pregnant, and Kyle dressed in yet another soccer jersey, this time one that proclaimed him coach of the Westside Warriors. He wore the Seminoles cap in this photo too.

"Young lady," I said sternly, turning to her. "Do the Jordans always have a lot of parties?"

"Well, not all the time," she said. "Sometimes Mrs. Jordan gets bored when Mr. Jordan is at work all day. So her friends come over and they watch MTV or listen to CDs. Or they go to the movies or the mall sometimes."

"I see. And what are Mrs. Jordan's friends' names?"

"Oh, Zak and Matt and Derek and Brittni and Kelly and Heather and some other names I can't remember."

"All right," I said, jotting the names down. "You stay here while I finish my inspection."

I walked quickly to the hallway off the living room, looking in each of the small bedrooms until I found the master bedroom.

Lissa and Kyle Jordan were apparently in their "black phase." A round king-size bed dominated the room, its black satin quilted comforter rumpled, with black satin pillows tossed about the room. A fancy black satin swag curtain kept any light from coming into the room. On the chrome night stand on one side of the bed there was a thirteen-by-eleven color photo of Lissa. It was one of those "boudoir shots" that were all the rage this year. In the photo, Lissa was wearing a French-cut black lace teddy, with one strap artfully allowing a stray breast to escape. Her lips were slightly parted and her eyes half closed in what looked like the throes of sexual ecstasy.

I walked quickly around the room, my fingers fairly

itching to open the dresser drawers and closets to search for some clue to this strange couple. But I didn't dare risk it; not with Lissa Jordan likely to return at any time.

In the kitchen, I opened the refrigerator. The shelves were crammed with beer cans and bottles of wine cooler, but I was gladdened to see that there was milk and juice too. At least these people had food for the children.

All three children huddled close to Traci on the living room sofa, the two girls sucking their thumbs and looking troubled.

"All right, Traci," I said, making nonsensical scratches in my notebook. "I'm not going to take these children into custody at this time. Listen, is your mama home?"

She nodded yes. "Do you live close to here?" She nodded again.

"Good. I want you to call her after I've left and tell her the lady from Child Services said you're too young to baby-sit by yourself. You understand? And when Mrs. Jordan comes home, you tell her the same thing. Tell her the lady from Child Services said to straighten out her act, or she'll have her children taken away from her. All right?"

"Yes, ma'am," Traci said. "I'm sorry."

"That's all right," I said. "Oh, one more thing. Were you unlawfully baby-sitting for these children on Saturday too?"

"Yes, ma'am," she said. "But Mrs. Jordan was home by six o'clock."

I marched smartly to the Hyundai then, started the engine, drove to the end of the block, parked, and congratulated myself.

21

CALLAHAN," A VOICE SAID softly. "Callahan. Wake uuuup, your dinner is here."

The smell of warm hamburger filled the car. I blinked my eyes open. Jocelyn was dangling a grease-spotted paper sack in front of my nose.

She got in the Hyundai and took a loud slurp from the biggest plastic cup I'd ever seen. There must have been a half gallon in that puppy.

I sat up as straight as I could and stretched. I'd dozed off in a funny position and now I had a crick in the small of my back. "Well, what did you find out?"

"Check this out," Jocelyn said. "Zak Crawford got kicked out of All Saints in March, for burning a cross on Andre Bernard's front yard."

I took a bite of my cheeseburger, slopping bits of bun and hamburger juice down my blouse. "Is Andre Bernard black?"

"Yeah," she said. "His family just moved to Atlanta from Jamaica in February, and he was going to be star forward on the All Saints team. Zak and his friends didn't like having a black kid starting, so they burned a cross in the Bernards' front yard. He bragged about it at school, and the word got around."

"Sounds like a lovely boy," I said sarcastically. "What does Zak do now?"

"He works as a lawn maintenance man for the apartment complex where he and his dad live. His parents are divorced and his dad travels a lot. He's some kind of salesman, I think."

"And Zak hangs out at the Jordans' a lot?"

Jocelyn sucked loudly on her drink. "Yeah." He cuts the grass and stuff, and he and Mrs. Jordan are, like, really tight."

"You found out a lot of stuff," I commented. "Who told you all this?"

"Different kids. I called a guy I dated when I was a senior, and he called some people. Stuff like that."

"Find out anything else?"

She considered for a moment. "Well, somebody told me Mrs. Jordan got married to Coach J when she was still in high school."

"When was this?" I asked. "Was it here in Atlanta?"

"No. Somebody said Coach was teaching at some private school in Florida, and Mrs. Jordan was a cheerleader, and she got pregnant, and had to drop out, but he married her."

I thought back to the framed photos I'd seen at the Jordans' house. "Coach J has a bad habit of sleeping with students, it sounds like."

"He's scum," Jocelyn said. "He killed Bridget, Callahan. I just know it. You gotta help me prove it."

"The police are working on it," I told her. "I told one of the detectives about Jordan, and they were going to look into it. Unfortunately, we seem to be turning up more suspects, instead of eliminating them. I'm not convinced that it wasn't Elliot Littlefield. Or this poor

Gordo Madison guy. Or even Pete Vickers, this nutty guy in Stone Mountain who wanted to buy the diary."

"You've got mustard on your chin," Jocelyn said, swiping at my face with a paper napkin. "Coach J did it. I know it."

"We'll see," I said. "What did Edna have to say?"

Jocelyn dug in the pocket of her shorts and brought out a piece of paper. "Yeah, she said your neighbor came through with the mystery phone number. It's a phone booth over in Cabbagetown. Where's Cabbagetown? I never heard of it."

"You wouldn't have," I said. "Cabbagetown is a little mill village surrounding the old Fulton Bag plant. The plant closed years ago. It's a pretty rough part of town now, although it's only about a mile from Littlefield's house. Wonder what Pete Vickers was doing over that way?"

"Beats me," Jocelyn shrugged. "Edna said to tell you she thinks she found the silver cup at an antiques mall in Chamblee."

"Great," I said. "That's fantastic. But Chamblee. That's a long way away from Inman Park or Poncey Highland, where I told her to look. I wonder how she tracked it clear out to Chamblee?"

"She said to tell you she called Hunsecker and left a message to tell him she thinks she's spotted it, but the antiques shop where the cup is at is closed. A sign on the door says the owner is on a buying trip to Maine."

"Shit," I said. "What else did Edna say?"

"She got the list from the lawyer. Edna says the lawyer said she unlocked the house for Littlefield, gave him her list of major pieces, and stayed for an hour or so, but she left because she got a call on her beeper. She said she went back by the house by six P.M., and Littlefield was just finishing up."

"So maybe Littlefield's alibi for Saturday isn't as firm as we thought. We've got both Littlefield and Jordan with big chunks of time unaccounted for that afternoon. And Vickers might have been in the area too."

Jocelyn picked up the hairbrush I'd used earlier and fluffed her hair, then checked herself out in the rearview mirror. "Gross. I look like one of those bag ladies who live in their cars. I gotta get a shower."

"Me too," I told her. "It's an occupational hazard."

"What do we do now?" she wanted to know. "Wait for Mrs. Jordan or Coach J to come home?"

"No," I said. "While you were gone I checked out the house. The baby-sitter says Jordan went to a Braves game after work and that Lissa said she'd be back in a couple hours. I don't want her to notice this car still sitting here when she gets back."

"So we go home?"

"You go home. I've got some people to see."

"Who?" she said.

"Nobody you'd know," I said. "Just some loose ends I need to check on."

22

L OOSE ENDS, I THOUGHT, AS I drove back
downtown, toward Cabbagetown. Loose ends will
trip you up every time. According to Edna's friend at
the phone company, the pay phone we were looking for
was in the parking lot of a mom-and-pop grocery store
at the corner of Memorial Drive and Estoria Street.
The twin brick smokestacks of the boarded-up hulk of
the old Fulton Bag textile mill shadowed the store and
everything in the neighborhood. The mill, which had
been in operation since Reconstruction days, closed for
good in 1981. The people of Cabbagetown, many of
whom had come to work in Atlanta right out of the hills
of Appalachia, were still scratching out a living, but the
houses were falling down, and the children who played
in the narrow trash-strewn streets reminded me of
underfed stray animals.

At Estoria Street, I pulled into the grocery store
parking lot. I got out of the van, walked over to the
phone booth, and checked the number. It matched the
one on Vickers's desk calendar. With the exception of
my van and a beat-up yellow station wagon, the parking
lot was empty.

Inside the store it was hot and smelled of roach spray and overripe bananas. Flies buzzed around a table heaped with sweet potatoes, onions, and cabbages. The girl at the counter, herself no more than sixteen, held an infant in her arms, feeding it a bottleful of fizzy orange drink.

I picked up a pack of gum and a package of crackers from a display of snack cakes, went to the cash register, and paid. The girl took my money wordlessly.

"I'm looking for somebody who might live in the neighborhood," I said, after she let my change drop to the counter. "Somebody named Darryl. Do you know anybody named Darryl who comes around here?"

"No," she said, her face expressionless.

"You sure?" I asked, offering a smile. "I really need to talk to him. I think he might have witnessed an accident my mother was in down the street last month. My lawyer says we'll pay his daily expenses to come to court to testify. But I need to find him."

"Don't know no Darryl," she said.

I got back in the van, unwrapped a stick of gum and thought about things. Good things come to she who waits, I reminded myself. So I waited.

For every hour I sat in the van I allowed myself a stick of gum. By nine o'clock I was good and sick of Doublemint. But I had company. The grocery store, smelly and understocked as it was, seemed to serve as a general store for the community. Cars pulled in and out, women came out of the store laden with paper bags, men with six packs of beer and cartons of cigarettes. By now the parking lot seemed full of teenage kids. Boys mostly. Sucking on quart bottles of malt liquor, perched or leaning against the hoods of cars, radios blasting. Late-model sedans cruised in and out of the parking lot, but there was no drive-through window, no hot french fries or milkshakes being sold.

I'd been away from police work for a while, which could explain why the attraction to the store seemed so odd at first. Now I remembered this corner and this store. Remembered it from a brief stay on the vice squad. I'd stumbled into a meat market for teenage hustlers.

At nine thirty I went into the store and bought myself a Miller Lite. The girl behind the counter acted like she'd never seen me before. I walked out slowly, pausing on the broken sidewalk in front of the store. Two kids, maybe ten and twelve, were sitting on the curb, taking turns playing one of those hand-held video games my nephews seem surgically attached to.

"Who's winning?" I asked.

The older kid looked up. He was barefoot, with dirty brown hair that fell across his eyes. "I got a perfect game goin'," he said. His pale face was sprinkled with freckles.

"That's a nice game," I observed.

"Friend of mine give it to me," he said. His pal snickered.

"Nice friend," I said.

"He's a fuckhead," the kid said, glancing at me to gauge my reaction. I shrugged. "Those things aren't cheap."

"I'm looking for somebody named Darryl," I said. "You guys know Darryl?"

The kids exchanged wary looks. "How much does a new game for one of those things cost?" I asked. "Twenty bucks?"

"Target's got Tetra for eighteen eighty-eight," the younger kid volunteered.

"Tetra sucks," the older one said. "Terminator's twenty-four bucks."

I unfolded a twenty and three ones from my pocket. "Twenty-three is all I've got," I said. "You guys say you know Darryl?"

The money was snatched out of my hand before I could draw it back. The older kid tucked it in the pocket of his ragged cutoffs.

"See the guy talking to that dude in the 'Vette?" He nodded toward a white Corvette that had pulled into the parking lot. A slim-hipped boy, maybe a little older, like sixteen or seventeen, was leaned over, his head stuck in the window of the car. He was tanned the color of mahogany and the only clothes he wore were a pair of tight-fitting jeans stretched over the cutest little butt I'd ever seen.

"That's Darryl."

"Does he have a lot of regular friends?" I asked.

"Yeah," the older kid said. "Darryl does pretty good. Except every once in a while his old lady sends his step-father over here lookin' for him, and if he catches him here, he'll beat the livin' shit out of Darryl."

"Darryl's no homo," the younger kid said. He had bright blue eyes and a mouthful of broken, rotten teeth. "He's okay."

"I'm sure," I said quietly. As we watched, Darryl pounded the roof of the sports car, accepted a beer from the driver, and waved as the car pulled back into traffic.

"Thanks, guys," I told my new friends. They nodded seriously.

Darryl had arranged himself across the hood of an ancient blue pickup truck, his back against the wind-shield. He watched me approach through half-closed eyes. His hair was probably naturally blond, but he'd helped it along with something that turned it a green-gold under the halogen street lights.

"How's it goin'?" I said, stopping and standing in

front of the truck, my hands jammed into the pockets of my skirt.

"Not too bad," he said. "What's the deal? You a cop?"

"Private detective," I said. "You know a guy named P. G. T. Vickers?"

His face registered a blank. "Drives a big Olds," I said. "Pete. Pete Vickers."

He smiled lazily, giving me the combined benefit of a cleft in his chin and those high cheekbones. "Yeah. Pete. He's a buddy of mine. So?"

"You usually see him on Saturdays?" I asked.

"Sometimes," he said. "What's the problem? His wife find out about his other hobbies?"

"Nothing like that," I said. "I was just wondering if you saw him last Saturday, like late in the day?"

"This gonna get Pete in trouble?" Darryl asked. He wasn't crying or anything, but I was touched at his concern for his "buddy."

"Out of trouble, is more like it."

"I seen him Saturday," Darryl said quickly. "He picked me up here around four. We shot some pool, hung out, like that."

I had a pretty good idea of what "like that" included, and I was fairly certain it wasn't a discussion of Confederate flanking maneuvers. Which was why Vickers had gotten so flustered when I'd asked for his whereabouts on Saturday. He'd been in the wrong neighborhood at the wrong time, for all the wrong reasons.

"You wouldn't lie to me now, would you?" I asked. Darryl looked like somebody who lied as a matter of habit, but it wouldn't hurt to ask.

"Shit no," Darryl said. "Me and Pete were together last Saturday. I won ten bucks off him, shooting pool."

"Thanks," I said.

While I was waiting to pull out onto Memorial Drive I decided to pay a visit to Littlefield's nosy neighbor, Mr. Szabo. I'd eliminated one suspect tonight. Now that only left a handful of others. I guess that could be called progress.

Stanley Szabo was sitting on his front porch listening to a Braves game on a transistor radio. I could see the shine from his bald head from the porch light.

"Mr. Szabo?" I called, as I climbed the front steps.

The wicker porch rocker he'd been sitting in creaked loudly as he pushed himself to a standing position. He picked up a pair of reading glasses from a small table and put them on, sizing me up.

"You're the girl detective," he said, making it a statement.

"Callahan Garrity," I said. "I guess you know I'm working for Mr. Littlefield. Could we talk for a moment?"

He gestured toward a rickety wooden chair beside his own, and I sat down.

"I was wondering if you saw anybody or anything out of the ordinary in the neighborhood last Saturday," I said. "Were you at home?"

"I was here all right."

"And did you see anything?"

"Told the police what-all I saw already," he said.

"Could you tell me?" I asked politely.

He sighed and scratched his belly. "Let's see. All kind of cars and coming and going commotion that day. Wore me out just listening to the car doors slamming."

"And you didn't notice anything in particular? No strange cars over at Mr. Littlefield's house?"

He shook his head. "Never saw anything but strange cars over there. That's why the neighborhood association got on him about those parties and such. Damned nuisance."

"Not too many of the neighbors like Mr. Littlefield," I said. "I understand your other neighbor, Mr. Dahlberg, has a big feud going with him."

"I keep out of it," Szabo said. "I mind my own business, missy. But now, that Littlefield, he goes too far."

"Jake Dahlberg told me Littlefield flew a Nazi flag from his front porch to make some movie people mad," I said.

"Jake had all kind of fits over that flag thing," Szabo said, laughing wheezily.

"Well, you can hardly blame him, since his father had a stroke and was paralyzed after he saw it," I said.

Szabo's eyebrows shot up. "Who told you that?" he asked. "Ed had a stroke all right, but it was two or three months before the movie thing. And he was already in a nursing home at the time. He wouldn't have known if Littlefield had flown the Goodyear Blimp from his front yard." He laughed that wheezy laugh again.

"Are you sure?" I asked, feeling my face growing red. I hate being suckered.

"Hell yes," Szabo insisted. "Jake put him in the nursing home not long after Miriam, that was the mother, after Miriam died. Jake moved in here right afterward, and Ed went over to Oak Haven, over near Emory. Ed raised hell about being moved out of his house, but he'd gotten kind of batty, wandering the streets in his undershorts, scaring the little kids. Ed was always a little batty, even when he had all his marbles. Hell of a pinochle player though," he said reluctantly.

"I see," I said coolly. "Maybe I misunderstood. Do you happen to know if Jake knew Bridget, the girl who was killed?"

"Sure he knew her," Szabo laughed, "I saw her hanging

around over there at Dahlberg's house all the time. They'd have a pizza delivered and eat it right there on the porch. Made Littlefield madder than anything too. I saw him run across the street one day, when she was sitting out there with Jake, he come up to the porch, grabbed her by the arm and jerked her clear across the street. And he was yelling at Jake to keep away from the girl."

"Did you happen to see Jake over there Saturday?" I asked.

"Nah," he said. "But I was in and out of the house four or five times. WSB was running a contest to win a trip to Panama City Beach. I kept going in to call every time they played the sound of waves crashing. Little nigra girl won the contest. Now what's a little nigra girl going to do at the beach?"

I wasn't really listening after that.

"They really hate each other," I said to myself. "Maybe Littlefield's not as paranoid as I thought."

"Paranoid?" Szabo said, his voice quavering with laughter. "He's a nut, that's what Elliot Littlefield is. A nut and a nuisance. And you can tell him Stanley Szabo said so. I hear he's going to prison this time, for murdering that girl."

"Maybe so," I said, picking my way down the porch steps. "Or maybe not." I turned around and gave him the Tomahawk Chop. "Go, Braves," I said.

"Attagirl," he answered.

23

THURSDAY MORNING, RUBY'S blood pressure was up and Neva Jean claimed she was down in her back.

"It's Patti Michaels. What should I tell her?" Edna asked, her hand over the telephone's mouthpiece.

I bit off a hunk of chocolate chip granola bar, chewed it, and leaned over to lace up my white, orthopedic-cleaning-lady shoes. The client on the phone was new, a real estate broker Edna had met at the beauty salon.

"Tell her I'm on the way," I said. "Tell her to leave the key on the ledge above the door."

"I thought you had to put together a report today for Elliot Littlefield," she said.

"I do. But I've been neglecting the House Mouse to run around all week looking for Littlefield's allegedly missing diary. Besides, I don't like being lied to, and I don't like being made a fool of. He'll get his report when I'm damn good and ready."

"You think he killed Bridget," she said. Her voice was muffled because she'd gone into the supply closet.

Edna came out and handed me a freshly laundered pink House Mouse smock. The starch fell off in white sheets when I tried to push my arms into the sleeves.

"He was guilty of that 1969 murder," I said. "I'm beginning to think he killed Bridget too and staged the burglary as a coverup. The damned diary was probably bogus anyway. I can't prove it yet, though. Jocelyn is still adamant that Kyle Jordan killed her sister, and with the other stuff going on, I'm beginning to think maybe we'll never find out who murdered the poor kid."

I filled her in then on what I'd learned about Gordo Madison, and the feud between Littlefield and Dahlberg, and how Dahlberg had lied to me about his father.

"Oh yeah," Edna said. "That reminds me. What did Kappler's office want yesterday? Did you ever call him back?"

I was taking a mental inventory of the cart's contents: rubber gloves, plastic bags, broom, mop, disinfectant, scrub brushes, scouring powder, glass cleaner, antihistamines, and my spray bottle of Fantastik. I love that stuff. The girls have threatened to have a monogrammed holster made for me, just for my spray bottle of Fantastik.

"What?" I said, shaking the scouring powder can to make sure it was full.

"Kappler," she said, exasperated. "What did he want?"

I really did not have the time to go into it. I dug the newspaper story about tamoxifen out of my purse and showed it to her. "There's a new, experimental breast cancer drug that sounds like it was invented specifically for me," I told her. "They're enlisting sixteen thousand women from all over the country for a trial of it. I called Kappler to tell him to get me in the study. That's all."

"Placebo," she said, reading aloud from the clipping. "Some women in this study won't be given the drug at all. And they won't even know it until this five-year study is completed. What happens if you get in the study and they give you a placebo? You could get another lump. The cancer could come back."

Gently, I took the clipping away from her and tucked it back in my purse.

"The cancer could come back anyway. I'm not losing anything by trying tamoxifen. But I could be losing the only chance I have to ensure that I'll eventually be cancer-free."

"I don't like it," she said, pooching out her lower lip, a sure sign that we were about to have a fight. "What does Dr. Kappler say?"

"He doesn't like it either," I admitted. "I talked to him first thing this morning. He doesn't want to enroll me in the study, but I told him if he doesn't do it, I'll just find another doctor who will."

She went to the back door and held it open for me. "You were even stubborn as a baby, you know that?"

"I'm not stubborn," I said. "Just high-spirited."

Edna gave me a swift but halfhearted boot to the butt as I passed her going out the door.

I was back again, moments later, holding my hands tight across my mouth, trying to suppress a gag.

"What?" she said, alarmed.

I ran to the kitchen sink and retched. Ran some cold water over the sink and my face, then retched again.

Edna was at my side in a second, holding my head for me, giving me a towel.

"What is it, Jules?" she asked, brushing the hair out of my eyes. "What's wrong?"

I buried my face in the towel and tried to suppress the memory of what I'd seen.

When I'd gotten out to the van I'd noticed Ping-Pong draped across the hood again. Damn cat, I thought. I'd gone up to brush her off, but stopped short.

Flies buzzed around as I approached, and a sickening smell wafted toward me. The cat was dead, its underside split open stem to stern, its Siamese fur blackened with blood, the legs sticking stiffly to the side. Someone had cut her open, then put her back on the van, as some kind of sick joke.

"It's Ping-Pong," I gasped. "Dead. On the van."

"What the hell are you talking about?" she asked, annoyed.

I sighed. I'd forgotten to tell Edna about Bridget's cat.

When I did her face went white. "Jesus," she whispered. "Who'd do something like that? The kids around here wouldn't hurt an animal, I don't think."

"It's kids all right," I said grimly. "But I don't think it's anybody from around our neighborhood. The tires are slashed too.

"I think Lissa Jordan and maybe some of her friends realized that we've been watching her house. I doubt they know Ping-Pong was Bridget's. They probably saw the cat on my car and thought it was ours. This same group of kids burned a cross on a black kid's lawn earlier this year."

"Goddamned juvenile delinquents," Edna said.

Edna glanced at her watch. We'd spent the morning dealing with this little crisis. "Wait here," she said. "I'll get my keys and take you myself."

Luckily, the trunk of Edna's land yacht is cavernous. We had enough room for the cleaning cart plus the entire staff of the House Mouse.

"Call Hunsecker," she said, right before she let me out of the car at Patti Michaels's house. "I don't care if they are kids. Anyone who'd do that to an animal is sick and dangerous." I nodded and got out.

When you get into the rhythm of it, cleaning a house isn't so bad, really. The best thing is that you're all by yourself, with nobody looking over your shoulder. I've got my own little method, my own little routines. And I'd had so much on my mind lately that I was happy to throw myself wholeheartedly into the job, and to resist thinking of poor dead Ping-Pong.

When I looked up, it was close to four o'clock. I took my Walkman off and went on a quick inspection tour. I hoped Patti was planning to entertain soon, because her home was so clean I felt like pasting a paper sani-strip from the top floor to the front door.

I was locking the door when Edna pulled into the driveway. Jocelyn got out and got in the backseat. "She was pulling up just as I was leaving to come get you," Edna explained as we loaded the gear into the car.

"Did you tell her about the cat?" I whispered. Edna shook her head no. I'd managed to distance myself from this maddening case for six hours, but now it was pushing its way back into my life.

"I'm scared, Callahan," Jocelyn announced. She'd huddled herself into a corner of the backseat, her knees pulled up to her chest. Her hair was uncombed and it looked like she'd slept in her clothes. "Somebody has been calling the house where I'm staying. They said if I don't mind my own business they'll bury me in the family plot with Bridget and the cat. What cat?"

Those little hairs at the base of my neck started to prickle. "What time did the calls come in?" I asked. "Was the voice a man's or a woman's? Did you recognize it? Who knows the phone number where you're staying?"

"What cat?" she repeated, sharply.

"Shit," I sighed. I tried to choose my words carefully. "Bridget had a cat, a beat-up old Siamese. Littlefield made me take it home yesterday. He was threatening to have it put to sleep. I meant to tell you about it, but I got tied up with other things. This morning, when I went outside, somebody had killed her. On purpose."

"Oh my God," Jocelyn whispered. "Oh my God."

"Just tell me what happened last night, about the phone calls," I said. I didn't want her dwelling on the fate of her sister's pet.

"I was asleep when the first call came. It must have been around two A.M. Then they called back every hour on the hour until I took the phone off the hook at six. It's a whisper, really, I can't tell if it's a man or a woman, and I don't know who it is," she said. "I left a message on my mother's answering machine, telling people that if they were looking for me, I could be reached at the other number until September."

Edna gave me that look again.

"You're right," I admitted. "I'll have to call Hunsecker. The Jordans must have realized you were watching them, Jocelyn. It's probably one of those kids that hang around at the house. When you left your summer phone number on your mother's machine, did you mention the address, too?" I asked, turning around to face Jocelyn.

"No," she said slowly, as it dawned on her what she had done. "But I said I was staying at Bonnie O'Bryant's house."

"Not anymore you're not," I said. "I think the calls are probably just kids trying to spook you, and the cat thing was an incredibly sick prank, but it's not safe for you to stay alone anymore. You better move back to your folks' house this afternoon."

"I can't," she said grimly. "Even if I wanted to, which

I don't. My parents left last night to stay for a week at some friends' house in the mountains in North Carolina. My mother said she needs to grieve. Hah."

"Call them and tell them what happened," I insisted. "I don't care how bad you hate your mother, your parents need to be home, and they need to know what you've gotten involved in."

It was my fault she'd gotten involved, of course, and I could have kicked myself, but the issue at hand was Jocelyn's safety, and not who to blame for a lack of it.

"They don't have a phone," Jocelyn said. "It's a mountain retreat. No phone, no television. Just piles of moldy old paperbacks and jigsaw puzzles with missing pieces."

"She'll have to come stay with us, Callahan," Edna said. "You got her into this, remember?"

Edna, of course, is never too busy to place blame.

"You're right," I admitted. "After we get home, you and I will go to pick up your stuff. Just exactly where is this house, anyway?"

"It's in Ryverclyffe, way up on the side of this big hill," Jocelyn said. "The Chattahoochee River runs right through the backyard. It's an awesome house."

"Maybe I'll leave my House Mouse business card."

"Oh man," Jocelyn said. "I almost forgot to tell you. After I finally got some sleep this morning, and I called and you weren't around, I decided to go stake out the Jordans' house again."

"That's it," I said. "You're grounded, young lady."

"No, listen," she said. "This is good stuff. Of course, at first it was totally boring. I listened to the radio and did my nails. After I read every piece of paper in the car, I ended up conjugating Spanish verbs."

"Wow," I said admiringly. Catholic schools.

"Yeah. And then, at about three o'clock, somebody in

a white Honda drops off Zak Crawford. And Mrs. Jordan comes out of the house, with all three kids, and they all get in her car and drive off. So I decided to tail 'em. God, it was so easy. First they stopped at this day-care place and dropped the kids off."

"Dropped 'em off, huh?" I mused. "Some meddling neighbor must have reported her for leaving the kids with an underage sitter."

"Anyway," Jocelyn continued, "then they went to the Kroger, and Mrs. Jordan went in and Zak waited in the car. I followed her inside. She bought some wine cool-ers, and some Buffalo wings from the deli and then, oh, this is gross. I can't say it in front of your mother."

Edna didn't even turn around. "I've raised four kids, helped deliver puppies and kittens and I used to help my own mother kill chickens, Jocelyn. Trust me, there is nothing you can say that would gross me out."

"Rubbers," Jocelyn said, her cheeks staining bright pink.

"Ribbed or fluorescent?" Edna asked.

"Gross," Jocelyn said, giggling. "Callahan, your mother is so funny. I wish my mother had a sense of humor."

"Oh yes," I said. "She's the Shecky Green of the AARP, Edna is."

"So after the shopping spree where'd they go?" Edna wanted to know.

"There's this little park in Dunwoody, where they have a playground and a soccer field. It's right on the river," Jocelyn said. "Mrs. Jordan pulled the car in there, at this little place that's surrounded by trees and sort of hidden. They spread a blanket under the trees, and they were drinking wine and laughing, and pretty soon they were making out, I mean, they were really into it, rolling all over the place . . . "

"Just a minute, please," I interrupted. "Where were you while all this was going on? I can't believe they were doing the nasty right there in front of little kids on the teeter-totter."

"Don't worry, they didn't see me," she said. "I parked on the other side of the park, then I jogged past. I was wearing this headband and sunglasses for a disguise, and when I was past, I stopped and drank from the water fountain, and they were not paying any attention to me, I guarantee. So then I jogged back to the car and watched them through my binoculars."

"Remind me to confiscate those things," I said. "And what did you see then, or can it be told in front of my aged and decrepit mother?"

"When things got really hot, they went and got in the backseat of Mrs. Jordan's car," Jocelyn said, breaking into another fit of giggles. "First they had to take the baby seat out and put it in the trunk, but the trunk wouldn't close, so finally, Zak just threw it on the ground and jumped in the back of the car."

"I hope you had the decency to put down the binoculars then," I said sternly.

"I'm not a peeping Tom," she said primly. "Besides, I had to park right in the sun, and it was about a gazillion degrees in my car, so I finally decided to leave."

"Good," I said. "That's the end of your career as a private investigator. That little red Hyundai of yours isn't exactly nondescript, you know. Somebody must have recognized it, or else one of the kids you called must have alerted the Jordans you were interested in them. I hesitate to ask, but before you went on your stake-out, did you find anything else about Kyle Jordan?"

"Just a little bit. Riviera High School is in Clearwater, Florida. But there was no answer. I guess they don't have anybody working there in the summertime. The other school is in Jacksonville, Florida, and it's private. The secretary said she remembered Coach J. He was popular with the students there, too, she said. She said it was a big scandal when that cheerleader got pregnant and Coach J ended up marrying her."

"So the rumor about Lissa was true," I said.

"Now all we have to do is prove that Coach J did it," Jocelyn said. "But how? How do we prove that he went to the house from soccer camp and killed Bridget and made it look like a break-in?"

"Good question," Edna pointed out. She'd pulled the land yacht into the driveway at home and cut the engine.

Pointing to the van, whose flat rear tires made it look like a kneeling elephant, Edna said, "I called Mario at the gas station. He said he'd send somebody over late this afternoon to fix those flats."

"Thanks," I said meaningfully. I was in no mood to fix one flat, let alone two.

"By the way," she said, pointing to the other car in the driveway, "Baby and Sister are waiting to tell you about their undercover mission. They wouldn't breathe a word to me. Said they'd wait until you got home."

The two elderly women were sitting at the kitchen table, staring at the black-and-white television. "Buy a vowel," Sister said loudly. "Get an *E*."

"Hello, ladies," I said loudly.

"Ooh, Callahan," Baby said. "Let me turn off this mess on television so we can tell you 'bout what we found out." She reached over and groped the control panel until her gnarled fingers found the off button.

"Let's tell Callahan and Edna about our visit," Baby shouted at Sister.

"That's some nice houses they fixed up for those people

to live in over there," Sister said. "And let colored folks live right there too. That's so nice."

"We done just like you said, Sugar," Baby said proudly. "Took some gospel tracts over to that Miz King and preached the good news about heaven and salvation. She invited us right in and we had some fine gospelizing. She done told us about her friend Josephina and her baby, burning up in that house fire. Miz King don't believe the little boy set that fire. She says Josephina slapped him so hard the last time he touched some matches that he had a handprint on his face for a week. He so afraid of fire he cried when they lit the candles on his birthday cake."

"Real nice house Miz King got there," Sister said, oblivious to Baby's conversation. "Course they got a lot of rules about can and can't. Can't have no clothesline outside. Can't park but one car in the driveway. Can't nobody else live there with them. Can't paint any different colors, or plant a little garden in the front."

"Can't have no barbecue grill, either," Baby broke in. "Now I think that's a shame. But Miz King, she say the Home for Hope people give her a house with good plumbing and a nice tight roof and good heat in the wintertime. So she say she don't complain about nothing, like if a little bit of water drips under the kitchen sink, or if they can't plug in a lamp in the living room."

"Why can't they plug in a lamp?" I asked.

"Miz King say that wall puts out smoke when they plug the lamp in. So they quit using it."

"Smoke? That sounds like a wiring problem. Did they report it to the Home for Hope people?"

"Miz King say Mr. Dahlberg, that's the man who runs it, he gets touchy about lots of complaints. Miz King don't wanna get in trouble, so she just leaves that lamp unplugged."

Edna popped the top on two cans of beer and placed them on the table in front of Baby and Sister.

Sister tried to push the can away. "Ooh. That devil alkyhol," she whooped. "Take that sin away." But Baby took a healthy gulp, leaving a foaming white mustache on her upper lip. "Don't taste like sin to me," she said loudly.

Then Edna sat down at the table with us. "Why on Earth are you asking all those questions about this Home for Hope thing?" she asked. "What's all this got to do with Bridget or Elliot Littlefield or Kyle Jordan or the price of tea in China?"

"Jake Dahlberg, the man who lives across the street from Littlefield, has this big blood feud going with him," I explained. "I'm supposed to have dinner with Dahlberg tomorrow night. The other day when I was over there, he offered to show me these houses his organization had rehabbed, and while we were there, this tenant, Mrs. King, mentioned that her neighbor's house had burned down, and the woman and her baby had been killed. Littlefield hates that project, he says they are trying to reghettoize Inman Park."

"Dinner?" Edna said. "What's Mac going to think about you having dinner with this man?"

"It's business, Edna," I said sharply. "And anyway, if it's any of your business, which it's not, I don't have to clear my social engagements with Mac. That's not what our relationship is about."

"Well excuuuse me," Edna said, lighting up. "But I bet the tables would be turned if you found out Mac was having dinner with some woman he'd just met, business or no business."

She'd win that bet.

24

I LEFT EDNA STANDING THERE, stalked to the back bedroom, and called Hunsecker at the copshop. Linda Nickells answered the phone. She said she'd see if he was around. "Sorry. He just left to go to dinner," she said briskly.

"Bullshit. I know he's there, Linda. Tell him it's important. Please tell him I really need to talk to him."

"I'll try," she said.

After five minutes on hold, Hunsecker picked up. "What the hell is so important that I couldn't go to dinner?" he barked.

"You need to listen to this, C. W.," I said, my teeth clenched as I tried to control my rising anger. "Jocelyn Dougherty, Bridget's sister, received a series of threatening phone calls last night. The caller threatened to put her in the family plot with her sister. Then sometime between last night and this morning, somebody slashed the tires of my van, and killed Bridget's cat and left it on the hood of my van."

"What have you and this kid been doing to stir up trouble?" Hunsecker asked.

"I've been investigating the theft of property from my client's home and she's been assisting me," I said.

"You've been meddling in a murder investigation," Hunsecker said. "I know you, Garrity. So who'd you mess with this time?"

I'd run out of ways of tap-dancing around the truth. "We've been running surveillance on Kyle Jordan. Remember, he was Bridget's soccer coach? After we learned that Jordan was Bridget's lover, we confronted him with that, but he denied everything, except for admitting that he'd slept with her, but only once. So we watched the house. It's a hangout for some kids from All Saints. And we discovered that Kyle Jordan wasn't the only one sleeping around. His wife, Lissa, is having a fling of her own with a kid who got kicked out of All Saints for burning crosses on a black kid's lawn."

I filled Hunsecker in then. He was dubious, but from the questions he asked, I could tell he intended to follow up.

"Anything else I should know about?" he asked caustically.

"I told Linda to have you call me," I said in my own defense. "We think at least one of the items taken in the burglary, the silver shooting trophy, is in a shop in an antiques mall in Chamblee."

"That's what your mother's message said," Hunsecker said. "How did she find it?"

I told him how a dealer Edna had talked to in Virginia Highlands had gotten a call from another dealer to ask if she knew anyone interested in Civil War–era antiques. "But the Chamblee dealer is in New England on a buying trip and the shop's closed," I said.

"We'll track her down."

"It's about time," I said.

"Go to hell, Garrity," Hunsecker bellowed. "Bring

that Dougherty girl in tomorrow, and we'll get her to make a statement about those phone calls. And in the meantime, you and that kid stay out of my murder investigation. You hear?"

Lightning cracked through the air as I hung up the phone, and the drizzle quickly escalated to a driving torrent.

"The windows," Edna cried. She and Jocelyn dashed madly from room to room, slamming down the opened windows. I went into the dining room and switched on the air-conditioner, crossing my fingers that it would work. There was a click and a rumble, and then a puff of cool air kissed my ankles near the vent on the floor.

"God bless central air," I said fervently.

"God bless warranties," Edna corrected me. "We didn't have to pay a penny for that new compressor."

She lowered her voice. "Jocelyn's in the kitchen ordering us a pizza for dinner. What are you planning to do with her after that?"

I knew what Edna was getting at. "There's no question that she can't go back to stay at the place she's been house sitting. And she can't stay at her parents' place alone either. She'll have to stay here, I guess, at least until we can get word to the Doughertys to get back here to Atlanta."

She nodded. "I told her she'd have to sleep over, but she says she needs to go back out to that house to get her clothes and contact lens solution and stuff."

"I'll run her out there after dinner," I promised. "I want to get that report and final statement typed up for Littlefield before we go. Then we can drop it off at Eagle's Keep on the way out to Ryverclyffe."

"You're getting off the gravy train then?"

"I'll tell him when I drop off the report."

Edna opened a bottle of red wine and I sipped a glass

while I typed up the report on my little portable electric typewriter. I hesitated about including all the details of what I'd discovered in the past week, but I like to give my clients value for the dollar. So I put it all in, including the part about how I thought the shooting trophy was in a shop in Chamblee and how I'd come to the conclusion that it was doubtful that an alcoholic schizophrenic could have pulled off the burglary and murder at Eagle's Keep without setting off the burglar alarm or otherwise getting caught. I also detailed our surveillance of Jordan's home, leaving out Jocelyn's presence. In the end, I had a three-page double spaced report, a statement billing Elliot Littlefield for forty hours worth of work and a pleasant buzz from the Chianti.

When the pizza came, I put the typewriter away and slipped the report in a brown envelope to protect it from pizza stains.

We deliberately talked about trivia at dinner, how the Braves were doing, what new movie Edna and Agnes were planning on seeing after dinner, chitchat that had nothing to do with murder or death threats or adultery.

"Let's go," I said, as Jocelyn picked a mushroom off a piece of pizza. She'd been eating the whole time we had, but she'd barely made a dent in the pizza slice Edna had served her. "I want to get this confrontation with Littlefield over with."

"You think there'll be one?" Edna asked, as she tossed our paper plates in the trash.

"I don't think he'll take my resignation gracefully," I told her.

We ran through the rain to the Hyundai, slamming the car doors shut just as another bolt of lightning tore through the dusky-colored sky.

"Thanks for letting me stay at your house tonight,"

she said shyly. "I haven't been nervous about staying at the O'Bryants' at all up until now. But those calls last night really spooked me. Every noise I heard I thought someone was trying to break in. And then the poor cat . . ."

"No problem," I said. "Have you got a pen? I want to write Littlefield's name on this envelope, in case he's not home and I have to leave it in the mailbox."

I grubbed around under the seat, thinking I might find one down there, but instead I came up with a handful of paper. Candy wrappers. I reached down again and brought up more candy wrappers, empty potato chip bags. Even an empty two-pound bag of Chips Ahoy cookies.

"Those are from when I was sick before," Jocelyn said. "I really need to clean this car, don't I?"

"Pull over to the curb here, will you?" I said, my voice even. She did as I asked. "Give me the keys," I ordered. Her face clouded, but she handed them over. I got out of the car, ignoring the rain pouring down my head and my back, and opened the trunk.

It was a junk food junkie's dream. She'd arranged all of it neatly, in small plastic baskets like the ones I keep at home for sorting socks. There were baskets of cookies, Chips Ahoy, Oreos. Baskets of candy bars: Mr. Goodbar, Snickers, Hershey bars. Another basket held boxes of miniature doughnuts and boxes of Little Debbie snack cakes. She'd been mainlining chocolate.

I slammed the trunk closed and got in the car again. She was weeping, her head and arms draped over the steering wheel. "I tried, Callahan, I tried," she said, sobbing. "I wanted to be good. You were so nice to me. I wanted to be good."

The glove compartment door fell open to the touch. The space where I'd earlier found hairbrushes and lipstick was now crammed with what looked like a lifetime supply of Correctol. There must have been twenty or thirty boxes, but I didn't count them. I felt a wave of nausea.

"You've been doing it again," I said flatly. "How long?"

She kept crying. I leaned over, jerked her head up by the chin. "How long, damn it? How long have you been bingeing?"

"Since, since the fu-funeral," she stammered, hiccuping and gulping for air. "Every, every night. I'd go to the store and buy my food. A lot of times I'd go back to Coach J's house and sit there and eat, and watch the house. I hate that bastard. Then I'd go to McDonald's. They have nice clean bathrooms, and the stall doors go all the way to the floor, so people won't ask you if you're all right."

She started to sob again. "Are you going to turn me in to the police? I'll pay for it, I swear."

I picked out a handful of boxes and looked at the price stickers. Each was from a different grocery or drugstore.

"You shoplifted this stuff," I said, disbelievingly. "You have money. Why would you steal laxatives?"

"I, I didn't want anyone to know," she blubbered. "They'd, they'd tell."

I turned the laxative box over and read the label. "Take two to four as needed," I read aloud. "How many of these things have you been taking, Jocelyn?"

"A lot," she cried. "I can't help it."

"Tell me how many," I repeated. "No more lies."

"Maybe forty or fifty," she whispered. "Not as many as before I went in the hospital. They don't work unless I take that many."

"Good Lord," I said aloud. The little con artist had

Edna and me completely fooled. Here we'd been thinking what a together kid she was, and she'd been bingeing and purging right under our noses. She'd taken enough laxatives to kill an elephant.

There was a gas station on the corner a block ahead. "Pull in to that Amoco station up there," I ordered. She wiped the streaming tears away, sniffled loudly, and did as she was told. At the gas station, I opened the glove box and emptied the laxatives into my purse. I took the keys again and opened the trunk. And then I took every cookie, candy bar, donut, and snack cake, and all those boxes of Correctol, and dumped them in the trash barrel by the gas pump. The junk food filled the barrel completely.

"I need it, I need it, I need it," I heard her screaming from inside the car. She pounded the dashboard and shrieked as though she'd been stabbed.

I walked around to the driver's side and made her switch places. On the way to Eagle's Keep I kept trying to think of something useful to say. I didn't know anything at all about this disease that had her in its grips. Didn't know anything about cognitive therapy or any of those other psychotherapy buzzwords. What I wanted to do was grab her by the hair and ask her why she wanted to kill herself with food.

Instead, calmly, I went over my plans. "We'll go to Littlefield's house. You stay in the car and lock the doors. I'm just going to give him my report, and tell him I've decided to remove myself from the case. I'll tell him I have another client." I glanced over to see her reaction, but she only sniffed and looked out the window.

"After that, we'll go out to Ryverclyffe and get your stuff. You'll spend the night with us. And tomorrow, I want to call your therapist and talk to him. You can't go on like this, Jocelyn."

She started crying again, and hunched her knees up to her chest. "Don't tell my parents, please," she pleaded.

I didn't want to betray her to her parents, but I didn't know what else to do. "We'll talk to your therapist," I reassured her. "See what he says."

25

ELLIOT LITTLEFIELD HADN'T mourned "my little Bridget" for long. Eagle's Keep was lit up like a Stewart Avenue used-car lot. There wasn't an empty piece of curb for two blocks. No way was I going to park and run through the rain to deliver my report. Instead, I moved the yellow traffic barricade in front of Jake Dahlberg's drive and pulled in there. We were friends, after all.

"Jocelyn," I said sternly. She sniffed and covered her face with her hands. "I'm going to run over to Littlefield's house. I'll be inside maybe five minutes. Can I trust you not to do anything stupid while I'm gone?"

"I'm okay," she mumbled.

I wasn't exactly dressed for a gala: white jeans, a navy blue Euclid Avenue Yacht Club T-shirt, and my new white Reeboks. But then I wasn't in a gala mood either.

Littlefield answered the door, laughing, a martini in his hand. The hallway in back of him overflowed with pretty, suntanned people in cocktail frockery. The host wore spotless white duck slacks, an open-collared shirt, and a navy blazer. His ascot must have been at the cleaners. He frowned at the sight of my rain-splattered personage. I held up the envelope with my report in it and fluttered it.

"This is really not a good time, Callahan," he said. He was talking without moving his jaws. It's a good trick. "I told you it could wait until tomorrow," he said.

"Actually, it can't wait," I said. "If you'll give me five minutes of your time, we can conclude our business, and I'll get out of your life."

He glanced around behind him. People were staring. Maybe they thought I was part of the entertainment.

"I don't understand all this urgency, but come along. We'll talk in the study." He hurried up the stairway; I was right on his heels.

In the study, he nearly snatched the envelope from my hands, ripping it open. He eyed the statement, adding up columns in his head. "Looks reasonable," he said, tossing it onto his desktop. Then he scanned the report, scowling when he read my conclusions.

"The police have this Madison person in jail," he said. "Why would you be shadowing this poor schoolteacher and his family?"

"Because I'm not certain Madison murdered Bridget, or took the diary, and neither are the police. They still haven't charged him with anything except the mugging. Evidence is pointing to someone else."

"And who would that be?"

"Elliot Littlefield, for one," I said.

He smiled sardonically. "You know, at first it amused me that you suspected me. I find skepticism attractive, usually. Now I'm really very annoyed with you, Miss Garrity. Not only have you not made any headway with finding my property, you've managed to implicate me in a murder for which I am totally innocent."

"Since we're discussing our innermost feelings, Mr.

Littlefield," I said, "I should tell you I'm quitting because I don't like you."

One of his eyebrows twitched, just slightly. "I have your report and your invoice. Your check will be mailed. I'd like you to leave now."

"I'm going," I said. "By the way, somebody killed Bridget's cat. Field-dressed her and left her on the hood of my car. The cops think it's somebody trying to scare me off this investigation."

I turned and regarded him carefully. "What do you think?"

He opened the door and stood back to let me pass. "I've had enough of your asinine accusations, Miss Garrity. I've got a houseful of guests to return to and a party to host."

The crowd in the downstairs hallway had grown thicker. I shouldered my way toward the front door, stopping only to help myself to a handful of stuffed mushroom caps and crab thingies from a silver platter being passed by a waiter.

Outside, the storm had lost its punch, the rain fizzled to a fine mist. I stopped to enjoy one of my purloined canapés, and from across the street, I saw Stanley Szabo, silhouetted in the light from his house, sitting on his front porch. I waved, and he returned the favor.

As I crossed the street I saw with relief that Jocelyn was still in the car. I was halfway afraid she might have bolted, but she was still there, waiting, listening to the radio.

I moved the barricade again, and backed out of the driveway, cautiously, to avoid hitting any of Littlefield's guests' cars. Jocelyn stared straight ahead. I turned on the radio to fill the silence in the car.

We were on Interstate 285 before I realized I didn't actually have a clue as to where I was going. "Directions?"

The road to the O'Bryants' was long and winding. With every turn the real estate got more expensive and more inaccessible. They'd chipped away part of a cliff side to build their home.

The front of their house was bathed by floodlights. Jocelyn unlocked the door, flipped a switch in the foyer, and the house lit up at once. She headed down a hallway to the right of the front door without looking back at me. "It should only take me a minute to get my stuff together."

I wandered into the living room and sat down to wait. Floor-to-ceiling picture windows gave a dramatic view down a ravine of the Chattahoochee River, which flowed by the O'Bryants' backyard. At least, I thought it flowed. Even with the floodlights, a heavy mist rolling off the water made it look something like Transylvania.

I leafed halfheartedly through a stack of magazines on the coffee table: *Field and Stream, Vogue, Bon Appétit.* With my index finger I traced a line in the dust on the tabletop. Wouldn't hurt to leave a House Mouse business card, I decided. We take our business where we can find it.

After a while I got tired of waiting. Teenagers. They pack a steamer trunk for an overnight stay. "Jocelyn," I called. "Let's go. I've got some stuff I need to do at home tonight."

"Coming," she called back. A moment later she emerged from the hall carrying a bulging overnight bag. "My room was kind of a mess," she said apologetically. "It took me a while to find everything I needed."

I pointed down the hallway. "Is the bathroom down here?"

I snapped the bathroom light on and sniffed. It smelled like a valleyful of Lilies of the Valley. In the cabinet under the sink I found an aerosol can of room freshener. I touched the nozzle. It was still wet.

Outside, after we'd locked up, I handed Jocelyn the car keys. "You drive," I said.

She took the hill at a creep, peering into the darkness to see the way.

"You're a good, safe driver," I said. "You know, if you really wanted to kill yourself, you could do it in the car. It would be a lot quicker, a lot less painful, and the people who love you wouldn't have to watch you do it."

"What do you mean?" she asked.

But she knew. "You went into the bathroom back there and tossed the pizza you ate for dinner," I said. "Don't bother lying about it. I'm a private investigator—remember?"

She jutted her chin defiantly. "You don't understand," she said. "I ate all that pizza. It was just lying there on my stomach. All that grease and fat and calories. I could feel my thighs and my butt just ballooning. I had to get rid of it, Callahan. The whole time we were on our way out here, I felt like I'd explode if I didn't get rid of it."

"Is that how you always feel after you eat?" I asked, alarmed.

She nodded miserably.

That's when I noticed the headlights. We'd been taking the winding road slowly and steadily because the pavement was still slick, even though the rain had stopped. The mist rising off the river that ran alongside the road made visibility touch and go. But the headlights in back of us seemed glued to our bumper.

"Blink your lights so this asshole will pass us," I instructed her.

She blinked the Hyundai's lights on and off three times. But the headlights got closer.

"Speed up just a little to give him room." But the car stayed right with us.

"How long has this guy been behind us?" I asked.

"I think he stopped at the bottom of the driveway to let us make the left turn," she said.

"Did you notice what kind of car it was?"

"Some kind of big gray car. It looks new and it has tinted windows. I couldn't see whether the driver was a woman or a man."

I thought for a minute. This was a lonely stretch of road. I hadn't seen any other houses around from the O'Bryants' house. The gray car's being there at the bottom of the hill was the kind of coincidence I don't like.

"Okay, Jocelyn," I said calmly. "I think these guys are following us."

"Well duh," she said. "I do watch television you know. What should I do?"

"Just keep it at an even speed," I said. "With the river right beside us like this, I don't want you to try to outrun him."

"Like I could," she retorted. "The fastest I've ever gone in this car is fifty miles an hour, and that's on flat road with only one person in it."

"Keep your eyes on the road," I repeated. "Does this street eventually intersect with Roswell Road?"

"It does, but not for another three or four miles," Jocelyn said. "Why?"

Before she could answer the gray car bumped us savagely, so hard the Hyundai skittered into the opposite lane. Jocelyn screamed, but yanked the wheel back hard right.

"He's trying to kill us," she cried.

"We'll be all right," I said. "If we get to Roswell

Road, there'll be lots of traffic, and the Fulton County Police precinct is right there. We'll find a cop. Pick up your speed just a little bit now."

She tapped the accelerator and the Hyundai scooted, but the gray car kept pace. I turned around to stare, but the car's tinted windows kept the driver's identity a secret.

I glanced over at Jocelyn. Her hands gripped the steering wheel and her face was contorted into a mask of fear and anxiety. Up ahead the road curved in a wide arc to the right, following a bend in the river. Jocelyn eased off the gas a little and the gray car let a few feet of distance fall between us. I relaxed a little. In the next second the gray car sped up again, and bashed us, harder. The Hyundai veered across the road. We hit a metal guardrail and then we were airborne.

We hit the ground with a bone-jarring crash. Then everything was still and dark.

I don't think I ever lost consciousness because I knew I'd hit my head on the dashboard. There was a warm trickle down my nose, from between my eyes. And my hands and knuckles were stinging. I held one up to my face, and I could see that it was crisscrossed with cuts from the broken glass of the windshield.

And then I felt wet.

We were in the river. Frigid water flowed through the smashed windshield. I looked over at Jocelyn. She was slumped over the steering wheel, not moving. I put my hand to her cheek, and it was warm. I could feel the rise and fall of her ragged breathing.

"Jocelyn," I said, loudly. "Jocelyn. Wake up. We're in the river." I struggled to extricate myself, but the seat belt was wet and my fingers were numb from the cold. I fumbled for the metal release and nearly cried from frustration. Finally, the belt clicked. I turned and knelt in the seat, trying to unfasten Jocelyn's belt. She stirred as I worked, and she wrenched away when I pushed her torso back away from the wheel.

"Wake up, Jocelyn," I screamed in her ear. She struck out at me, trying to push me away until I caught her wrist and held it in mine.

"It's Callahan, Jocelyn. We've had a wreck. We're in the river. We've got to get out and get to shore. Understand? Are you hurt?"

She opened her eyes, but her pupils looked funny. She was in shock. The water was waist high in the car now. I tried my door, but something was jammed against it. I reached over, shoving Jocelyn back again, to try her door, but it too was jammed. It was pitch black. My window was rolled down halfway, and I managed to roll it down the rest of the way. I hauled myself through the window, perching with one leg in and one leg out of the car. With my right leg, I felt around in the water. It was icy, but the current didn't seem to be ripping too badly. Gingerly, I let myself all the way down, gasping at the coldness. When my feet met bottom, I stood up. The water was moving, but it was only chest-high where I stood. Clinging to the edge of the car, I inched my way around to the other side. At the left front edge of the car, my foot slipped on the moss-covered rocky bottom, and I plunged headlong into the water.

Somehow though, I managed to grab hold of the car's bumper and pull myself upright again.

After forever, I could make out the dim outline of the driver's side window, and the slight figure sitting there. I reached in and felt for her. "Jocelyn," I screamed again, my teeth chattering so loud they nearly drowned out the scream. "Wake up now. You've got to help me get you out."

I felt an arm snake out of the car, and slowly, she

twisted and managed to get her upper body half out of the window. I half-dragged, half-carried her out the rest of the way.

Dry, and standing under her own steam, Jocelyn Dougherty probably weighed less than one hundred pounds. But wet, in shock, limp and dazed, she was lead weight and felt twice as heavy. Somehow though, slipping and sliding, we made it to the riverbank.

As soon as I loosened my grip on her waist, she sank to the weed-covered bank in a heap. I flopped down beside her, wrapping my arms around both of us, trying to generate some warmth. We were bloody, soaked, and chilled to the bone, but we were alive.

26

I DON'T KNOW HOW LONG I crouched there in the weeds at the side of the road, torn between wanting to flag down a car for help and being terrified that the driver of the gray car would come back to finish us off.

Desperation finally flushed me out of hiding. I stood in the middle of the road, arms flung wide, and closed my eyes to the headlight glare of an oncoming car.

My rescuer didn't seem terribly surprised to see a wet, bleeding woman standing in the road. In his late forties, he was huskily built, wearing a dress shirt, tie, and a baggy business suit. To me he looked like the cavalry. He turned on the car heater and made me stay in the car while he went back for Jocelyn. I heard her whimpering before I saw him struggle up the riverbank, carrying her in his arms like a discarded bundle of rags.

He loaded her in the back seat, took off his suit jacket and draped it over her. Then he got back behind the wheel. "Where to?" he asked. "Only reason I came across you was I made the wrong turn somewhere back there and got lost."

Disoriented, I couldn't think how to tell him to get to Johnson Ferry Road, where Northside and St. Joseph's hospitals compete for the city's sickest, fully-insured patients. Clenching my teeth to control the chattering, I told him to keep following the road until he saw the street lights of Roswell Road.

Thank God for dumb luck. Somehow, we made our way back to the land of fast food, all-night supermarkets, and instant teller machines. After ten minutes, he pulled up to the entrance of the north precinct of the Fulton Police Department, lifted Jocelyn out of the back, and came around to my door.

He looked embarrassed. "I'm gonna have to sort of let ya'll go in under your own steam," he apologized. "My ex-wife's got a warrant out for me for back child support and right now I don't need any more hassle in my life. You understand?"

There was a wooden bench beside the front door to the copshop. "Just leave her there," I said. "You've been wonderful." He set her down on the bench and touched my arm. "Sorry." Then he sprinted to his car and drove off.

The police dispatcher on duty took one look at Jocelyn and me, and in an instant, the precinct lobby was swarming with cops.

"I'm a private detective," I told the sergeant on duty. "We were run off the road and into the river back on Old Riverside Road. It's a red Hyundai. I'm all right, but my friend here is in shock and she may have a head injury."

They gave me a blanket to wrap up in and Jocelyn a ride to Northside Hospital. Before I'd give them my statement, I made them let me call Edna.

"We're all right," I said as a preamble. After I told her what had happened to us, she came unglued for a moment. But only a moment. "Call Hunsecker and tell him what happened," I told her. "Ask him to meet me up here at Fulton County. See if you can sweet talk him into coming by and picking up some dry clothes for me. Then head over to Northside's emergency room. Call me as soon as you know something about Jocelyn."

The police dispatcher, a five-foot-tall middle-aged white lady named Marylee, rescued me from the sergeant. She went off shift at eleven but not off duty, making me strip off my wet clothes and outfitting me in a set of pale-blue drawstring pajamas, the kind they issue to prisoners who are being kept in the precinct holding cells. When I was dressed, she unlocked a vacant office and insisted that the sergeant could take my statement there, rather than in the crowded, noisy bullpen. Then she brought me a steaming mug. "Cup-A-Soup," she said, apologetically. "French onion. I don't dare give you the coffee here, it'd kill you for sure."

I sipped the soup slowly, answering the cop's questions, grateful for being warm and dry.

By the time Hunsecker and Linda Nickells bustled in, I'd told everything I knew about our encounter with the gray car. Worry was etched on Hunsecker's face. "Are you all right?"

I touched the welt on the bridge of my nose, felt the small abrasions that covered my forehead, cheeks and chin. "Don't I look all right?"

The Fulton County cop slipped out of the room, and Hunsecker took his vacant chair. Nickells kept standing, leaning against the wall.

"Your mama wore him out on the phone," she said, laughing. She held out a paper sack. "Here's your clothes."

"I don't ever want to mess with that lady again,"

Hunsecker agreed. "She had a point though. I blew off all the stuff you were trying to tell me, because I resented your remarks about my private life. That's bad police work, and I'm ashamed to say it."

"Callahan understands," Nickells said gently.

He glanced down at the incident report he had in his hand, the one the sergeant had handed him before leaving the room. "Any idea who ran you off the road?"

I gave it some thought. "Well, I saw Littlefield tonight. I sort of got carried away. I told him ya'll weren't convinced Gordo Madison killed Bridget. I quit the case but told him I didn't intend to quit investigating until I found out who killed Bridget."

"Goddamn," Hunsecker moaned, running his hand across his face. "You got a big mouth, Garrity, you know that?"

"I know it," I said. "He pissed me off, C. W. The car that ran us off was a big gray sedan with tinted windows. That's all I know. It wasn't one I've seen before. It was waiting for us at the bottom of the hill when we left the O'Bryants'."

"We haven't given up on Littlefield," he said. "We have somebody working on getting all his phone records; to see if he'd been trying to sell any of the stuff taken in the burglary. Before I came out here, I sent somebody over to his house, to find out if he left the party tonight, or if any gray cars are parked in the vicinity. And we'll be questioning that soccer coach, too. We ran a check on him, by the way."

"And?"

"Nothing. He may have an overactive set of hormones, but he's never been arrested for anything. The principal at All Saints told me Jordan is an excellent biology teacher and the kids love him. He's aware of the relationship between Jordan and the dead girl. He says he counseled Jordan, and he swore it was a one-shot deal that was over."

"Over," I said woodenly. "It's over because somebody killed Bridget. Because she thought she was pregnant."

"There you go again," Hunsecker complained. "If you can't make up your mind who did it, you better shut up altogether and go home and let us do our job."

Linda Nickells came to my defense. "Aw, C. W., ease up on her. She's had a rough night."

"Thanks, Linda," I told her. "What do you see in him, anyway, if you don't mind my asking?"

She winked. "I guess he's a father figure. For an old fart, he's not too bad."

"Old fart," Hunsecker said bitterly. "Linda, tell her about Gordo Madison."

"He's back in the prison ward at Grady Hospital," Nickells said. "He started having seizures again. Poor old guy."

I stood up and stretched. It felt like I'd tried to run the hundred-yard dash with a concrete block in each hand. I ached all over. "I'm going to go get out of these jail clothes," I announced.

Marylee knocked on the door then, and poked her head in. "There's a phone call for you. Pick up this phone and dial three one."

It was Edna. "Jocelyn is going to have a bad headache tomorrow, and some interesting bruises. Otherwise she's fine. I lied and told them I was her grandmother so they'd treat her. I'll take her back to our house as soon as I get done filling out all the paperwork. How are things at your end?"

"Dandy," I said, not bothering to suppress a yawn. "As soon as I get changed, I'll hitch a ride home with Linda and C. W."

"Did they send a posse over to roust Littlefield?" she wanted to know.

"They're questioning him now, and they're going to talk to Jordan too," I said. "Can we finish talking about this tomorrow? I'm whipped."

"Are you sure you're all right?" she asked. "I'd feel better if you'd come over here and let one of these doctors look at you."

"Mom, I'm fine," I snapped. "I'll see you at home."

As I was hanging up the phone there was another tap at the door. I turned and Mac was standing there.

"Hey," I said weakly.

"Hey your own self," he said, glancing at Hunsecker and Nickells. "I heard you took a dip in the 'Hooch. Everything all right?"

"I'm tired," I said. "Otherwise, as I keep telling everybody, I'm fine. Did Edna call you?"

He came over, tilted my head up, and gently touched the bridge of my nose. "We'll have matching scars now," he said. "You'll grow to like it. It's a good conversation starter. Yeah, your mother called and gave me orders to come get you and drag you to the emergency room. She knew you wouldn't go on your own."

"I'm not going," I said stubbornly. "How about taking me home, instead?"

Mac looked to Hunsecker for approval. "You don't need to hold her for questioning any more?"

"We ought to hold her for orneriness," he said, "but she's too mean to keep around for long. Get her out of my hair, would you?"

I dozed on the ride home. Mac woke me up when we got there, took me in the house, and fended off Edna's questions while he trundled me off to bed. He kissed me lightly and was gone.

27

WHEN I WOKE UP around ten the next
morning, coffee was made, but Edna was
gone. She'd left a note though, telling me she was
filling in at the Coopers' for Ruby, who had another
doctor's appointment, and reminding me to keep an
eye on Jocelyn.

Coffee in hand, I tiptoed into the den. The television
was on, with the sound turned down. Jocelyn, wrapped
in blankets, was watching Oprah Winfrey.

"Edna said to check you for brain damage," I said,
taking both my hands and probing her skull. "Looks like
the same puddin' head you had to begin with."

She sat up. Her face had its share of cuts and bruises
too, and her right wrist was bandaged where a piece of
glass had cut her.

"Some ride last night, huh?"

"I've never been so scared in my whole life," she
replied. "If you hadn't gotten me out of the car, I would
have drowned, wouldn't I?"

I considered it. "Probably not. You were shocky, but
the water was only about chest-high. You're a pretty
tough cookie; you would have made it without me."

She pointed the remote control at the television and clicked it off.

"I've been thinking about what I did last night."

"What?"

"You know. Lying to you. Barfing and trying to hide it. Last night you told me if I wanted to kill myself I should get it over with, instead of making everybody watch me do it slowly. But when I was lying on that riverbank last night, wet and freezing, wondering if that car would come back and shoot at us, or who knows what, I realized I don't want to die. I'm tired of all this crap. I don't want to do this to myself anymore."

"Then stop it," I said. It seemed easy to me.

"I want to," she said. "But I don't know if I can. I think I need help. When my parents get back to town, I'm going to talk to them about it. And I want a new shrink, too."

"You might have to go back in the hospital again," I pointed out. "How would you feel about that?"

"I think it sucks," she said.

"Yeah, well, life sucks sometimes. But you might have to."

"I know."

"Glad to hear it," I said. "Want some breakfast?"

She disentangled herself from the blankets and stood up slowly. "Oww," she said. "I'm sore all over."

"Me too." I turned her toward the kitchen. "Coffee's made, cereal's in the pantry, there's fruit on the counter. I'm going to go wash the rest of the river off me."

Hot water and soap did wonders for my morale. But I was oddly keyed up, full of energy.

Hunsecker and Nickells were out. I left a message. Twice I dialed Littlefield's number and twice I hung up after one ring. Leave it to the cops, I urged myself. It's their job, not yours.

The kitchen was clean. I got it cleaner. Jocelyn watched me scrub without comment for a while. Finally she couldn't stand it any longer. "What are you doing?" she asked. "Why are you cleaning house instead of trying to find out who ran us off the road and tried to kill us?"

"That is the cops' job," I said firmly. "And you, especially, are through with detecting. I never should have let you tag along. After a head injury like the one you had last night, you're supposed to stay quiet for a while."

"That sucks," she moaned. "I'm fine. I want to nail Jordan. We must have been getting close to him, or he wouldn't have tried to kill us last night."

"I don't think it was Jordan," I said.

"Who was it then?"

I could have bitten off my tongue. Like Hunsecker said, someday I've got to learn to keep my mouth shut. But it probably wouldn't be today. Keeping quiet was playing hell with my nerves. But there was another pesky loose end I wanted to check out in the meantime.

My insurance agent was delighted to hear from me. "Make any decisions on that group policy yet?" he wanted to know.

After I promised to discuss it with the girls, he gave me the number of the independent claims adjuster his company used. "Name's Gillespie. What he doesn't know about fires, they haven't discovered yet," he promised.

K. C. Gillespie had to drop off a roll of film to be processed, then he promised to meet me at Josephina's house.

The only way I was able to leave Jocelyn at home was

to lie. I told her I was going to see my agent about some insurance business. Really, it was only a half-lie. And I promised to take her with me if I went out again later in the afternoon. "In the meantime," I reminded her, "you better get on the phone yourself. The cops will have had your car pulled out of the river by now; call and find out where it is. Then you better call your insurance agent and start talking repairs and estimates and deductibles. If Edna comes home, tell her I'll be back in about an hour. And if C. W. Hunsecker calls, tell him I'll call back this afternoon."

A red Ford pickup truck with a camper top was parked in front of the burned-out house on Gormley Street. The driver, a heavyset man with an impressive set of white muttonchop sideburns, was sitting with the cab door open, shoving his feet into a pair of tall black rubber boots.

"Callahan?" he said, standing and holding out a callus-worn hand. I shook. He gestured with his head toward the house. "Looks like a bad one. Woman and a baby died; isn't that right?"

I was surprised he knew the details, but he showed me the police radio in the truck. "I monitor fire calls all over the metro area," he said.

He insisted I borrow a pair of his boots before we toured the house.

A discarded piece of yellow crime scene tape lay forgotten on the concrete stoop of the house. I stood aside to allow Gillespie to lead the way.

The acrid carbon smell in the house was intense, even though most of the front wall of the house was burned out and the roof had gaping holes, allowing the sun to shine into the blackness. We picked our way through the small living room. "See this?" Gillespie said, pointing to a place where the floor had apparently caved in.

"The sofa burned so hot and so fast it just burned right through the floor joists and fell in." Looking over his shoulder I could see a blackened oblong lump with metal springs extruding from it.

"Does that mean someone maybe left a lit cigarette on it, or a kid might have been playing with matches?"

"It could," he agreed. "It could mean a bunch of things."

From the living room we went to the kitchen. A blackened stove and refrigerator, surreally melted, stood against a back wall. From a hook in the ceiling hung a crisply dried out house plant.

"Fire didn't start in here," he announced, turning to go back to the hallway.

"How do you know?" I asked.

"Walls are still standing, ceiling is intact," he said. "The front part of the house was totally involved when the firefighters got here, and they got here pretty quick. They put hoses on the back, before it could do more damage."

I followed him and stood in the doorway of a small back bedroom. The walls were scorched, the bedclothes sooty and water-soaked, but I could see a double bed with the sheets still rumpled. A pink crocheted baby blanket lay on the floor nearby. A closet held women's blackened clothing.

"This is where the mother and baby were sleeping," I said. It was more a question than a statement.

He nodded. "Smoke got to 'em before they were awake."

One thing puzzled me. "How was the little boy able to get out alive? He was only four."

"That happens a lot," he said. "Smoke and poison gases rise. Little kids are closer to the ground, which is where the cooler oxygen is." He looked around the room soberly. "If this lady had put up a ten-dollar smoke detector, she and her baby might still be alive today."

"She'd never had her own place before," I said softly. "It probably never occurred to her."

We looked in on the other bedroom; it too was smoky and water-stained, but a small cot covered with a blue Mickey Mouse bedspread told us we'd found little Oscar's bedroom. A battered toy chest overflowed with stuffed animals and Ninja Turtle action figures.

The house was small. The tour was short. Gillespie dug a small knife out of the pocket of his overalls and poked at the walls in the living room. He walked around the outside of the house, sniffing and kicking at the blackened grass.

"Could the fire have been deliberately set? Like with kerosene or something?"

He didn't answer my question. Instead, he went back into the house again. In the corner of the living room, in a wall near the hole in the floor, he found what he was looking for. A melted lump of metal.

"Here's your probable cause right here," he said. He got up and went back in the kitchen, using the knife tip to unscrew a smoke-blackened wall socket. He cut a hole in the soggy Sheetrock and pulled the electric receptacle out.

"See that?" he said grimly. "It's copper."

"Is that against the electrical code or something?"

"No, it's right up to code," he said. Then he took his knife and flicked at a slender piece of silvery wire. "Except when you use it with aluminum wiring."

"Is aluminum wiring bad?"

He folded the knife and put it away. "Aluminum is cheap is what it is. But if you use aluminum receptacles with it, it's all right. Whoever wired this house used copper receptacles."

"Why would they do that?"

"To save a little money, maybe. Not much, you'd probably only save around fifty to a hundred bucks. Or maybe somebody just didn't know what they were doing."

"What caused the fire?" I wanted to know.

He pointed back to the living room, to the sofa wall. "Something, maybe a television or a lamp, was plugged in near that sofa. Corrosion between the two metals set in, and the receptacle began to get hot. Eventually it started to smolder in that wall, and then it flared up, probably late at night, after the family had gone to bed. The sofa acted like a wick, and the rest of the house went too."

I felt sick. I had to get out of that sad little house. Away from the smell and the soot and the sight of soggy, melted toys and a life's dreams up in smoke.

Outside, I leaned against the van and looked up at the cloudless blue sky. When Gillespie came out, he had the copper receptacle in a plastic bag.

"That's it then?" I asked. "Bad wiring?"

He opened the truck door and stowed the bag on the seat. "That's for the arson boys to decide," he said. "Mine is an opinion, that's all. I'll take this thing and drop it off to Don Mann at the fire department, to make sure his guys don't miss it."

He stood by the truck door. "You get what you needed?"

I glanced back at the house. A strong wind could knock down what was left of Josephina's house. The street was quiet. Its residents were at their jobs, stretching toward their dreams of a middle-class existence. "If somebody wired that house, cut corners to save money, knowing it could cause a fire, is that considered arson? If somebody dies, could it be prosecuted?"

"District attorney can prosecute anything he wants," Gillespie said. "That doesn't mean you'll get a conviction. Georgia juries are funny about arson. A lot of people don't see much wrong with burning something down. Especially if there's insurance money involved. The attitude is, let the Yankee insurance companies pay for it. Even in Atlanta, where you've got fairly enlightened juries, arson's not easy to prove. Most juries want the cops to hand them somebody with a match in his hand and a smile on his face."

I thanked Gillespie and gave him my business card. Then I went home. Suddenly there was more than dinner on the menu for my date with Jake Dahlberg.

28

IGOT MYSELF ALL SPRUCED UP for dinner at
Jake Dahlberg's house; short, black-knit, off-the-
shoulder T-shirt dress, a silver concha belt, silver flats,
and some dangly, silver, cowboy-boot earrings. I even
wore makeup, which I applied more out of nervous
energy than from the desire to look good. As long as it
was a day for settling up, there was something I wanted
to settle with him.

Dahlberg's eyes swept me up and down. With the tip
of his finger, he stroked my bruised cheek. I flinched at
his touch. "What happened?"

"It's nothing," I said. "Comes under the heading of
work-related injury."

He looked puzzled but didn't pursue the matter.

His living room was an essay in minimalism: taupe
walls, white woodwork, bleached wooden floors. The art
was modern oil paintings, splashes of bold primary colors,
and some lumpy-looking bronze sculptures. The chairs
and sofas reminded me of so many black punctuation
marks, and the windows were large curtainless expanses
of glass. The whole world could see in, if it wanted to.
Some cool jazz, nothing I recognized, was playing.

He showed me to an apostrophe chair. "I'll get you a drink," he suggested. "Gin and tonic all right?"

"Actually, I'm a bourbon person," I said. "With water, on the rocks."

The house was chilly. I rubbed my bare arms, trying to wish away the goose bumps.

He came back in, handed me my drink, and sat down on the big, squashy sofa with his own drink, a gin and tonic.

"Dinner's about fifteen minutes away," he said. "So how's the case coming along?"

I didn't want to discuss my case. I didn't even want to be in this house anymore. I'd planned my speech just so, dressed for drama, built up my indignation. I thought I was primed for a big scene. But my anger had mostly ebbed. I wanted to walk away from the whole thing.

He sat across from me. Dark-haired, his smooth-shaven face radiating intelligence and sensuality. I loved the way he dressed; khaki-colored pleated linen trousers and some soft, full shirt in the same hue of khaki, his tanned ankles showing above a pair of soft leather-soled shoes. He even smelled good, like trees, or forests.

"What?" he said, leaning forward. "What's wrong, Callahan?"

I took a healthy swallow of the bourbon. Sometimes artificial courage is better than no courage at all.

Matter-of-factly, I laid it all out for him. Told him I knew the house on Gormley Street had burned down, and two people had died, because his organization had cut corners.

To his credit, Jake didn't try to dodge the blame.

"You're right," he said, shrugging. "It was my call, God forgive me. Josephina's and the Kings' houses were the first ones for our project. We had thirty thousand budgeted for the rehabbing, and I thought it would be plenty.

"Then we found out Josephina's floor joists had dry rot. We had to jack the house up and pour a new foundation. The roof of the Kings' house had to be stripped bare. Then it rained before we could get the new roof on, and the plywood underlayment buckled and leaked. We were over budget. And then the foundation that had been our major donor decided that they wanted to have a grand ribbon cutting on move-in day, a month away. I was desperate. So I called in the subs and told them we had to get the costs down, that I didn't care what it took. Most of the cuts were harmless, cosmetic things: one coat of paint instead of two, the cheapest grade of vinyl flooring, kitchen and bathroom cabinets that were seconds. We canceled the storm windows we'd ordered. Things like that. But it wasn't enough. When my electrician said we could save money by using aluminum wiring, I hesitated. But he said the city inspectors wouldn't notice, because the Sheetrock guys would cover everything up before they came. I told him to go ahead."

I gripped my glass with both hands and stared at the pale amber liquid. "You knew it was a fire hazard."

He nodded. "I didn't know exactly what could happen, but when he made it a point that the inspectors shouldn't see it, I knew it was wrong. I just thought we'd go back later, after we got more money, and make it right."

"Couldn't the ribbon cutting wait?" I asked. "Couldn't you explain that you'd run out of money and needed more funds to finish?"

He sat his drink down on the coffee table. "I can see you know nothing about nonprofits," he said wearily. "They put money in projects with the maximum visibility, and they put it into projects run by administrators who've proven they can get results. Just do it, that's the rule. If I'd told them the truth, they would have pulled their support, another eighty thousand in grants we'd applied for to do the next phase."

"You could have gotten other sponsors," I suggested.

"No," he said flatly. "We had to prove the first phase would work. Nothing breeds success like success," he said, his voice mocking. He leaned forward, hands pressed together, prayerlike.

"This program is so important, Callahan. We're saving lives. Saving families, getting people off the streets, out of shelters, putting them in their own homes. This is a pioneering program. Other organizations from as far away as Seattle are coming to Atlanta to see how it works. A filmmaker is doing a documentary about Valeria and Juan King. We have four more houses under contract. Four more families to help."

The bourbon was really good. I couldn't tell whether it was Wild Turkey or Maker's Mark. I do hate cheap whiskey. I saw a green Blazer glide slowly past the house. It had been by once before, while I was waiting for my drink.

I was finished with the drink now.

"Will you help those families like you helped Josephina and her daughter?" I asked.

"That's not fair," he said, flushing. "I never, ever believed that family was in real danger."

"You didn't really care about that family," I said angrily. "None of this is about helping homeless people. All those ridiculous, dehumanizing rules about clotheslines and cars and unauthorized residents. It was all to make you look good. Your practice was struggling. The foundation was supposed to make you a big name in the right kinds of circles. And I don't believe you didn't know that wiring was dangerous. After the fire at Josephina's house, you must have known, but you tried to cover it up, blaming it on a kid playing with matches, or on Josephina herself. And what about the Kings? There's an outlet in their living room that smokes, but they're too afraid to report it. How long will it be before you do something about that? Or do more people need to die so you can 'help' four more families?"

"The work order is already in for the Kings' house," he said, pleading. "What happened to Josephina was tragic, and I take the blame. But does the program have to suffer because I made a mistake?"

My empty glass was making a puddle on the top of the stainless-steel table next to my chair. I smoothed my skirt and stood up. Time to go.

"You're a murderer, Jake Dahlberg. I called the arson squad today. They've got one of the copper receptacles from Josephina's house. I suppose you'll be hearing from them. And Mr. Szabo set me straight on the flag incident at Littlefield's. Your father never saw that Nazi flag. You hate Littlefield so much you'll say or do anything to destroy him. Killing Bridget would have accomplished that neatly. I can see you like things neat," I said, gesturing to his immaculate decor. "But cops have a way of messing up your life when they investigate you for murder. Jake, I'm sorry about your dinner, but under the circumstances, I don't think I can swallow anything else you have to offer."

Suddenly he jumped to his feet. I backed away involuntarily. He grabbed my arm. "How can you believe I'd kill Bridget?"

I yanked my arm away. "After seeing that house today, I believe you're capable of anything."

* * *

Moral indignation caught up with me three blocks from Jake Dahlberg's house. And I always get hungry when I'm feeling righteous. It wasn't terribly late, maybe Tinkles would scramble me an egg or something.

The green Blazer was parked on a side street near the Yacht Club. I parked right behind it and locked my doors. These are scary times.

Mac was sitting alone at the bar, his chin propped on his hand, sipping a Killian's Red, watching the Braves whip up on the Dodgers.

I sat down beside him, and he looked up, surprised. "I thought you were having dinner with a friend tonight."

"He thought so too," I said.

Tinkles walked up to take my order. "Jack and water," I said.

"Let's go over there and talk," I said, when the drinks came. We moved to a booth, away from the blare of the television.

"I saw you drive past the house. Twice," I said. "Is this a game I don't know?"

"You missed the other two times," Mac said. He was clearly unrepentant. "I could see you through the window, sitting there, chatting, sipping your drink. I wanted to kill that guy. Stupid, huh?"

"That's an understatement," I said. "What the hell is the big idea, following me around, then cruising back and forth, like something out of an old grade-B movie? Who the fuck do you think you are?"

"Who the fuck do you think I am?" he whispered hoarsely. "Don't I mean anything to you? One night you drop by and hop in the bed with me and we're talking about living together. The next thing I know you're seeing somebody else. What the hell is going on with us, Callahan?"

I took a long swallow of my drink and kept both hands on the glass because they were itching to slap the face across the table from me.

"It was a business thing, goddamnit," I said. "Not that I owe you an explanation."

"You're right," he said, pushing his chair back and getting up from the table. "You don't owe me a thing. Not a goddamn thing." He threw some money on the table and stalked out.

I sat there, stunned. I had no idea how things had escalated so fast, from casual conversation to a rip-roaring fight. I got up and walked quickly out the front door.

I found him sitting behind the wheel of the Blazer. Just sitting there. "What?" he said when I opened the passenger's side door and got in.

"It was a business thing," I said lamely. "Swear to God. It's too complicated to go into."

"And there was no attraction between you," he said quietly. "You got all tricked out like that for a business meeting."

He had me. "Okay," I said, sighing. "Maybe I was sort of attracted to him, at first. I love you, Mac, I really do. I've always told you, I'm a one-man woman. But just because I'm on a diet, that doesn't mean I can't go to the store, does it?"

He laughed a little bit. "Interesting metaphor. So why didn't you stay for dinner?"

"I probably never intended to. I just found out he was responsible for the death of a woman and her baby. I had to let him know I knew, to tell him he wasn't off the hook for their deaths."

"And that's it."

I put a tentative hand on his knee. "That's it. But you can't go around following me, you know. I'm a big girl. I can take care of myself. And I hate the idea that you don't trust me."

He put his hand over mine. "I do trust you. It's just that sometimes I don't know where I stand with you. Things with us are so, so, temporary, I guess is the word. We're like a couple of kids, shacking up here or there, wherever we get the chance. I'm too old for that shit. I like to know where I'm sleeping every night, and who's going to be there. I want us to live together. Is there something wrong with that?"

Here it came again. And this time I couldn't dodge it. "It's not that I don't want us to be together," I said. "I do. But I need to be able to live my life a certain way. Sometimes I do stuff that's sort of dangerous. But it's stuff I'm trained to do. Stuff I'm good at. But you'd worry, I know you would. And I can't be always leaving a note to tell you I've gone out and I don't know when I'll be back."

"I know what you do for a living," Mac said. "I've never interfered in it, have I?"

He hadn't, but then most of the time he had no idea what I was up to, because I made it a point to be vague about such things.

"And don't forget, my house is the House Mouse office too. I need to be someplace central for the girls and our clients. And what about Edna? I can't just walk off and leave her with that house to run. She'd never admit it, but it would be too much."

"We've been through this already," he said quickly. "Edna and I get along pretty good. She could move in too. There's loads of room in the cabin."

"Very sweet," I said. "But very impractical. Besides, Edna'd never move way out to the sticks. Have you considered moving in with me? We could use a man around the house."

"Rufus," he said simply. And it was true. The big, goofy black Lab would be miserable in the city, with no fields to run in and no creeks to romp.

No wonder I'd avoided this issue for so long. "So where does that leave us?" I asked. "I want to be with you, you want to be with me, but we're still about forty miles apart."

"Sounds like we're right back where we started," he agreed. "Listen. Come home with me. Just for tonight. I'm getting up at five-thirty to go trout fishing up in Helen. Supposed to meet B. J. halfway. Why don't you go with me?"

I shook my head. "I'd like to, but it's been a long week. Jocelyn's still at the house, and things are heating up with the case. I wouldn't feel right about leaving her home, after what she went through last night. I'm planning on sleeping in tomorrow."

He got out of the Blazer and walked me back to the van, glancing up and down the street. "No gray sedans. I'll follow you home anyway, just to make sure."

I shook my head. "Didn't we just discuss this?"

"Humor me," he said. "Pretend I'm not there."

29

FRIDAY MORNING I WAS UP and out early. We'd been asked to bid on the cleaning of four model homes in a new subdivision in Gwinnett County. The job would be a piece of cake; some mopping, a little vacuuming, our girls could take care of it in thirty minutes a week.

When I got home, Jocelyn was in the den, poring over a Georgia State University catalog I'd sent away for. I'd been toying with the idea of going to law school. The only flaw in my plan was that I didn't much like lawyers, and didn't really want to practice law. I just wanted to know what lawyers know, to get the upper hand.

She put the catalog down hastily when I walked in.

"Any calls?"

"A couple of your cleaning clients called. I left their names and numbers on the notepad in the kitchen."

"No word from Hunsecker?"

"Nope. I've got my car taken care of. They're going to tow it to the garage my dad always uses."

"Good. Did you have some breakfast?"

"Cereal and orange juice," she said proudly. "No

Correctol. I ran too, but only a mile or so. I got kind of nervous that I might see that gray car again."

In the kitchen, I stared at the phone, willing it to ring. To distract myself, I fixed a ham sandwich. And ate it standing up, staring at the phone.

When I turned around I saw Jocelyn standing in the kitchen doorway. I recognized the faded T-shirt and cut-offs she wore. They were mine from the days when I could still squeeze into a size eight. They were miles too big for Jocelyn, of course.

"I'm going bonkers just sitting around your house," she complained. "Can't we do something?"

"Like what?" I asked. "Hunsecker already threatened to throw my butt in jail if I don't keep out of his case."

"I don't know," she admitted. "How about going back to Coach J's? They won't recognize your van."

I shook my head. "No way. They know somebody's been watching their house. Besides, we haven't gotten one damn thing out of all your surveillance."

She walked over and nibbled at a potato chip on my plate. "What about my finding out that Mrs. Jordan is screwing Zak Crawford? That's something, isn't it?"

I thought about it for a while. "Might be."

"Maybe it was Zak Crawford," she said.

I smiled indulgently. "Why would he kill your sister? Did they even know each other?"

"They both played soccer. Coach J could have paid him to kill her," she suggested. "He thought Bridget was pregnant. He knew it would wreck his marriage. So he killed her, or he had her killed, and made it look like a burglary."

"Maybe." I wasn't convinced.

I gave Hunsecker another call. I was already regretting tipping my hand to Dahlberg. No telling what he might do now. "He came in and got his messages and left again," the secretary said. "He told me if you called, to tell you he's in a meeting all day with the district attorney."

"Please just have him call me," I said, and hung up.

"Well?" Jocelyn said, expectantly.

"I'm thinking," I told her. "Do you know where Zak Crawford lives?"

She picked up the phone book and flipped it open to the C listings. "All the kids at All Saints have their own phones," she said, running her finger down to the end of the page of listings for Crawfords, all the way down to the Zs.

There was no one home. "Did you say he works somewhere?" I asked.

"I think he does lawn maintenance at the apartment complex where they live," she said.

This was not good news. We wouldn't want Zak coming home for cookies and milk while we were tossing his apartment. While Jocelyn was writing down the address, and calling to see if anyone was home, I went into the supply closet and got us two fresh, pink smocks. I tossed one to her. "This is totally against my better judgment," I said. "Put it on."

"Gross," she said, holding the smock with her fingertips, as though it carried a contagious tacky germ. "I'll look like a stick of bubblegum in this."

"Stay home," I said casually. "I'll go by myself."

She buttoned the smock and handed me a piece of paper with the address.

We drove every street, every cul-de-sac in the Willoughby Woods apartment complex, looking for the rusted out green Vega, or signs of ongoing lawn care. But the complex was quiet, parking spaces mostly empty. Not a creature was stirring except for the House Mouse.

The rental office was beside the community club, which was beside the pool and tennis courts and the weight room.

I tied a bandanna around my head and got out of the van. "Are you sure they'll buy this?" Jocelyn asked dubiously.

"If they don't, they don't," I said. "What are they going to do, arrest me for impersonating a cleaning lady? Besides, you said Zak's father travels a lot. He's probably out of town right now. And Zak doesn't seem to be around either."

The rental agent on duty wasn't much older than Jocelyn. She had blond hair, swept back in a severe knot at the nape of her neck, and Kewpie doll lips. Her eyes swept over my charwoman ensemble: pink smock, white slacks, orthopedic shoes, and a stupid, self-effacing smile.

"Uh, I'm Julia Kidd from the maid service," I said, humbly. "Mr. Crawford was supposed to leave the key to his apartment. Is this the rental office?"

She squared her shoulders, pulling a small index file box from the edge of the desk. "Let me check," she said. She leafed through the cards, frowned, then did it again.

"You must have the wrong complex," she said, rewarding me with a sympathetic smile. "There are several other large complexes along Chamblee-Dunwoody. Try Winston Woods or Verdant Valley, why don't you?"

"No, ma'am," I insisted. "My work order says Mr. Alex Crawford's apartment, Willoughby Woods, building 300, unit D. He ordered our Neat as a Pin special, the $49.99 one where you get the complimentary pine potpourri bathroom freshener."

She shook her head and showed me the file box and the C section. "I know Mr. Crawford, his son Zak works for us. But you can see, he didn't leave you a key."

"Uh oh," I said woodenly. "He paid in advance, and I'll catch holy you-know-what if it's not done when he gets back."

She gave my plight some thought, then got up and walked into an inner room. I heard her unlocking, then opening a cabinet, then heard the musical jingle of many keys. She came back and pressed one into the palm of my hand. "Bring it right back when you're done," she said sternly, "or I'll be the one to catch holy you-know-what."

I decided to press my luck. "Is Mr. Crawford's son home today? I wouldn't want to disturb him or anything."

"Don't worry," she said. "He's edging and trimming today at Mountain Manor, our property in Stone Mountain."

"Thanks," I said fervently. "You saved my fanny."

We parked the van in an unobtrusive spot by the building next to the Crawfords' just in case.

Alex Crawford obviously spent a lot of time on the road and very little at home. Unit D had a stale, musty bouquet, with undertones of sweaty gym socks. In the living room, mini-blinds covered the windows and the sliding glass door that lead to a small balcony. The furniture was serviceable brown plaid; the kind men rent when they're outfitting their first post-divorce apartment. A large smoked glass coffee table wore a thin veneer of dust and a stack of unopened mail.

Jocelyn stood in the entryway and gaped. "I've never broken into a place before," she whispered. "What happens if somebody comes home?"

I walked over to the sliding glass doors and unlocked them. "We're on the ground floor here. If you hear somebody coming, run out here, hop over the balcony railing and make yourself scarce. I'll be right behind you. But don't worry, we're not staying long."

The galley-style kitchen was a mess; overflowing trash can, the sink full of dirty dishes. A long hallway lead toward the back of the apartment.

The father's bedroom was neat and impersonal, the bed made, closet arranged just so. We gave it a cursory glance.

Zak's bedroom had that cruddy, lived-in look. One whole wall was a collage of *Playboy* pin-ups. The other sported heavy metal rock concert posters with images of screaming rockers, death heads, writhing serpents, and the like. A compact disc player was hooked up to a pair of speakers that looked like they could blow the walls down.

The waterbed had no sheets, only a wadded up blanket. The floor was littered with clothes, CDs, shoes, and empty beer cans. More clothes spewed from open dresser drawers.

"Geez," Jocelyn said. "My mom would kill me if my room looked like this. Where do we start? And what are we looking for?"

"Just look," I said, lifting the clothes in each drawer. "We'll know when we find it."

We found a small plastic bag of moldy-smelling marijuana tucked on the floor under the dresser, and approximately nine pairs of filthy blue jeans scattered around the room. Everything else seemed pretty routine.

"Look, Callahan," Jocelyn said, finally. She'd unearthed a footlocker from a mound of dirty clothes in one corner of the room. "It's locked," she said.

"Not for long." Most cheap footlockers have locks a

baby could open. I myself perfected the art in my college dorm, so that I could borrow my roommate's clothes.

That locker was the only orderly object in Zak's room. He'd arranged things in stratas. The top layer consisted of carefully folded woolen sweaters. The middle layer was made up of old soccer jerseys, baseball caps, team photos, and other mementos of the sporting life. The good stuff was on the bottom. It always is.

"Oh my God," Jocelyn said, as the bottom layer was unearthed. She reached out a hand to touch, but I slapped it back.

"That's the Civil War revolver taken from Littlefield's house," I said. "It's evidence in your sister's murder." I looked around and found a T-shirt on the floor nearby. Gingerly, I picked up the revolver and lifted it out of the trunk. Then I picked up the cavalry officer's saber and the carbine longarm and laid them beside the revolver. The only thing left was a package wrapped in pink silk.

"Get me the rubber gloves out of my cleaning caddy," I told Jocelyn. I pawed through the sweaters and the soccer jerseys one more time to be sure, but I was fairly certain Lula Belle Bird's diary wasn't there.

With the gloves on, I unfolded the pink silk, which turned out to be a lace-edged Frederick's of Hollywood teddy. Inside was a framed photograph of Lissa Jordan, in a considerably more risqué pose than the boudoir shot she'd presented her husband, half-wearing what looked like the same teddy that the photo was wrapped in. There was a small stack of letters too, five in all, written in a childish handwriting on cheap pink stationery.

Lissa Jordan should have spent more time in English class and less time in cheerleading. The spelling was egregious, the grammar abominable, the contents chilling. The gist of her correspondence with Zak was concerned with her growing desire for his taut (spelled tot), hot body, and for her desire to gain revenge on Kyle, to make him sorry that he'd ever screwed around on her with that scheming little bitch Bridget.

Jocelyn's lips pressed together firmly, but she kept reading.

Kyle Jordan apparently hadn't been nearly as clever with his affair as he'd thought. Lissa Jordan had followed him twice to his assignations with Bridget, once at her parents' home, on a schoolday when both were playing hooky, another time at a Motel Six just off I-75.

She'd stalked Bridget too, her three little kiddies tucked in car seats in the back of the Camaro. She'd followed her from Eagle's Keep to Little Five Points, to Sevananda, to the neighborhood pizza joint. "Tonight I nearly made roadkill out of the bitch," she wrote. "I'd have done it too, but I was afraid it might screw up the paint job on the Camaro, and piss Kyle off."

Another night, Lissa had followed Bridget into a multiplex cinema at the mall, sitting behind her during a midnight showing of *The Rocky Horror Picture Show*, fantasizing about stabbing her rival, there in the dark.

The last note seemed to be a pep talk of sorts. "We will be strong and silent for each other," she told him. "For Megan, Jessie, and Trevor, we will do what must be done.

"Remember what the Led said," she urged. "If you listen hard, the truth will come to you."

I recognized Lissa's scrambled version of "Stairway to Heaven" immediately, and so, apparently, did Jocelyn, who was reading over my shoulder.

"What a moron," she said, pointing to Lissa's next verse:

"If there's a butthole in your hedgehog, don't be alarmed now; it's just a sprinkling for the May Queen."

"How do you know the words to 'Stairway to Heaven'?" I asked.

"I listen to the oldies station," she said. "Besides, it's sort of like a classic, you know?"

"I know," I said. "I just didn't think someone like Lissa Jordan and Zak Crawford would know anything about Led Zeppelin."

"They killed Bridget," she said, her face pale, serious. "Why?"

Carefully, I wrapped the letters back in their pink silk envelope. "Reading between the lines, I'd say it looks like Lissa was obsessed with keeping Kyle. She thought Bridget was a real threat to the family. She probably seduced Zak just to get him to help her kill Bridget."

Jocelyn stood up slowly, and stretched. She was dry-eyed. "I'll get a bag to put this stuff in."

"No. We leave it here."

"What if Zak finds out we were here? He'll burn the letters and get rid of the guns and stuff. We'll never be able to prove they did it."

"We leave it here," I repeated. "We entered this apartment illegally, without a warrant. I'm talking breaking and entering, Jocelyn. None of this stuff would be admissable as evidence during a trial, because we found it by breaking in. The cops have to find it, and they have to get a judge to give them a search warrant to look for it first. That's how the law works."

"The law stinks," she cried. "They'll get away with it."

I was putting the footlocker's contents back together again, trying to remember which sweater had gone where. "No they won't," I said.

We made the phone call from a convenience store at

Chamblee-Dunwoody and Interstate 285. I sent Jocelyn inside for a Slushie. When the secretary in the homicide division picked up the phone, I started talking in a low monotone.

"Anonymous caller," I said. "Write this down. Murder of Bridget Dougherty. Tell cops Zak Crawford. Hocked silver cup. Rest of the stuff hidden in his apartment. Willoughby Woods. Girlfriend is Lissa Jordan. They did it."

Then I hung up the phone, and we ran for the van, laughing like a couple of lunatics. The Slushie was cold and sweet. My butt still hurt.

A navy-blue Buick with a radio antenna on the hood was parked in front of my house.

"That's the cops," I told Jocelyn. "Hunsecker must not have gotten the anonymous tip yet. Here's the deal: we've been out checking antique stores, looking for the rest of the stuff from Littlefield's house. Understand? If he asks, you know who Zak Crawford is, you saw him with Lissa at the Jordans. But that's all you know, right?"

"Got ya," she said.

Linda Nickells sat at the kitchen table with Edna, who had her hair up in rollers. The two of them were talking shop.

"I just use a relaxer," Linda said, touching her shining, dark hair. "No color, because that makes it break. And I'm real careful how I comb it after it's washed."

I pushed open the kitchen door noisily.

"Hey, Linda," I said. "How's it going? Been here long?"

She looked up at the kitchen clock. "Not bad. I've been here about ten minutes, talking to your mom."

Nickells nodded at Jocelyn, who waved and beat a hasty retreat in the direction of the den.

"She's still kind of shook up from the accident last night," I explained. "Headachey. Where's C. W.?"

Edna got up and got the aspirin bottle from the kitchen cabinet. "I'll see if she needs dosing," she said.

"C. W. just got out of his meeting with the D.A. He's still trying to track down your gray car. We checked at Littlefield's. There were two silver Honda Accords, and a gray Volvo wagon, but no big gray sedans. Kyle Jordan drives a black Chevy pickup truck, and his wife has a white Camaro."

"A lot of kids hang out at the Jordans' house," I said, trying to sound casual. "Jocelyn knows the names of some of the kids we saw. There's one kid, Zak Crawford, who spends a lot of time alone with Jordan's wife, if you know what I mean. And then there are three or four other kids who hang around."

"Littlefield called," Linda said abruptly. "He was complaining that you were harassing him, and making false accusations and stuff."

"What did you tell him?"

"I told him you have a big mouth and the police have no control over what you do, and suggested he call the state agency that licenses private investigators, if he has a problem with you."

"Thanks a lot," I said.

I debated whether or not to suggest she look at Zak Crawford's whereabouts on Saturday. Then I remembered her crack about my big mouth.

"If you can manage to keep it to yourself, I'll tell you something else," Nickells said. "We talked to Jordan again this morning. Turns out he wasn't at that soccer camp all day last Saturday."

"Where'd he go?"

"Seems like the coach suspects his wife was fooling around on him," she said, grinning. "One of the kids saw him leaving the camp around one-thirty P.M. After we leaned on him a little he admitted it was the truth. He called home and the baby-sitter answered. So he drove home, and the wife was still gone. Then he cruised the neighborhood, all her friends' houses, the mall, the neighborhood pool, nothing. He's really pissed. So he goes back to camp, and when he calls home again, the wife is there. She tells him she went to the movies with a friend."

"Did Jordan believe her? Did you check it out?"

"We're working on it," Nickells said. "C. W. told me not to tell you anything else. I shouldn't have told you this much. Get Jocelyn to put together a list of those kids' names for me. Phone numbers too. Call me."

"I will," I promised.

"Tell your mama good-bye for me," Nickells said. "I like her. She reminds me of my Aunt Alice. The lady who raised me. Tough old biddies. Both of 'em."

30

I WAS JUST BASTING THE CHICKEN with
Edna's secret barbecue sauce when the phone rang in
the kitchen. "Somebody get that," I yelled. "I don't dare
leave this grill."

But after it rang a second and a third time I turned
the grill off and ran for the phone myself.

It was Hunsecker. "Understand you've been looking
for me," he said.

"Yeah, uh, I have been," I said. "So how's the case
going?" I didn't want to tell what we'd found at Zak
Crawford's apartment if I could avoid it.

Edna walked into the kitchen then, her hair wrapped
in a towel turban. "It's Hunsecker," I mouthed.

She sat down at the table and dealt herself a hand of
solitaire.

"Big anonymous tip came in today," he said casually.

"Yeah?" I said, innocently. "What kind of tip?"

"Somebody called to suggest that the cops search an
apartment on Chamblee-Dunwoody for evidence in
Bridget's murder."

"Really?" I said, sitting down. "Whose apartment?
Did you guys search it?"

"Some kid who'd been kicked out of All Saints," he said. "Friend of Lissa Jordan's," he said. "We checked it all right. Got a search warrant, went over there. Nobody home. We got the manager to open it up. Know what we found? Nothing but a lot of dirty clothes and not enough marijuana to roll a single joint."

My heart sank. Zak had been home. "That's it?" I said.

"Just about," he said. "You know anything about this Crawford kid?"

"Not much," I said. "According to Jocelyn, the kid might have been having an affair with Lissa. Maybe you should check it out."

"Might do that," Hunsecker said. "We do know there's a gray Lexus registered to Alex Crawford, the kid's old man. But the father's on a business trip to the West Coast. Can't be reached. And nobody's seen the kid today. So what did you want to talk to me about?"

"Oh yeah," I said. "Jake Dahlberg. The guy who lives across the street from Littlefield. He's responsible for the fire that killed that woman and baby at the house on Gormley Street last week. He admitted as much to me."

"I've got a message here from the arson squad," he said. "Guess that's what they were calling about."

He paused a moment. "Garrity," he said, his voice lowered, "if you've been screwing around in the Crawfords' apartment, I'll have you charged with breaking and entering so fast your head will spin."

I was tempted to tell him everything. But I couldn't, not just yet. I blustered my way out of the conversation and hung up as quickly as I could.

"Shit," I said, pounding the table. "All the stuff is gone. Zak must have figured out we were there."

Edna played the black ten on the red jack. "If

Hunsecker finds out you were there, your ass is grass, Jules."

I reached out a hand to show her a play, but she slapped it away. "Hunsecker said the car that ran us off the road is registered to Zak's father. The father can't be reached and nobody knows where Zak is."

"Don't worry," said a voice behind us. "I've got the proof that they did it."

Jocelyn stood in the doorway, barefoot, dressed only in an oversize T-shirt. She held a folded up sheet of pink paper in her hand. "I took it when you weren't looking," she said, apologetically. "I had to be sure we could prove they did it."

I stalked over to her and snatched the paper out of her hand. It was the "Stairway to Heaven" letter. "Goddamnit, Jocelyn," I said. "I told you. This isn't worth anything unless the cops find it in their possession. Now all it does is tie us to a charge of breaking and entering."

"It's okay," she said stubbornly. "I figured it out. We'll go back and plant it in his car, and you can call the cops again, like you did today. We'll still be able to prove they did it."

"No, no, no," I said, exasperated. "We can't plant evidence, Jocelyn. It's too obvious. One anonymous tip might be plausible. Two, a judge would never believe. I just hope Zak doesn't count those letters to see if they're all still there."

Edna took a long puff on her cigarette, stubbed it out, and gathered her cards into a stack.

"Call Hunsecker back," she said. "Explain what happened. You've got the one letter. Give him that. Maybe you could plant it back at the apartment. That kid has tried to kill you two once. What's to stop him from doing it again?"

Jocelyn gave me that beseeching look. "No way," I said. "Hunsecker is Mr. Straight. If he knows for sure that we broke in there, none of the stuff, the letters, the guns, the saber, could be used as evidence against Zak and Lissa. There still might be a way to nail them, and I don't want to screw up the cops any more than we already have."

I opened one of the kitchen cabinets, got out a Tupperware lettuce crisper, took the letter and sealed it inside the container with a satisfying burp of the lid. Then I put it in the refrigerator, in the back of the bottom shelf.

"We'll figure out what to do with this later," I said. "Let's eat."

The chicken had gotten extra-crispy on the grill, but none of us felt much like eating anyway. We all decided to make an early night of it.

After Edna and Jocelyn had double-checked all the windows and doors and gone to bed, I went back into the kitchen, got the oatmeal box down out of the pantry, and fished inside until I felt the touch of cool metal. I took a dishtowel and wiped down my new 9-millimeter Smith & Wesson semiautomatic. The stainless steel gleamed dully, and I flicked away a crumb of oatmeal from the black plastic grip. I was still getting used to my new, high-powered pistol. Last year, after someone had easily taken away my little .22, I'd decided, after much debate, to move up in firepower. I wasn't planning on using it unless I had to, but if I did decide to fire, I wanted the firee to know he'd been shot, and that I was serious.

I had to think to remember where I'd hidden the gun's clip. Finally I spotted the Earl Gray tea canister on the top shelf of the pantry. Once I'd checked to make sure it had all fourteen rounds, I rammed the clip home and slipped on the safety, then put it in the pocket of my nightgown. I was still feeling jumpy, so I fixed myself a Jack Daniel's and water and took it to bed with me. I put the gun on the night stand and opened my book. But after a few pages and a good slug of bourbon, my eyelids finally gave up the good fight.

Barking; the insistent, frenzied yapping and snarling of a small dog jolted me awake. I instinctively reached across the bed to the night stand, grabbed my gun, and ran toward the back of the house.

I knew that dog. It was Homer, our next door neighbor's ill-tempered Boston terrier. Mr. Byerly's lawn mower had been stolen from his garage in May, so he'd recently let Homer have the run of the yard, to scare off petty thieves. From the kitchen window I saw the lights blink on next door and heard Mr. Byerly's back door creak open. "Homer, here, boy," he called. But Homer was barking furiously now, not about to give up his stance. I snapped the patio light on, but nothing happened. The backyard was bathed in inky darkness.

"Callahan?" Edna's voice called from her bedroom. "What the hell's going on?"

"I think Homer has somebody cornered out there," I yelled. "Call the cops and stay where you are. I've got my gun. I'm going outside."

"Homer," Mr. Byerly called. "Here, boy." I could see him, a tall gaunt figure in his print pajamas, brandishing a toilet plunger against the unseen invader.

I opened the kitchen door. "Mr. Byerly," I yelled, "get Homer and go back inside. The police are on their way."

"Where's Jocelyn?" Edna called. "She's not on the sofa."

"Dear God," I muttered to myself. I sprinted down the hallway toward the den and was halfway there when the explosion came, a tremendous *WHOOF* that vibrated the floorboards under my feet. At the same time I heard the sound of shattering glass coming from the basement. Smoke came pouring out of the floor vent by my feet.

"Jocelyn," I screamed. She wasn't in the den, the covers had slipped to the floor. Then I heard another sound, the sound of running water. The bathroom door opened and she stepped out, bleary-eyed and clearly terrified. "What's going on?" she whispered. "What's happening? Was that an explosion?"

The hall lights flickered out then. I gripped her by the shoulder and moved her along the hallway toward the front of the house. Edna met us in the hallway, her hair in curlers, a robe thrown over her cotton gown. "The back of the house is on fire," she said. "We've got to get out."

I propelled both of them toward the front door. "Out," I said. "Quickly. I think it started in the basement. Hurry."

The three of us stumbled blindly in the dark, fumbling with the double locks on the front door. Outside, we ran for the sidewalk, then turned to watch yellow-orange flames leaping up over the roof of the bungalow from the back of the house.

Suddenly we heard a series of shrieks, piercing, anguished cries. "Help me, help me, Jesus, I'm on fire." A woman, her clothing in flames, hurtled into the yard, then dropped to the grass. Behind her came a man, his silhouette outlined by the flames licking at his pants, his shirt, even his long hair.

From nowhere, we saw a second man running from the street toward the two fire-engulfed figures. "Get down," he screamed, "get down." He ripped his shirt off, and tried to blanket the woman in it, but she rolled on the ground, writhing and screaming in agony.

Edna was shrugging out of her robe just as I turned to her. I ran over and threw the robe on the young man, frantically trying to beat out the flames with the thin cotton fabric. "Help me," he sobbed, "help me."

The woman was still flailing on the ground, rolling away from her rescuer, screaming for him to get away. "Lissa," he hollered. "Hold still. Hold still, dammit. It's Kyle. Hold still."

Kyle Jordan, bare-chested, cradled his wife in his arms, sobbing as he tried to peel away the scorched jeans that had melted onto her long, shapely legs.

It didn't register until then that the blackened, singed shape, lying on my lawn, wrapped in my mother's bathrobe, was Zak Crawford.

Their screams, high, keening wails, nearly drowned out the sirens of the fire trucks and ambulance that careened down our street.

"You're burned," Edna cried. "Look at your hands and arms."

I'd been so busy trying to beat the flames off of Zak Crawford that I hadn't noticed what the stinging sensation was. But she was right. The palms of my hands looked like raw hamburger and the hair on my forearms had been singed.

"Fire's out," announced Mr. Byerly, strolling up with a snarling Homer in his arms. Our neighbor was still dressed in his pajamas, but he'd thrown a raincoat over them in the name of modesty, and a soft felt hat was squashed down on his high, hairless forehead. We swiveled around to look. A cloud of gray smoke hung in the air, but the flames had subsided and the firemen were rewinding their hoses and loading equipment onto their truck.

"I'm afraid to look any closer," I said. The bungalow was small, humble by other people's standards, but it was the first and only house I'd ever owned and I loved it fiercely.

"Fella over there gave it a couple good blasts from that hose and that fire was gone," Mr. Byerly said, nodding at one of the firemen. "He tells me gasoline actually doesn't do that good a job for burning a house down from the outside. It lights fast, then burns itself out just as quick."

"Did you see how much damage there was?" I asked anxiously.

"Not too awful bad," he said. "Me and Homer walked around to the edge of the backyard. Still pretty dark, but the walls are all standing. I'd say you're gonna need to plant some new grass, and Miss Edna's azaleas got all burned up. Looks like the back will need some siding, or paint, at least."

I took one of Homer's paws in mine, wincing at the sensation of his nails on my hand. "Is he all right? You know this little pissant probably saved our lives."

Mr. Byerly puffed his chest out. "Homer's too smart to get burned up. He had ahold of that lady's leg and chased her clean over to the side of the yard. He took off lickety-split for home when those windows blew out."

"Good boy," I crooned, scratching his ears. He bared his teeth at me. "I'm gonna buy you a big ol' sirloin steak tomorrow, Homer. You can take a dump in my yard or hump my leg any time you feel like it, from now on."

"Shut up about the dog," Edna fussed. "You're going

to the emergency room right this minute to see about those burns."

Thirty minutes later, Edna, Jocelyn, and I were sitting in the waiting area at Grady's emergency room, all of us dressed in the pink House Mouse smocks we'd gotten out of the van. The cops on the scene had refused to let us back in the house for clothes.

Kyle Jordan sat in a hard plastic chair across from us in the waiting room, his three sleepy children spilling out of his lap. All of us tried to avoid making eye contact. Except Jocelyn.

"I'm going over there to talk to him," Jocelyn announced, standing up to go. But Edna grabbed the hem of her smock and yanked her back. "Those babies' mama is in there, burned to a cinder. You set still and be quiet now."

She looked up at the waiting room clock for the third time in five minutes. "If they don't come out and get you pretty soon, I'm calling your sister, Maureen, at home. She'll get you seen in a hurry."

Maureen works the day shift in Grady's emergency room, but on the surgical side. My hands were throbbing now. "They'll see me as soon as they can," I said through clenched teeth. "My hands are nothing." But they hurt like bloody hell.

I tried to concentrate on watching an old episode of "The Andy Griffith Show" on the television mounted near the waiting room ceiling, but it was one of the later ones with Ken Berry instead of Don Knotts, and my heart wasn't in it. Just as I was about to relent and suggest that Edna call Maureen, C. W. Hunsecker and Linda Nickells strode through the waiting room doors. C. W. nodded curtly at us, said something to Linda, and she disappeared into the treatment area.

He came over and stood in front of me, and gave me a cockeyed let's-make-friends smile. "Caught yourself a couple of flame-throwers, huh?"

"Actually, my neighbor's dog caught them," I said. "All I did was try to get us out of the house in one piece."

"Her hands and arms are badly burned," Edna piped up. "Can't you get somebody to take care of her, Captain Hunsecker?"

He said something flirtatious to the admitting clerk sitting behind a frosted glass window. She blushed, giggled, then picked up the phone. After she hung up, she gestured to me. "You can come back now, Miss Garrity."

Edna and Jocelyn got up to go too. "Just the patient," the clerk said. "You two will have to wait out here."

As Hunsecker led me toward the treatment room, the waiting room door opened again and a harried-looking woman in her forties rushed in. Her frosted blond hair was askew and she had makeup smudges under her eyes. "Somebody called. My son, Zak Crawford, is here. He's been hurt. I have to see him."

The clerk shook her head, sending her shoulder-length earrings tinkling like a drunken chandelier. "He's in treatment in the burn unit right now. I'll let the doctor know you're here and he'll speak to you as soon as he gets a minute."

I wanted to hang around to hear more, but Hunsecker nudged me. "Let's go," he said.

A cute black intern with a single diamond stud in his ear and a name tag that read like an eye-chart pronounced my burns first-degree. Since I couldn't remember when I'd last had a tetanus shot, he jabbed me in the arm with a needle, then quickly bathed my hands in a cool saline solution and wrapped them in a gauze dressing.

He handed me two tablets and a paper cup of water. "Tylenol, for the pain," he said. "Now you're ready to go."

I guess he'd surmised from my appearance that I was one of the thousands of indigent patients Grady treats yearly. "Do you have a MARTA card? I can get the clerk to give you a token for the train."

"Thanks anyway," I said, touched. "My mother's waiting outside for me. But could you see if you could find Captain Hunsecker and ask him to come see me?"

"No problem," he said.

Hunsecker stood outside the treatment room door before coming in. "You decent?"

"Come on in anyway," I said. "We could both use a laugh."

He leaned warily around the doorway, then came all the way inside, glanced at my hands, then sat down on the only chair in the room, a backless stool.

"How are Zak and Lissa?" I asked.

"Zak's got mostly second-degree burns on his legs and torso, some third-degree burns on his hands, arms and neck," Hunsecker said. "He still had the empty gas can in his hands when the fumes ignited prematurely. We think the pilot light on the hot water heater in your basement did the job. Lissa was luckier. That little dog had her by the leg and she was trying to get away, so she dropped the gas can and was trying to make a run for it when the gas flared up. It was when she went back to try to help Zak that she got burned. The gas had spilled onto her clothing, so they ignited as soon as she got near the flames. She's got second-degree burns on her thighs, abdomen, and arms. They'll both be all right. I've seen lots worse crispy critters."

I shuddered at his description. It would be a long

time before I could forget the smell of seared flesh. "Has either one of them given you a statement?"

Hunsecker crossed his arms over his chest and gave me his silent chief profile. "You know I can't tell you that."

Linda Nickells came busying into the room then. She had a cold can of diet Coke with a straw sticking out of it. "Drink," she ordered. The icy stuff was heaven on my parched throat. I nearly sucked the can dry in one swallow.

"Lissa's talking a mile a minute back there. Zak's got his own version of the night's events. You feel like taking a walk?" she asked me.

A uniformed cop guarded the door of the treatment room next to mine. Nickells nodded at him, and he opened the door. Hunsecker shot Nickells a warning look, but Linda ignored him.

The gauze-wrapped figure stretched across the bed bore little resemblance to the ponytailed kid I'd seen partying at the Jordans' house. Zak Crawford's face and neck were smeared with the same white goo I had on my hands. His hair had burned off in patches, his eyebrows and lashes were singed off. What showed of his face was an angry red and his eyes were swollen shut.

I winced despite myself. There were IV tubes running to his bandaged groin and one to his foot. The blonde from the waiting room had a chair scooted up close to the bed. Her face was pale and her eyes were redder than they'd been before.

"You're Miss Garrity," she said.

"Shit," Zak muttered.

"She probably saved his life," Linda Nickells said, turning to Hunsecker, who'd followed us in. "Okay if she stays?"

"Ask him," Hunsecker said, gesturing toward the bed.

"Fuck," Zak whispered.

The blonde rubbed wearily at her eyes. "I'm Audrey Crawford, Zak's mother," she said. "It's all right. She can stay."

Hunsecker switched on a tape recorder that was sitting on the bedside table. "Let it be noted that the suspect has agreed that Callahan Garrity, a licensed private investigator, should be present during the statement. Go ahead," he said.

"We left Lissa's car down the block from her, the detective's house," Zak said tonelessly. "With the keys in the ignition, so we could peel off in a hurry."

Hunsecker interrupted again. "Lissa Jordan's white Camaro was impounded tonight. A search of the unlocked trunk turned up an antique pistol, a rifle, and a package of letters."

"It was all Lissa's idea," Zak continued. "She's the one who wanted Bridget dead. I barely knew the chick. Like, last Saturday, we drove by that mansion, the one in Inman Park, a whole bunch of times. We saw the old dude leave. I thought Lissa'd get tired of it. Then she's, like, 'Let's go in. Let's kill the bitch.' I go, 'No way.' But Lissa wouldn't let up. Finally she says she just wants to go to the door and, like, tell Bridget off. But she made me go with her. And when Bridget opened the door, Lissa went apeshit. She pulls this freakin' gun. I didn't even know she had a gun. So Bridget starts screaming for us not to hurt her and Lissa, man, she hits her upside the head with the gun. But Bridget's crying and trying to run away. So when Lissa sees this big metal doorstop thing, she goes, 'Hit her. Hurry up before somebody hears and calls the cops.' And man, Bridget's screaming like shit. So I hit her, you know, in the head? And she went down. We were scared shitless. So Lissa says, 'Take her upstairs. So nobody will see her.' So she makes me carry Bridget upstairs, while she runs around the house and grabs stuff to make it look like a burglary. And I took her and put her on this bed."

"Was she still alive at this point?" Hunsecker asked.

"I thought she was dead," Zak said. "But Lissa comes up and starts screaming, 'She's still alive. You gotta kill her. You gotta.' Now I said, 'No way. I'm outta here.' But Lissa pulls out this short knife-thing she'd found, and she stabs her. So then we left. Lissa had to get home before Kyle got back from soccer camp."

Audrey Crawford was sobbing quietly now, bent over double, her back shaking.

"You're telling us that Lissa killed Bridget?" Hunsecker said. "You sure, Zak?"

"For sure," Zak answered quickly. "She was alive when I took her upstairs. Swear to God."

Hunsecker glanced at Nickells and then at me. Lissa had obviously given a different version during her statement.

"What happened to the stuff you took from the house?" Hunsecker asked.

"We had the shit in this plastic garbage bag, but I guess the point of that sword tore a hole in it, because something fell out. Lissa was really pissed."

"And the other stuff—the silver trophy and the diary, and the dagger—what happened to them?"

A ghost of a smile passed Zak's swollen lips. "I pawned this silver cup thing. Got forty bucks for it. Lissa had a shit fit when she found out. We threw the dagger in the river."

"What about the diary?" I asked, unable to keep quiet.

Hunsecker glared at me.

"That old book thing?" Zak said. "We thought it was just a piece of crap. I left it in the trunk of my car."

"Is it still there?" Hunsecker asked.

"Somebody ripped off my car," Zak said. "On Thursday. I was going over to Lissa's house, and it overheated. So I walked to a gas station and a buddy came and picked me up. The next day when I went to get it, it was gone. Ripped off. Bet the fuckers stripped and burned it."

"Is that why you got your father's car?" Nickells asked.

Mrs. Crawford looked surprised.

"Yeah," he said wearily. "He always leaves it at the same park-and-ride near the airport. I got a spare key. So I went down there and boosted it. I do it all the time."

"And then you took a ride up to Ryverclyffe and tried to kill Jocelyn and me," I said angrily.

Hunsecker shut off the tape reporter. "Out," he said.

Nickells gave me a gentle push.

In the hallway, I leaned against the wall for support. "You believe any of that?" I asked Nickells.

"Parts of it are probably true," she said.

"Shit," I said. "This is unbelievable. They kill a girl for reasons neither of them understand, and then these two morons pull a burglary. The most valuable thing they steal is stolen by another moron, who probably burned up the only thing of value in the whole car. Unbelievable."

"Very few of our criminal clientele are brain surgeons, Callahan," Nickells pointed out.

"True," I admitted. "But I still don't understand how Zak and Lissa knew we, uh, somebody, knew that the letters and stuff were in Zak's apartment."

"Dumb luck," Linda volunteered. "Lissa said she was driving up to Zak's when she saw you two coming out of the apartment. She drove on past, and when she saw you leave, she took her skinny little fanny in there and got the stuff. When Zak got back, she says it was his idea to burn you out. He thought he'd get rid of you and the missing letter all at the same time."

"I'm just thankful they were such amateurs," I said. "The last way I want to die is in a fire. But how about Jordan? How did he get to my house so fast?"

Linda snorted. "He was there all along. When his wandering wife left the house tonight, he figured she was going to go shack up with the boyfriend. So he loaded the kids in the backseat of his car and followed her. He had no idea the house he was watching was yours. He thought the gym bag Zak was carrying had his clothes in it. He planned to wait outside and confront Lissa when she came out again. Catch her red-handed, as it were."

I looked down at my own gauze-wrapped hands, which now looked like large white oven mitts. "Red-handed is right."

31

WE FINALLY DID GET a new roof on the house, and yes, in an indirect way, Elliot Littlefield did pay for it.

Not that he meant to. Nooo. To put it in the simplest possible terms, Littlefield stiffed me for my fee. Big time.

Old Mr. Byerly was right about the damage to the bungalow. It wasn't nearly as bad as we'd feared. Thank God, Lissa Jordan and Zak Crawford were the world's stupidest would-be arsonists. The gasoline burned the grass in a ten-foot swathe around the patio and blistered and charred the clapboard siding on the back of the house, so we had to replace it. And the roof. And the basement windows and the hot-water heater. The insurance paid for most.

And yes, for the month the house was being worked on, Edna moved in with her friend Agnes and I moved in with Mac and Rufus. We ran the House Mouse out of Agnes's basement rumpus room and aside from the lingering odor of mildew in my clothes, things worked out better than we'd expected.

I take two small white tablets twice a day every day. I

hope it's the tamoxifen and not a placebo that I'm taking, but if not, I recently discovered that Edna secretly says her rosary every night before she goes to bed. That's fine with me. I figure any old hoodoo will do.

From what I hear, the dysfunctional Dougherty family is in the process of healing too. Jocelyn and her mother worked out a compromise. She's in college at Agnes Scott, a small liberal arts women's college in Decatur, only a few miles from her parents' home, and she lives in the dorm there. The whole family is going through therapy. Jocelyn comes by every now and again, to sample some of Edna's cooking and to get a lesson in biscuit making. She's slowly gaining weight and the big news is that last month she had her first period in over a year. Little things mean a lot.

Zak Crawford and Lissa Jordan still haven't gone to trial for Bridget's murder yet. Lissa's attorney is claiming she has one of those talk-show illnesses: the women who love too much syndrome. And Zak's attorney is claiming that heavy-metal music lyrics drove him to violence. Don't you love the 1990s?

Elliot Littlefield may finally do time for the Sunny Girl murder. With all the publicity around Bridget's murder, a "mystery witness" came forward and admitted he and his girlfriend had been in the bedroom next to Littlefield's when Sunny Girl was killed. Littlefield hasn't gone to trial yet either. But the judge in the new trial, Byron "No Bail" DeLavelle, revoked his bond after the district attorney reported that Littlefield had been badgering the witness, an old acquaintance, not to testify against him. Eagle's Keep has a big *For Rent* sign out front.

Home for Hope has a new director. Jake Dahlberg resigned his post after city fire inspectors declared the agency's houses a fire hazard. Dahlberg was never charged with anything relating to the deaths of Josephina and Maria Rosario. I understand all the Home for Hope residents are being put up in the Holiday Inn while their houses are being retrofitted.

I was driving down North Druid Hills Road one rainy Friday recently, when I saw a tow truck hooking an abandoned car to its winch. And it got me thinking. Six or seven phone calls later, I was picking my way between shiny new Cadillacs and crunched-up Volkswagen beetles at K & A Towing down in southwest Atlanta.

The manager of K & A was a sawed-off little guy named Karl Kaziersky. He lead me down the rows of cracked asphalt. And there it was, parked between a battered black Mustang convertible with kudzu growing up through the floorboards and a mustard-colored Chevette: a rust-covered green Vega.

"This is it," I said. "My baby brother's car."

"Tow fee, plus storage fees, that's gonna run you two hundred and eighteen dollars and thirty-seven cents," Kaziersky said, unmoved by my emotion at finding my brother's long-lost car.

I had to detour to the nearest instant teller machine to get the cash, which he insisted on. It cleaned out our savings, but I didn't care. I counted the twenties, tens, and ones into his hand, which he quickly closed over the bills.

"You got the pink slip?"

I hadn't thought of that. "My brother had it in his wallet when he died in the airplane crash," I said, improvising. "This Vega is the only thing my mother has left to remind her of Junior."

He shoved his fist in his pocket and the bills disappeared. I walked around to the trunk and tried it. Still locked. "We think Junior might have left some family pictures in the trunk," I said. "But it's locked."

"So use the keys," he growled.

"The plane crash," I said simply. "They were in his pockets."

"There's a crowbar in the office," he said. "Help yourself."

The All Saints gym bag was on the bottom of a snarl of dirty clothes and tools, with the pieces of a broken plastic foam cooler on top. I picked the gym bag up, held it in both hands, and walked quickly toward the van.

My hands shook as I unzipped the bag. Inside I found a small brown leather volume, no bigger than a woman's billfold. The cover was cracked and the yellow pages brittle. They crumbled to the touch. The page I opened to was covered, nearly every inch of it, with Lula Belle Bird's tiny ladylike writing. It zigged and zagged over the pages, starting on the thinly drawn red lines, then inching up the margins, and back in between the lines. I could make out a word, occasionally, but after fifteen minutes of trying to unlock the secrets of seducing the Confederate army, I was none the wiser.

In the back of the diary, however, I found some modern writing: a bill of sale, dated May of 1992.

I found Lula Belle Bird's distant relative in a leafy green hollow of Gilmer County, in a tiny redbrick house set in the shadow of a falling-down old white clapboard farmhouse. I rang the bell, but there was no answer.

I walked around to the back of the house. A stout lady in a straw hat was down on her knees, pulling weeds in her vegetable garden.

"Mrs. Sparks?" I called.

Startled, she looked up, then struggled slowly to her feet. She wiped her hands on the rickrack-edged apron she wore and put her hands up to smooth her gray hair.

"Yes, ma'am," she said pleasantly.

Mattie Mae Sparks's cheerful red face crumpled into a frown when I told her what I'd come for, and what I'd brought.

I held out the diary. But she wrapped her hands in the apron and stepped away from me.

"No, ma'am," she said. "I sold that old writing desk for one hundred and twenty-five dollars to that man from Atlanta. That was my late husband's granddaddy's desk. But the children bought me a lovely new desk from Haverty's Furniture for Mother's Day. Pecan veneer with antique brass handles. I had that old desk sitting out on the front porch. That Atlanta man drove by and saw it, rang my doorbell, and offered me cash. I was tickled to get it. I'd forgotten that book was in there, but he paid for it, and I believe it belongs to him now."

"Mrs. Sparks," I said. "This diary is worth a great deal of money. Thousands. And Mr. Littlefield should have told you he'd found it. It's your family heritage."

"Not my family heritage," she said quickly. "Us Wards are Pentecostalists. It's the Sparkses that were Methodist. Worldly, you might say. Lula Belle was my husband's great-great-aunt. His mama told me a long time ago about Lula Belle moving to Richmond and shaming the family. Miss Etta didn't feel right having that book in a Christian home, so she always hid it in the bottom of that desk drawer. Now it's gone, I reckon it can stay gone."

The stubborn expression on her face told me she considered the matter settled.

"Good or bad, this is considered history, Mrs. Sparks," I said, pleading. "Maybe you should donate it to a university or a museum or a library, where scholars could study it."

She still looked dubious. I gave her the diary, and she quickly tucked it into her apron pocket, an unclean thing offensive to the eyes of a God-fearing Pentecostalist. "We'll see," she said.

Months later, sipping coffee and reading the *Constitution*, I came across an item that made me laugh so hard I spit coffee out my nose.

"What's wrong with you?" Edna said, dabbing at the coffee droplets that had landed on her crossword puzzle.

"Look at this," I said, laughing and gasping for air. I pointed to the headline on the story: "Bible College Sells Civil War Diary for Record Amount."

"Lula Belle Bird's diary?" Edna said. "I thought you told me it belonged to some old lady up in the mountains. How'd a college get ahold of it?"

"Mattie Mae Sparks donated it to the Living Word Evangelical Bible College in Nahunta, Georgia," I read. "But they deemed it antiscriptural and decided to sell it off and use the funds to buy more gospel-centered literature. Two-hundred and eleven thousand dollars should buy a whole lot of tracts."

"Who's the buyer?" Edna asked.

"Brown University, in Providence, Rhode Island," I said. "Says here they already have the greatest collection of Abraham Lincoln material in the country."

"Damn Yankees," she sniffed.

Welcome to the
World of
KATHY HOGAN TROCHECK
and the Callahan Garrity mysteries

•

"Kathy Hogan Trocheck keeps readers
on the edge of their seats."
Atlanta Journal-Constitution

Irish Eyes

In her former life as an Atlanta cop, Callahan Garrity trusted no one more than her partner, Bucky Deavers. Now, when her old friend asks her to go to the annual St. Paddy's Day bash, she can't say no. Looking for fun, Callahan gets the shock of her life instead. Bucky is shot in a liquor store on the way home. Stunned but clear-headed, the tenacious PI turns on all her skills to find the culprit. What she discovers, though, are accusations that Bucky might be working both sides of the law as an accomplice in a string of robberies.

With her friend's life and reputation hanging in the balance, Callahan and her feisty band of House Mouse employees kick the investigation into high gear, using their unorthodox methods to get answers. This time, it will take every skill they've got to pierce the veil of secrecy surrounding an Irish police organization and prove that the case is more than it seems.

•

"An entertaining, suspenseful romp."
Publishers Weekly

Midnight Clear

It's a few days before Christmas and sometime sleuth/full-time cleaning lady Callahan Garrity has things under control for a change, until her ne'er-do-well brother, Brian—missing for over ten years—appears with his toddler daughter, Maura. Trouble has always followed Brian, and now he's in deeper than ever because he's kidnapped Maura from his estranged wife, a vengeful shrew with the law on her side.

When his ex-wife is found dead, the cops suspect Brian. Though he's many things, Callahan knows Brian is no murderer. To save her brother and her holiday, Callahan, along with her House Mouse employees, will crisscross yuletide Atlanta—going everywhere the search for the truth leads.

> "Will make you laugh, make you cry,
> make you mad, and make you wonder
> right up until the very last page."
> *Boston Globe*

Strange Brew

Cleaning lady cum sleuth Callahan Garrity has cautiously watched her seedy bohemian Atlanta neighborhood morph into a trendy haven for yuppies. But just as she fears, too much cappuccino and new money can be a bad mix.

When the young owner of a microbrewery looking to score prime real estate turns up dead, neighborhood local Wuvvy, an aging flower child and the brewer's bitterest foe, becomes the prime suspect. Digging for evidence to clear Wuvvy, Callahan isn't prepared for the succulent secrets she finds—shocking truths that force her to reassess old friendships and an old love—as even deadlier developments surface.

"A tidy mystery with . . . polished writing
and industrial-strength suspense."
Sue Grafton

Heart Trouble

Callahan Garrity has her hands full trying to expand her House Mouse cleaning business. So she's reluctant to take on a client in need of detective services, especially when that client is the most notorious woman in Atlanta—Whitney Albright Dobbs. Whitney is a wealthy socialite who hit and killed a young black girl while under the influence and just kept driving.

Whitney's light sentence has set the city's racial tensions on simmer, and Callahan is not especially keen on helping her track down Whitney's soon-to-be ex-husband's hidden assets. Against her better judgment though, Callahan launches a full-out search for Dr. Dobb's dollars. But it only takes a glance to see that more than Whitney's alimony is at stake. When more people show up dead, it takes all of Callahan's grit—and a lot of help from the House Mouse team—to outsmart one mean, mad killer.

•

"A fast-paced, highly entertaining caper."
Louisville Courier-Journal

Happy Never After

Callahan Garrity is a former Atlanta cop, a part-time sleuth, and full-time owner of House Mouse, a cleaning service that tidies up after Atlanta's elite. She and her coterie of devoted helpers can ransack a house for clues faster that it takes a fingerprint to set.

Callahan needs all the help she can get trying to keep Rita Fontaine, a washed-up 1960s teenage rock star, out of jail. It's nothing less than murder when Stu Hightower, the vain, temperamental president of a thriving Atlanta recording company, is found dead in the designer den of his posh home. His only companions are the slug in his heart and Rita, dead-drunk and looking guilty. Callahan believes in Rita's innocence because, after all, Hightower has made more enemies than records in his career. But discovering who hated him enough to kill him could send her floating lifeless down a river of lost dreams without a paddle.

•

*"If Happy Never After were a song,
we'd all be dancing in the streets."*
San Jose Mercury News

Homemade Sin

Some people might call Callahan Garrity nosy, but she prefers to think of her tendency toward snooping as a healthy interest in the truth. So when news of her cousin's murder reaches her, Callahan shakes off her House Mouse cleaning uniform to don her detective's cap. It's not that she doesn't have confidence in the Atlanta police—she used to be among their ranks—it's just that the crime seems too incongruous with Patti's suburban life to be an accident.

Callahan's search takes her on a convoluted trail starting with Patti's priest, who may have provided more than spiritual counsel, through Atlanta's inner city and into the shady deals of Patti's recently prosperous husband. The pieces start to fall into place, but not everyone is as fond of the truth as Callahan, because the closer she gets to it, the harder it is to stay alive.

•

"The prose is tart and lively,
the storytelling swift-paced, and the large cast
and multiple plot lines deftly handled."
Atlanta Journal-Constitution

To Live and Die in Dixie

Callahan Garrity, housecleaner deluxe and occasional private investigator, has no idea what kind of mess she's getting herself into when she agrees to work for a prominent antiques dealer. During her days on the Atlanta police force, she'd heard about Elliott Littlefield's sordid reputation, but she's only cleaning his house, after all.

No sooner does her crew begin the job than they discover the bloodied body of a young woman in a bedroom. Then Littlefield hires Callahan to recover a priceless Civil War diary stolen by the killer. Deadly serious antiques collectors, right-wing radicals, and impulsive teenagers make the case a bit more difficult to tidy up than Callahan anticipates . . . and a whole lot more dangerous.

•

"A madcap mix of humor and homicide."
Clarion-Ledger (Jackson, MS)

Every Crooked Nanny

After ten years of cleaning up Atlanta's streets, former cop Callahan Garrity trades in her badge for a broom and buys herself a housekeeping business. She's on the job when her clients discover that their pretty nineteen-year-old Mormon nanny has disappeared . . . along with jewelry, silver, and a few rather sensitive real estate documents.

Soon Callahan is involved with a job messier than any she's ever encountered while wearing an apron. Illicit love triangles, crooked business deals, long distance scams, a dead body . . . it's going to require some industrial-strength sleuthing on Callahan's part if she wants to solve—and survive—this one.

•

"A breezy debut."
New York Times Book Review